BEHIND THE BARON'S MASK

RESOLVED IN LOVE - BOOK 1

PENNY FAIRBANKS

ALSO BY PENNY FAIRBANKS

Resolved in Love Series:

Behind The Baron's Mask

Healing The Captain's Heart

Finding The Artisan's Future

Embracing The Earl's Dream

The Harcourts Series:

Anna's Decision

Dalton's Challenge

Caroline's Discovery

Patrick's Arrangement

Harriet's Proposal

The Harcourts: Another Generation Series:

A Convenient Escape

The Hidden Heiress

An Unexpected Bloom

The Necessary Lesson

An Impossible Fate

For my husband—my real life hero.

CHAPTER 1

"Truly, Cecilia, you must not fuss," Mrs. Edna Richards snapped.

"But Mama, I hardly think such an extravagant gown is necessary," Cecilia protested, ignoring the warning in her mother's voice. The small hands at her back stilled over the gown's ties.

"Continue, Violet. Remember, this is your only new dress this year. We need all the advantage we can get if we are to make a decent match before Season's end. And you *will* make a match, one way or another." Mrs. Richards's words came out through gritted teeth, cold and harsh.

Cecilia hung her head and clasped her hands in front of her. "Go ahead, Violet."

Her maid obeyed and tied the back of the gown.

Seemingly satisfied, Cecilia's mother left the bedroom, her rustling skirts the only announcement of her departure.

"I apologize, Miss Richards," Violet whispered as her nimble fingers finished the job.

"There's nothing to be done. I know she is right. Though I doubt a few extra pearls and ruffles will find me a husband."

Cecilia, far too embroiled in her worries to censor herself in front of her maid, knew she sounded as bitter as she felt. Besides, Violet had proven herself to be a loyal and caring servant many times over in her years of service with the family.

"If I may be so bold..." The maid's voice was quiet as she stepped before Cecilia to continue adjustments.

"Please do." Cecilia smiled at the young woman. Violet had earned a fond spot in Cecilia's heart. Though they could never truly be equals, Cecilia always appreciated her maid's thoughts, which never strayed beyond their respectful boundaries.

"I do hope you find whatever it is you seek." The words came out rushed and Violet's head remained low as she fussed over the dress, pinching and prodding at seams and ruffles.

"Thank you, Violet. I do, too. Lord knows Mama and Papa are desperate to rid themselves of me. And I am quite of a mind to be rid of them as well." She mumbled the last part, thinking back on the incident with her mother just moments before.

The sound of fabric swishing and sliding filled the room as Violet turned Cecilia this way and that to ensure every flounce was in place.

"I should think you won't have any trouble catching every eye in the room with this dress, Miss Richards." Violet took a step back to view Cecilia in her brand-new gown, as if she were admiring an exhibit of fine paintings at Somerset House.

A blush prickled under Cecilia's skin. Indeed, the elegant gown had just been delivered from the modiste that morning. She hated to admit the devilish satisfaction she'd felt as Juliet moaned over the beauty of the dress when it had arrived. Unfortunately for Cecilia's younger sister, no amount of begging Mrs. Richards for the privilege of wearing the gown had worked.

As their dear mother had put it, Cecilia needed the boost of a beautiful dress far more than Juliet did. And besides, the dress had been painstakingly made to Cecilia's exact measurements.

Cecilia's excitement over her new gown had quickly faded, however. It marked simply another of her parents' many ploys to land her a worthy husband. Their anxiety grew more apparent by the day, as did Cecilia's.

At the start of her third Season, she could now be considered on her way to spinsterhood. But Cecilia would cling to her hopes until the very last moment. Her growing unease told her that moment would arrive all too soon.

Her sister's recent presentation had further reduced Cecilia's chances; everyone considered Juliet the handsomer of the Richards sisters.

And with Juliet out, Mrs. Richards had made it abundantly clear that this gown would be Cecilia's only new dress of the Season. Her parents had not expected to pay for full *ton*-worthy wardrobes for both daughters at the same time. Several of Cecilia's older gowns had now been refurbished.

"I'm afraid you pay me too high a compliment, Violet. I only wish to catch the right pair of eyes…" Wearing the exquisite dress now, Cecilia couldn't help feeling a little optimistic. The smooth cream satin and delicate embroidery perfectly complimented her dark blonde hair.

She smiled down at her body wrapped in this breathtaking work of art, running her fingers over the fabric of her skirt. Her hopes of finding her perfect match had dwindled to nearly nothing over the last two Seasons yet she refused to simply settle for any man with a title or fortune who might show her a sliver of interest, as her parents hoped she would.

Her reputation had suffered somewhat because of it. But perhaps tonight...

"Let's finish you up now, Miss Richards. It would not do well to keep your family waiting." Violet's voice nudged Cecilia out of her thoughts. It was for the best. Cecilia had no business engaging in wishful thinking.

Violet fluttered about Cecilia as she administered the final touches, ensuring that every bead and curl maintained its proper place. Violet's beaming smile surprised Cecilia. She hesitantly stepped toward the long looking glass in the corner of her room. The reflection showed someone quite unlike her true self.

The gown itself was of course perfect and far more extravagant than she was used to, yet somehow Cecilia felt that it became her. The charming ringlets of hair that framed her face, the sparkling headdress, the jewels that graced her neck all aided in transforming her into a truly elegant young woman. An unfamiliar grip of excitement caused Cecilia's heart to leap in her chest.

"Y-You've outdone yourself, my dear Violet," Cecilia mumbled, unable to take her eyes from the looking glass.

"You do yourself a great disservice, Miss Richards. The hard work is all yours. I merely dress up your charm and beauty." Violet's green eyes danced with mirth and pride. If Cecilia hadn't known better, she could have sworn that Violet stood before the looking glass admiring her own reflection.

"My, my, Violet. With such a silver tongue you could very well be a poet," Cecilia giggled.

The maid blushed and cast her eyes to the floor. "You are too kind. Shall we present you to the master and mistress?"

Cecilia took one last lingering look at herself and nodded. No doubt her parents would be eagerly waiting to see if the expense of this gown had paid off. She crossed the room and was at the door when a cry from Violet caused her to jump nearly out of her gloves.

"One last thing, Miss Richards! You mustn't forget this." Violet held an expertly crafted white half mask in her hands.

"Ah yes, it would be a shame to be turned away from Lady Henshell's door after all the effort Mama and Papa took to secure us tickets." Cecilia nearly scoffed at the idea.

Her parents had made a great fuss about the many connections they'd pressed in the hopes of gaining entrance to the first fancy dress ball to welcome the new Season, hosted every year by the much-loved Lady Henshell. For her own petty satisfaction, Cecilia allowed them to sail about London, begging scraps from the *ton*, knowing full well that her dear friend Rosamund, Lady Henshell's daughter, had already insisted upon Cecilia's attendance along with the rest of the Richards family.

At the present moment, Cecilia could only shake her head at their ridiculous behavior, retrieve the mask from Violet, and make her way downstairs to the drawing room.

"Sissy!" A flurry of pale pink fabric rushed across the room and smothered Cecilia in a hug before she could fully enter the room.

She wrapped her arms around her younger sister, chuckling at the longstanding nickname. Cecilia had been too difficult of a name for little Juliet, so she'd been Sissy ever since.

"You look absolutely stunning!" Juliet pulled back to take in Cecilia's ensemble.

"As do you, Jules." Now that Cecilia had a better view, she could see just how well her little sister had grown into a breathtaking young woman. Her sweet pink gown, dotted with pretty rosettes, brought out a touch of color in her pale skin and perfectly suited her white blonde hair.

"Oh don't you just adore this dress?" Juliet broke free and twirled before Cecilia, allowing her skirt to flutter about her.

Cecilia laughed at the display. In many ways Juliet would always be the same silly girl she'd grown up with.

"Still, I do wish Mama would have let me steal your dress. It's an absolute dream." Juliet pouted and crossed her arms, but she couldn't keep the playful gleam out of her blue eyes.

"Perhaps you can wear it later in the Season, with some alterations of course," Cecilia offered, gesturing to Juliet's clearly shorter frame.

"How lovely are my dear girls!" Both young women turned to see their father approach, arms outstretched as if to proudly display his daughters though no guests were in the room.

The uncomfortable pit of resentment that had been eating away at her stomach for months retreated just a bit. As frustrated as she'd been with both her parents' treatment of her and their antics about town, Cecilia knew that James Richards simply wanted to secure a better future for his family and the generations to come. Unfortunately for Cecilia as the eldest child, much of that burden fell to her shoulders.

"Neither of you will want for a single dance tonight, I wager." The obvious pride in his voice told Cecilia he genuinely meant it. Even still, she wished that the conversation need not always turn to making matches or finding partners on the dance floor. She knew the grand goal well enough.

"Thank you, Papa! And you look very dashing yourself." Juliet quickly returned the compliment.

"Please, dear, do save your flattery for the ball." Mrs.

Richards's voice sliced through their companionable chatter, shooting an unpleasant glare at her husband.

Cecilia pursed her lips when she saw her father's face fall ever so slightly. Their mother's disdain for their father had been a fact of life for Cecilia and Juliet, but Cecilia still hated to see her well-meaning father looked at with such scorn. Though she knew almost nothing of their courtship story and had no contact with their relatives, Cecilia knew her mother's family had been notably wealthier than her father's family. Cecilia suspected that Mrs. Richards felt herself to be above her husband in any number of qualities.

Mrs. Richards's eyes slid up and down each girl's dress. "You both look very well. Cecilia, the gown suits you." She swept out of the room after administering her assessments, not looking back to see if her family followed.

Cecilia glanced to Juliet who looked just as surprised at the high praise from their mother. Mr. Richards ushered them out of the drawing room, motioning for them to don their masks, and to the front door where Mrs. Richards already waited, the tapping of her gloved finger against her skirt the only indication of her impatience.

A footman held the door open for them and assisted the family into the coach. The young ladies were careful not to crush their gowns in the crowded carriage. Cecilia peered out the small window as their coachmen expertly guided them through the London streets until they arrived at Berkley Square.

She sighed wistfully as they pulled up to the beautiful town home of Baron Henshell. The Richards's home was certainly nothing to scoff at, but there was no denying the fact that her family lacked the true mark of elite Society—a fact that never went unnoticed by her parents.

The sounds of merriment sent a thrill through Cecilia's chest as the coachman opened the doors and assisted them out onto the street. Despite her many growing concerns, she'd been looking forward to this event. She adored dancing in all its forms, but a masked dance added an extra layer of intrigue and excitement.

The Henshell family hosted this masked ball every year at the earliest sign of spring in London, when most families had settled into their town homes and dusted off the drowsy country lifestyle. It was a truly grand event, designed to welcome the *ton* back to London and bring the Season into full swing.

Cecilia also knew there would be a good chance she would be asked to play. Her pianoforte skills were quite known and she was often asked to play at events, but the nerves still overcame her and caused her fingers to stiffen over the keys. She had to work harder for an audience than she did when practicing at home, though she could typically keep her listeners from realizing this fact. Perhaps her mask would aid in relieving some of the nerves.

Immaculately dressed servants led the Richards family into the Henshell home. Though they were not late by any stretch, the ballroom already held more than two hundred of Society's best. Chandeliers illuminated the grand space and dancers spread out along the shining floor, dresses of many lovely shades swirling with grace. Cecilia's heart thumped to the sound of the music, aching to join.

"Come, let us make our rounds," Mrs. Richards announced, snapping Cecilia out of the beauty of the scene. She nearly protested but her mother looked even more severe than usual with a black domino sweeping over her dress and a matching mask. If she did her duty now without any fuss, hopefully she would be able to take her place on the dance floor sooner rather than later.

"My dears, I will be in the card room." Mr. Richards

quickly excused himself from their company, as he usually did.

"But Mama, how can you introduce me to anyone if we don't know who they are?" A hint of a whine threaded through Juliet's voice and her eyes behind her half mask darted eagerly to the dancers enjoying a lively cotillion. Cecilia noticed that many eyes, of both men and women, snapped to Juliet. A few, it seemed, even glanced her way as well.

"Hush now. It is simple. We need not know identities. We may simply strike up conversation with suitable ladies and perhaps discover acquaintances or make new connections." Of course, Mrs. Richards was adept at forging valuable relationships with all the right people.

Juliet couldn't hide her pout and Cecilia tried to covertly elbow her sister in the side. But it did not escape their mother's notice. Most things did not.

Mrs. Richards sighed, her exasperation clear. "You will both dance, I promise you. As many dances as your feet can manage. But we must first make our presence known amongst these fine ladies."

Juliet followed behind their mother reluctantly but obediently and Cecilia brought up the rear. She scanned the crowds, both those on the dance floor and those standing to the side conversing and enjoying refreshments. Though she thought she saw some familiar dresses or figures, the disguises truly muddled her senses.

Mrs. Richards led the young ladies about the room in a succession of curtsies, floating from one small gathering of attendees to the next, discussing inconsequential matters and gossiping about who was here and who wasn't.

They did indeed discover several acquaintances beneath the masks of all varieties, who naturally asked after Juliet's debut and subtly inquired about Cecilia's prospects. Though

Juliet was thrilled to share her experience as a young woman officially out in Society, Cecilia shrunk away from any questions directed at herself.

Once, she too had been thrilled to finally attend the glamorous balls and dinners she'd heard so much about and to have gentlemen call upon her for carriage rides or walks in the park.

But with two years of balls and dinners and rides and walks with nothing to show for it—and seemingly all of Society's eyes waiting to see who she might turn down next —Cecilia now preferred to give a quick but gracious response and turn attention back to Juliet's lovely dress, her many accomplishments, her unending charms. She hoped her sister's first Season would be far more successful than her own had been. In any case, she was determined to do her part to make it so.

"Cecilia, is that you?" A bright, melodic voice called out to Cecilia from somewhere behind her. She turned to see a tall young woman in an elegant pale green gown and white full-face mask making her way through the crowd.

"Rosamund?" Cecilia hazarded a guess, squinting as if she might be able to see through the mask. But the woman's voice and graceful bearing all but revealed her identity.

"My dear, you are positively radiant!" Rosamund declared, confirming herself to Cecilia.

"And you are most stunning," Cecilia returned as she curtsied.

"Oh, come now," Rosamund chided, taking Cecilia's hands in her own and placing a quick kiss on her cheek. Though Rosamund was a very close friend—second only to Juliet—Cecilia still knew that her place as the daughter of a landed gentleman without titles put her far below the daughter of a baron. Rosamund, however, had the luxury of not caring for such distinctions.

Mrs. Richards quickly excused herself from her current conversation and turned both herself and Juliet to the attention of the hostess's daughter.

"How did you recognize me?" Cecilia asked.

"Well, I thought something about your presence seemed familiar, and of course once I saw your company I knew it could be none other than the three finest ladies in all of London." Rosamund beamed graciously under her mask. "We are thrilled to have you here."

"The pleasure is ours, of course." Mrs. Richards and Juliet curtsied.

The domino could not conceal the glee in their mother's eyes. If Cecilia had thus far failed in her duty to the family by way of finding a husband, at least she'd managed to befriend Lady Henshell's daughter. Mrs. Richards loved to exploit this tidbit of information when making her many connections, as Lady Henshell was greatly respected in all the finest circles.

"I'm glad to have found you, Cecilia." With greetings done, Rosamund turned Cecilia away from her mother and sister, her voice grave.

"Whatever is the matter?" Concern drew Cecilia's brows together behind her mask.

"I grow weary of these musicians and I believe they could take a rest in any case. Would you do us all the honor of gracing the pianoforte with your impeccable talent?" Though she could not see her friend's expression, the imploring tone in her voice was clear enough.

Cecilia laughed quietly. Rosamund need not beg her for anything. Cecilia was happy to oblige her charming friend. But, as Cecilia had come to learn, Rosamund did enjoy a show and made anything a performance if she could manage it.

"Already? I've only just arrived, and I haven't danced a

single set yet." Cecilia already knew that she would play, but that didn't mean she wouldn't tease her friend a bit first.

"Please, you must! You know everyone adores your playing! I promise to introduce you to every fine gentleman I know here and you'll wish for another pair of legs for all the dancing you'll be asked to do," Rosamund wheedled, grabbing Cecilia's hands and squeezing them with sincerity.

"Wouldn't Mama and Papa be so very pleased about that! Do lead the way."

CHAPTER 2

*H*enry could not fathom how Solomon had convinced him to attend this cursed ball. It was certainly the largest event he'd attended in a long while, and hopefully it would be the only gathering of this size he would be dragged to for the rest of the Season.

"It amazes me how dour you can manage to look even behind your mask," Solomon huffed under his own half mask.

"It is only because you know me so well." Henry fought to keep the annoyance out of his voice.

"I appreciate you humoring me this once, oh great Lord Neil." Solomon laughed and patted Henry squarely between the shoulders, nearly causing him to stumble up the stairs to the grand Henshell home.

There was nothing for it but to sigh and hope the night would pass quickly enough, or that his gregarious friend could be torn from the dance floor at a reasonable hour. The sound of the musicians playing a rollicking tune for the dancers set Henry on edge as they passed through the foyer and down the hall toward the ballroom situated at the back of Lord Henshell's town home.

He suspected that Solomon would insist he dance at least one set, pointing out suitable partners amongst the thick crowd of well-dressed women. He could always escape to the card room, but even there Henry didn't feel at home. As they entered the ballroom, the thought of home reminded Henry of the book languishing on the desk in his study, waiting for him to fill it with more words.

"Drat, I forgot how effective these costumes could be," Solomon murmured by the doorway, trying to see through the boisterous activity. "Well, we shall simply have to take the opportunity to make some new acquaintance." He picked a direction and strode forward confidently, disguised eyes turning to watch his poised figure weave through the crowd.

An easy enough feat for the Earl of Overton, Henry thought to himself, a stinging tinge of jealousy shooting through his chest for the briefest moment. Being best friends with Solomon Catley, Earl of Overton and a top Society beau to boot, could at times put one's own life and manners into harsh perspective.

Rather like a lost dog, Henry followed Solomon about the room, bowing to introductions as Solomon easily engaged in conversation. Henry dutifully answered questions directed towards himself and remarked on mundane details such as the fortuitous weather as of late. Unfortunately for Henry, each time he found himself easing into the simple banter, Solomon marched on to the next group of gentlemen.

But luck finally struck as they came upon none other than Lord Henshell himself, the portly man enjoying a refreshment of champagne and laughing at some joke or tale relayed by the masked man who currently claimed his attention.

"My lord! Do save some drink for your guests, I beg you."

Solomon beamed as he and Henry approached Lord Henshell. Though Solomon outranked their host as an earl and Lord Henshell a baron, the jab landed playfully and elicited a nearly uncouth cackle from their friend. If Henry and Solomon had learned anything of the Baron of Henshell in their years of friendship forged through membership at Boodle's, it was that the man could and would drink to his heart's content.

"Overton, Neil, thank Heaven you are here. I could certainly use some help in making this delightful champagne scarce." Lord Henshell greeted the two men, quickly ignoring whichever poor gentleman had been hoping to make an impression on him.

They settled into friendly conversation and Henry found himself unwinding slightly. To say that he hated company would be a mistake. He simply chose his company very carefully—and at such a gathering as this, he could not tell where he might find a comforting presence. Save for Solomon, of course, and now Lord Henshell. A few more lords of their acquaintance joined their number and Henry felt more at ease within this small circle.

"Neil, how are you doing these days?" Lord Henshell asked as the group cycled through topics of interest.

"Quite well. Locked away in my study reading anything I can get my hands on, as usual." Henry swallowed as he lied.

Being a writer was his greatest joy, far more than being the Baron of Neil or having a great estate or being invited to all the best events hosted by the *ton*. Writing was his life and love. Though it was an eccentric hobby, he gladly whiled away his hours in his study, scribbling word after word, creating thrilling scenarios for intriguing characters with his imagination.

Indeed, as soon as his pen placed the last period on the page, Henry began work on his next adventure. He'd turned his most recent manuscript in at Frye Publishing just last week and they would ensure that it was fit for publication while he continued writing. Though it was just a few pages long yet, Henry had been loath to leave his work to attend this masquerade.

But no one aside from Solomon knew this. It was unusual for a man of Henry's standing to pursue such fancies, especially when an abundance of far more interesting pastimes could be had. Most of Henry's acquaintances knew and eventually accepted that he would never be found in a gambling hell or in the audience of a boxing match. They learned to leave him to his own devices in his library, where he did read a great deal. He simply left out any discussion of his primary occupation—writing a series of adventure novels.

Fortunately or unfortunately for Henry, Solomon—his dearest friend since their boarding days at Winchester—really did know him too well. Now that he was at the ball and in pleasant company, Henry could feel the tension slowly slipping from his cramped shoulders, all too often hunched over his writing desk. And it was Solomon, after all, who recognized Henry's gift for storytelling and convinced him to finally put his thoughts on paper, and then quietly passed his first manuscript along to Anthony Frye himself.

"We should consider ourselves lucky that Neil agreed to join us tonight," Solomon chimed with a laugh, clapping Henry on the shoulder. Henry knew Solomon jested but all the same he was glad that his blush could not be seen behind his full-face mask.

As the other men shared updates of their own lives, the music ceased. Dancers lingered on the floor and the guests on the sidelines craned their necks to determine the cause of the silence. The Master of Ceremonies came forward and announced, "Lady Henshell has selected a special performance by a very accomplished guest to be played on the pianoforte."

"Let's take a closer look, shall we?" Solomon elbowed Henry and nodded toward the band at the back of the room, the pianoforte barely visible between the press of shimmering dresses and sharply cut coats.

"Do we really need a closer look at a performance designed to delight our ears?" Henry retorted, perfectly content to remain with his companions.

"Must you always be so troublesome, dear Henry? A young and exceedingly talented pianoforte player has been talked of in town, and I have had the privilege of hearing her play at a number of dinners last Season. I simply wonder if it might be the same young lady." Considering the debate ended, Solomon made his way into the crowd.

Henry quickly caught up and asked, "And, if the lady is masked, how do you presume to know it is her?"

"I like to think that I possess a trained ear and can determine if she is one and the same."

"Do you have a particular interest in this young pianoforte player?" Henry knew the likely answer to this question, and the caution in his voice betrayed his suspicion, but he asked nonetheless.

"Heavens, no," Solomon scoffed. He sounded nearly offended that his friend would even consider the possibility. "But part of the entertainment of this ball is using one's intelligence to mentally unmask the revelers, is it not? I have my guess as to this lady's identity, and I should like to see if I am correct."

Henry could only shake his head and chuckle. Of course, everything with Solomon was a game or contest, either with himself or any unlucky man fool enough to test him. His attitude toward being leg-shackled anytime soon seemed unchanged.

They secured a spot closer to the pianoforte, but the crowd certainly hadn't thinned. Though Henry was of slightly taller than average height, he still struggled to see. Solomon, on the other hand, had an unrestricted view. Even with what he could see, the pianoforte was at an unfortunate angle for him to get a better look at the player. It was just as well. He needn't see to enjoy the music.

But as the young lady approached the instrument, a murmur swept through the crowd. Curious, Henry peered around the other guests. The glimpse he caught surprised him. Though he couldn't see much more than her back as she sat on the bench, he had to admit that the gown she wore was beautiful and she carried it with elegance. The soft cream fabric shimmered as she moved and her blonde curls glowed in the candlelight of the grand chandeliers. Whoever she was, she possessed a most becoming poise.

Despite the indication from Solomon and the Master of Ceremonies, Henry could feel his eyes go wide behind his mask as the music tumbled from her hands. The young woman's gift for the pianoforte stole his breath from his body. Her fingers flew over the keys with grace and precision, not a single note out of place. He didn't doubt that it was one of the most beautiful performances he'd ever heard.

And despite his earlier protests about seeing the performance instead of simply hearing it—as was the main purpose of music— Henry could not remove his eyes from her form as she played, swaying ever so slightly to the music. As the piece came to an end, her head turned just enough for Henry to see her side profile, hidden of course by a white half mask. But he could see the smile that tugged at the corner of her mouth as the last notes faded into silence.

Polite applause greeted the young woman as she rose from the instrument and Henry lost sight of her. But Solomon had seen all.

"A truly spectacular performance, wouldn't you say?" He peered at Henry through the gaps in his mask, his eyes dancing with mischief.

"Indeed. Breathtaking," Henry murmured, knowing that something he did not like was running through his friend's mind.

"The musicians will be starting back up shortly. You should dance at least one set, and I think I know just the young lady." Solomon grinned before darting away into the crowd.

"Wait!" Henry called out, but it was too late. His heart thudded in his chest, deeply embarrassed that his friend had noticed his interest. If it could even be called that.

As something of an artist himself, Henry appreciated fine music and the talent it took to practice and produce it. He would have thoroughly enjoyed the performance, regardless of who played the piece. But it was in Solomon's nature to weasel as much fun as he could out of any situation. Unfortunately, Solomon's fun was presently at Henry's expense.

Henry stood rooted to his spot, anxiety coursing through him, until the other guests began flowing around him and he realized he would soon be crushed under the feet of dozens of dancers if he didn't move out of the way. He stumbled toward the outskirts of the dance floor and he could feel beads of sweat forming at his temples.

This was not at all what he'd agreed to when he came out with Solomon tonight. Conversation, refreshments, perhaps a dance with someone of his choosing. He did not appreciate Solomon attempting to play matchmaker and forcing him into an unexpected situation. As he frantically scanned the room, Henry vowed to have some strong words with his friend. If he survived whatever was about to happen.

Thanks to Solomon's height and auburn hair, it wasn't difficult for Henry to spot him weaving through the guests toward him. "I hope you have not done what I think you've done," Henry whispered sharply as Solomon rejoined him.

The other man's coy smile was answer enough, but Solomon still defended himself. "It couldn't possibly be so horrible as you make it sound, Henry. You could use a little intrigue in your life once in a while. And what is tonight all about, if not intrigue?"

"Solomon, you kno—"

"She disappeared quickly but I managed to find where she's sitting. We must hurry, the next set will be starting soon." Solomon winked, cutting Henry's complaints off. With a firm hand on Henry's shoulder, Solomon steered them both across the room.

"But Solomon, do we know anyone in common who could even make the introduction?"

"Do not try to weasel out of this. Those rules are laxer at mysterious events such as this. Part of the fun is not knowing who you might come across, so no one will think you a rogue for not making a typical introduction."

Henry's jaw clenched. Guests swept past him in a blur, the different colored dresses melting together as his nerves thrashed against this unwanted, impertinent situation. The two men approached a small group of women seated together along the wall. There she was. The young woman who could make magic out of thin air.

"I'm off to fetch a drink. The rest is up to you," Solomon whispered in Henry's ear as they came up to the group and dashed away just like he'd done before. The ladies looked up at Henry, now alone.

A beat of awkward silence passed before Henry remembered what Solomon had cornered him into. He couldn't very well just stand there all evening, staring. "Good evening, madam." He turned his attention to the pianoforte player. "I greatly enjoyed your playing. May I ask for the next set?"

"I would be delighted," the mystery woman agreed, holding her hand out for Henry to take. He obliged, a shiver running through him as their gloved fingers made contact. As Henry lead her to the floor to join the set, he spied Solomon near a footman bearing glasses of champagne, chatting with a young lady.

They immediately fell into step together. Clearly musicality lived in everything the woman did. Henry could tell within seconds that she was also a very practiced dancer.

After a few moments of nothing but music between them, the young lady finally spoke, quiet and polite. "Thank you for your kind words earlier. Have you been enjoying your evening?"

Henry coughed. "It was indeed a splendid performance. My evening has become all the better for it." His voice came out gruffer than he intended, his nerves drying out his throat.

"You are too kind. It is simply a favorite pastime of mine." The young woman graced him with a humble smile. Henry sensed that she really did not view her talent as being particularly special, just something she enjoyed privately and occasionally shared. Not unlike himself.

"Ah, I understand and appreciate the sentiment."

"Oh?" Her head tilted to the side, soft curls bouncing slightly. "Are you an artist?"

Henry faltered, nearly crushing the poor woman's feet as his mind worked quickly to determine how much he should share. He ultimately erred on the side of caution. "Of a sort, you could say."

If she noticed his struggle, she didn't let on. She simply gave a small nod at his discretion.

"Isn't it wonderful to have a creative outlet? I do think more people would benefit from such hobbies that allow their minds and spirits to wander into other realms besides this physical one. Yet no one seems to put much store by it except for the great masters, and only those masters are really respected for their craft." She spoke softly, a wistful lilt to her voice.

Henry's heart flipped in his chest and he suddenly realized the anxiety that had seized it just moments ago had been replaced by another sensation, though he could not fathom how to describe it. How silly, he thought to himself—a writer unable to describe something.

"Yes, that is unfortunately true. It seems our world is full of small people with small minds. They don't know how little it costs to broaden one's perspective."

His own words surprised him. He certainly hadn't been intending to share any deep life insights. But the young woman nodded with an understanding smile.

"Too right you are. For some reason those wonderful adventure novels by that promising new author have come to mind." She paused thoughtfully, the corner of her mouth turning down slightly as she puzzled over her own words.

A sudden chill stole over Henry. He had no doubt she must be thinking of his anonymously published series. But why would she connect them with Henry's critical statement?

"Is that so?" Half of him did not wish to hear what the masked lady would have to critique about his work. But the other half needed to know, needed to understand what his writing lacked. Henry only hoped that he managed to keep the nerves out of his voice.

"I quite adore those books myself." The young woman hurried to continue. She seemed to sense that Henry had grown tense, but she didn't question it. "The hero is dashing, the adventures are exciting and terrifying and humorous and heartwarming all at once, and the writing is so eloquent. But…"

She paused again, her blue eyes narrowed as she pondered how to phrase her thoughts in a respectful way.

"But...something is missing?" Henry found himself offering, surprised by his own assessment.

"Yes, that's it." The young lady agreed with a grateful smile. "The stories are all full of brave, intelligent, reckless, honorable men who go to unimaginable lengths to right the wrongs that have been done in their world. But I can't help noticing that there are so few ladies with whom I can relate or aspire to be like. Ladies who can stand next to the hero against a foe or offer comfort. Perhaps such situations have simply never crossed the author's mind, but I think the books would be just perfect if they did. Women long for adventure and escape just as much as men do."

It was Henry's turn to pause. His brow furrowed under his mask as he let his dance partner's words sink in and take root. Perhaps his perspective did require some growth after all. He had to admit to himself that he had not given much consideration to writing female characters. But the young lady's observation was bright and astute. He ardently wished that he could thank her.

"That is very interesting. I'm sure the writer would have been happy to hear your thoughts on the matter."

A small smile painted her lips and her eyes sparkled. "I would very much enjoy having someone I could share such thoughts with, though I fear it is difficult to find such like-minded gentlemen. Save for yourself, of course."

Henry swallowed as a blush tinged his cheeks under his mask. "Indeed. Having similar interests is crucial for any long-term relationship if it is to be happy and fulfilling for both parties. And both partners should feel free to share their thoughts and interests with each other. That will make for a worthy match."

Silence followed Henry's statement and he realized after

refocusing on the lady's frozen face that perhaps he had been far too forward with his thoughts. Something about these masks must have loosened Henry's tongue.

"That is simply my opinion, at least. I am far from an expert in the matter," he mumbled.

"No, I think you absolutely have the right of it." The woman's voice sounded nearly dazed and she stared at Henry with interest. She appeared to be seriously considering his words. But she squeezed her eyes shut and returned to her previously unaffected and sweet demeanor, deftly changing the subject.

Though Henry had never been a particularly strong dancer, often struggling to keep conversation while minding his feet, he found that he needed little concentration for the movements now. Each step seemed to flow into the next with ease as he enjoyed both simple discussions and comfortable silences with his partner.

He couldn't stop himself from noticing the many charming nuances of the woman's countenance, from her perfectly bow shaped upper lip to the way her ringlets framed her round face. The glimpse of dark blue eyes behind her mask stirred his curiosity. If only he could see all her features put together properly.

Above all, Henry clung to every word she said. At times he struggled to hear her above the music and the general cacophony of noise that crowded the room, but something about the quiet timbre of her voice seemed to put him at ease. And she was clearly an intelligent and responsive woman with an appreciation for beauty. Something told him that so much more bubbled below the surface of this conversation that the current situation did not provide sufficient opportunity to discover.

The time slipped by and suddenly Henry found himself bowing to the young woman as she curtsied to him and turned away, swallowed by the throng of guests. For a wild moment he considered following her and asking her name.

But Solomon quickly squashed this impulse. He materialized at Henry's side and urgently whispered, "Come, it is time we take our leave. I cannot stand to be in this room another moment."

Alarmed, Henry allowed himself to be led out of Lord Henshell's ballroom. As they reached the double doors, he spared a glance back, hoping to catch a shimmer of blonde hair or cream satin. But there were far too many people for him to analyze in the mere moment he had before he and his friend quit the room.

It was just as well. Whatever interest the girl had sparked would remain trapped within these walls. True to his goal of secrecy, he'd never told her his name.

CHAPTER 3

"*S*issy? Are you meant to be practicing or daydreaming?" Juliet's voice startled Cecilia out of her reverie. She certainly meant to be practicing, but her mind had wandered back to a sore subject that had been heavily occupying it as of late.

"I see I've been found out," Cecilia admitted sheepishly, turning herself around to face her sister. She still sat at the bench, but her hands lay limp in her lap, the sheet music before her turned to the middle of a piece. It did not help Cecilia that after her perfect performance at Lady Henshell's ball nearly two weeks past, her hands seemed to freeze up whenever she approached the pianoforte.

"Still no word on your mystery gentleman?" Juliet sat next to Cecilia, the fabric of their dresses rustling against each other.

Cecilia smiled ruefully. Of course Juliet would have already known. "Luck is not on my side, it would seem."

Juliet took one of Cecilia's hands in her own and patted it gently. "You know I love you so, my dear sister, but perhaps it is time to move on from this train of thought. What good can come of dreaming about a man who wouldn't even give you his name?"

The words jolted through Cecilia, an equally embarrassed and disappointed knot forming in her stomach. Juliet had always been bold, willing to speak her mind, and lively—much to the chagrin of their mother, governesses, and schoolteachers. Yet the truth of the words, and the gravity with which she delivered them, still stung. She glanced over to her sister and saw only concern.

"I appreciate your candor, Jules. I know you must be right.... Yet I cannot shake this feeling that he was exactly the man I've been looking for these past two years. He had such a soft-spoken charm and he seemed so interested in everything I had to share about music and art."

Her head dropped down to her chest, defeat sinking in. "I simply cannot believe that none of our connections at the ball knew his identity or could even make a guess."

"Is it really so difficult to believe? You weren't forthcoming with your identity either." The motherly tone in Juliet's question clearly carried an implication Cecilia did not like. "You yourself begged Miss Henshell to leave your name out of your performance. I do believe only myself, Mama, and Miss Henshell knew it was you. And even now you refuse to claim responsibility for your playing."

Cecilia's cheeks flamed. Juliet's point did not go unheard. When had her little sister matured into such a sound thinker? Still, Cecilia knew she must defend herself.

"It is that very fact that allowed me to play so splendidly that night. No one knew it was me, so I felt as though I was simply playing here in the drawing room as I always do. Even though I'm asked to perform during dinners and dances, I'm always beset by nerves and it impacts my ability.

And even if that weren't the case, it would be exceedingly rude of me to presume to show off.

"And I fear that if I do claim responsibility, I will forever be held to that standard at every future event and that is an expectation I cannot force myself to meet. It would kill the joy of the art for me." With a voice to finally give them life, the words tumbled out of Cecilia.

She herself had only come to this conclusion slowly since the night of the masquerade. After the first few days of stilted playing, she realized that putting on the best performance of her life somehow put more pressure on her. And the question of the masked man she'd danced with only added to her clouded mental and emotional state.

Juliet sighed and shook her head slowly. "I suppose I can appreciate that, but you know I've never had any great love for the pianoforte or most other dear female accomplishments. I can't say I truly understand your predicament but I respect it."

She squeezed Cecilia's hand as if to emphasize her support. "I would just hate to see you waste away waiting for someone who may as well be nothing more than a mirage. Especially when there are many fine men who would happily ask for your hand—if only you'd let them."

Juliet's knowing look caused Cecilia's blush to deepen and she again rose to her own defense. "You know very well that most of those 'fine men' are only looking for a wife who will produce an heir and keep out of his business. I do not desire such a match in the least. There must be at least one man in all of London who hopes for a true companion in his wife, someone he can share himself with and she do the same. And I believe I danced with him that night..."

Though she had started strong in her argument, Cecilia could feel her despair—not just with this man but with her situation as a whole—breaking down her resolve.

"I do so admire your romantic ideals, Sissy. I wish I shared them—or any inclination toward marriage that seems so innate in our sex. Mama and Papa truly drew the short straw with this pair of stubborn daughters." Juliet chuckled, but there was little true humor in it.

"But you have been absolutely glowing since you made your debut. And you were quite popular for dances at Lady Henshell's ball. Are you so sure no one struck your fancy?"

For as close as they were, Cecilia and Juliet were opposites in many ways. But she was indeed correct. Their parents had been struggling to marry Cecilia off for two years, with another year shaping up to be just as unsuccessful. And Juliet still seemed disinclined to give them an easier time.

Cecilia had to admit that her sister's almost complete lack of interest in marrying at all did concern her greatly. At least Cecilia did wish to marry, but only to marry the right man, regardless of her parents' opinion on his rank. After all, marrying for social standing had not brought her parents any latent happiness.

So far the many elite men of the *ton* whom Mr. and Mrs. Richards would have been thrilled to have her marry had failed to set off that desperately desired spark in her. Cecilia had not lacked for suitors in her first Season, and even in her second.

But Cecilia knew the hope they carried during her first Season of finding a good match dwindled smaller by the day. Her mother's patience in particular grew dangerously thin. Cecilia knew she was on borrowed time, that her parents were near their wits end. Mrs. Richards had once been content with watching the suitors come to Cecilia and reveled in her eldest daughter's natural popularity. Her increasingly active role in managing Cecilia's appearance, behavior, and social calendar had not gone unnoticed.

Juliet was another tale entirely. She had always been a clever and independent girl, oftentimes to a troublesome degree. But even Cecilia had expected, or at least hoped, that she would mature into a slightly mellower young lady before her first Season. Juliet had certainly matured, as this conversation indicated, but she had matured even further into her own beliefs of independence.

"It is really not so different than your own convictions. I love being out in Society. The dances, the dinners, the socializing. I know for most women the goal is to marry. For me the goal is to enjoy every moment on my own terms. I don't know if there is a man in all of England who would allow me that after we were wed."

Juliet's expression grew dark. A lump rose in Cecilia's throat. She hadn't realized how deeply this issue troubled her sister, nor how hypocritical she'd been for expecting Juliet to mold herself to ideals that did not suit her.

"It seems we are both in quite a bind," Cecilia whispered. "There is only one thing that can sooth our worries now."

Juliet shot a sideways glance at her older sister and raised an eyebrow. Based on how many times Cecilia had seen that same expression over the course of their lives, she would have happily placed a wager that Juliet had been born with it.

"An ice from Gunter's!" she cheered, springing off the bench. Juliet's momentary shock was quickly replaced by a beaming smile, her eyes sparkling with excitement. There was nothing in the world that a sweet treat couldn't fix, at least for a moment.

"Ah, just in time!" Mr. Richards's booming voice caught them at the bottom of the stairs, freshly changed into comfortable walking dresses. He'd just stepped out of the library.

"Papa, we were just on our way to Gunter's," Cecilia explained quickly. After her suggestion to Juliet, she found that she desperately needed to get out of doors and distract her restless mind with the hustle and bustle of London.

"Surely you wouldn't mind some company then." Their father beamed, his exceptionally good mood radiating in every word. He disappeared back into the library. The sisters exchanged nervous glances with each other.

A few moments later he emerged from the library, followed by two gentlemen. "My lords, I am delighted to introduce you to my daughters, Miss Richards and Miss Juliet." The two sisters curtsied respectfully. "And these fine men are the Earl of Overton and the Lord Neil." The two men dipped their heads in acknowledgement.

The atmosphere immediately changed as soon as introductions were made. Juliet went stiff next to Cecilia and the younger woman scooted even closer to her side. From the corner of her eye, Cecilia could see that Juliet's naturally doe-like eyes had become even bigger, and they were glued to the taller of the two men, the one with dark reddish hair—the well-known Earl of Overton.

Mr. Richards chuckled, looking between Juliet and Lord Overton. "I suppose I didn't need to make an introduction between the two of you. But there, it is official now."

The realization suddenly dawned on Cecilia. Juliet had mentioned this man in the days following Lady Henshell's masked ball. He had asked for a dance shortly after Cecilia had been whisked away onto the floor. But unlike Cecilia and her partner, they'd had the good sense to exchange names. Though Juliet hadn't expressed any particular interest in him over the other numerous gentlemen she'd danced with.

"Juliet, Lord Overton has requested your company on a

carriage ride today. Though I don't suppose he would be opposed to a stop at Gunter's for your ice?" Mr. Richards posed the question to the earl.

"Of course not." He smiled graciously. "My friend Lord Neil is happy to accompany us wherever we may choose to wander."

The other man simply cleared his throat and looked down the hallway toward the front door. He clearly had no interest in playing chaperone but he'd been dragged along somehow.

"Why don't you make a true outing of it and take Cecilia along!" Mr. Richards declared, taking Cecilia by the hand and pulling her forward.

She could feel her ears and cheeks burning. Of course, she knew exactly what her father was trying to do. Her parents would be thrilled if they could get rid of both daughters in one fell swoop. And to a baron and an earl, no less. It would be a dream come true for them.

"Oh please do, Sissy. Wouldn't that be so fun?" Juliet suddenly transformed back into her usually cheerful self, clinging to Cecilia's elbow. But Cecilia could see the plea in her sister's eyes. Juliet did not want to go on this outing for whatever reason, but if she must then she did not want to go alone.

And realistically, Cecilia knew that if her father pressed it, she had no choice. "I'm sure we'll all have a grand time," she acquiesced.

THE CARRIAGE RIDE to Gunter's felt every bit as awkward as Cecilia imagined it would. Lord Overton engaged Juliet in conversation and Juliet responded with a cheer that only Cecilia could see through.

Lord Neil, on the other hand, appeared entirely uninterested in either joining their conversation or striking one up with Cecilia. He simply gazed out to the passing streets and buildings and people. Cecilia did the same. On the one hand, she supposed she couldn't blame him. She too was an unwilling participant in this excursion. But if they were lumped in together, the least he could have done was try to put her at ease as any well-mannered man should.

Cecilia hardly remembered the ride to Gunter's being so long, nor the waiter being so slow to bring their ices out to them as they waited in the carriage under the shade of the trees. The sweet dessert did soothe her frazzled mind a bit, but the trip had turned out very differently than she'd hoped.

Lord Overton and Juliet continued to chatter and, as Cecilia glanced out of the corner of her eye at her sister seated next to her, she noticed that her smile and interest appeared more genuine as time went on. Those two were slowly being sequestered into their own world. The man across from her, however, ate his ice as morosely as possible, a feat that Cecilia had not known could be accomplished. Clearly, it fell on her shoulders to turn this event around.

"Lord Neil, are you enjoying your ice?" Cecilia put every ounce of grace she could muster into her voice.

He coughed suddenly, seemingly caught off guard by the question, or by the reminder of Cecilia's presence. "Yes, indeed." He quickly checked his coat to ensure that he hadn't spilled on himself.

"Forgive me, but your name sounds familiar. Do I know you from somewhere?" The question that had been poking at the back of Cecilia's mind finally came out. The more she'd pondered over it on the carriage ride, the more she felt certain that she must have heard his name before.

"Oh, I think not." He coughed again, and his jaw clenched. His eyes remained fixed on his slowly melting ice.

"Do tell, my lord. Are you one of those famous Corinthians everyone in town so admires?" Cecilia knew it was a bit forward of her to press, but her reluctant companion had something to hide, and her curiosity impelled her to bend the rules.

"Quite the opposite," Lord Overton laughed, turning his attention to their conversation. "My good Lord Neil is a humble man. So humble that he rarely emerges from his study or library save for when I'm around. He's best known for being one of the most reserved gentlemen in the *ton*."

Of course! It seemed so obvious now. Cecilia certainly knew of Lord Overton and they had even attended a few mutual events during her past two Seasons though they'd never been formally introduced. But now she knew where she'd heard her reluctant companion's name before. Cecilia almost always heard of a mysterious Lord Neil discussed alongside Lord Overton. And while many in Society respected Lord Neil for his quiet and stoic poise, that respect did not always shield him from whispers about his unusual reclusive nature.

But finally Cecilia found something that could steer her in the right direction with the sulky man before her.

"You must do a great deal of reading in your library then, Lord Neil. Which books have captured your attention these days?" She asked with a gentle smile, hoping to coax at least a little amiable conversation out of the baron.

"I read all sorts," was all he offered, eyes narrowed at his ice.

"Those adventure novels written by that anonymous fellow have certainly been gaining popularity, haven't they? Do you know of them, Miss Richards?" Lord Overton intervened yet again, with an almost mischievous glance at the baron. He seemed practiced at drawing discussion out of his friend, or at least trying.

"I highly doubt she's read any," Lord Neil mumbled in response, glaring over the side of the carriage.

Cecilia jerked back at his response, surprised by the scorn she heard. Why should it seem so unlikely to him that she would read those works?

"Ah, do you think I'm not well read, my lord? I read all sorts as well, including those books." Cecilia could barely keep the spite out of her voice now. There were few things that bothered Cecilia more than being thought a vapid woman, something that all the men that had come and gone from her life seemed unable or unwilling to understand.

"Sissy..." Juliet hissed, surprise momentarily overtaking her normally pleasant expression. For once, it was Juliet's turn to censure her sister.

"I-I did not mean that." Lord Neil's eyes finally made contact with Cecilia's, and guilt immediately squeezed her chest. Gone was the boredom and frustration she thought she'd seen earlier. Now he looked panicked and embarrassed.

"Of course he didn't!" Lord Overton cheerily attempted to correct the course of the conversation. "Lord Neil has been a champion of this series since its very first installment. Unfortunately, he has not found many ladies who seem interested in such thrilling tales. They find them too harrowing."

Cecilia swallowed and mumbled, "I suppose I must confess I also have not met many other women who read adventure novels." She turned her face down, allowing her bonnet to shield her shame, unable to bring herself to look into the face of the man she just terribly insulted. No amount of ice from Gunter's could soothe the heat pooling in her face and neck.

"You have interesting taste," Lord Neil responded curtly. Cecilia's mission of making at least a pleasant acquaintance for the duration of the outing was turning into quite the disaster.

"The stories are not too harrowing for you, Miss Richards?" Lord Overton's question seemed simple on the surface, but the look in his eye sent a shiver through her. He was giving her an opportunity to defend herself.

"They are indeed harrowing, but that's what I enjoy about them. I wish more ladies would give them a chance. They're a breath of fresh air and they offer the excitement we could all use from time to time."

The explanation sounded horribly weak after her ill-mannered accusation, despite its truth. She lowered her head again to avoid seeing the judgement in Lord Neil's and Lord Overton's eyes, paying excruciating attention to the ice in her hands.

"Oh yes!" Juliet chirped. "When my sister isn't practicing pianoforte she can be found tucked away in some corner with her nose in a book." The younger woman turned to Cecilia with a charming smile. Cecilia silently thanked Juliet for trying to salvage the situation by steering the discussion back towards more pleasant waters.

"Pianoforte, you say?" This time Lord Overton sounded genuinely curious. "I do believe I have had the honor of hearing you play at past events."

"I am sure you have. Cecilia is often asked to perform when she is invited to dinners and dances," Juliet answered once again.

Cecilia's stomach churned and she shot her sister a warning glance. She still did not wish to have her performance at the masked ball exposed, especially now that she had made a fool of herself in front of an earl and a baron.

"And what of you?" Lord Overton turned his attention back to Juliet. "Do you have any particular pastimes you enjoy?"

"I fear I do not share the same level of artistic skill as Cecilia. If I must remain indoors, sketching will entertain me. But I much prefer to be out and about in the open air, especially in such charming company." She gave a demure smile, eyes flickering up to Lord Overton's face, before continuing. "And when Papa allows it, I enjoy taking our little tilbury for a drive."

Juliet's voice lilted perfectly, both modest and engaging at the same time. Cecilia had always admired the ease with which her younger sister could flatter just about anyone.

"You two make quite the interesting pair of sisters." Lord Overton nodded approval at his own statement. He seemed to have forgotten entirely about Cecilia's earlier disgraceful outburst. Lord Neil, it would appear, had not. His gaze remained on the world outside of their conversation, his ice quite abandoned.

The rest of their party soon abandoned their treats as well and took up Lord Overton's suggestion to walk about Berkeley Square before returning to the Richards home. Cecilia heartily accepted the idea, eager to get out of the confines of the carriage where she had no choice but to directly face Lord Neil.

With a footman following behind at a respectful distance, the two pairs strolled past the shops of Berkeley Square. Naturally, Lord Overton took Juliet's hand through his arm and lead her down the street. Lord Neil silently offered his own arm to Cecilia—nothing more than a mere courtesy. Though they were physically closer than they had been in the carriage, her hand resting gently on his arm, Cecilia was glad that she could distract herself by observing the scenery, her bonnet obscuring her view of the baron at her side.

They walked in silence, but something about his presence —perhaps the feeling of his arm beneath her hand, or the way he walked—struck a chord within Cecilia. But she knew that any interest, no matter how slight, she may have had in the man would go nowhere. Surely he would be only too happy to never see her again. And even if he did wish to, he could only serve as a temporary distraction from the true focus of Cecilia's heart and mind: her charming masked gentleman.

CHAPTER 4

$\mathcal{T}$he sound of Henry's pulse rushing in his ears drowned out all his other thoughts. His arm burned where Miss Richards's small hand rested on his coat sleeve. He became aware of every step he took, wondering if they were too long or too short or if he even walked in a straight line.

Henry could not believe his unfortunate luck to be caught in yet another unexpected situation with a stranger. Though this time he could not fault Solomon. After Lord Henshell's ball, Henry had thoroughly chastised Solomon. His friend gave a heartfelt apology and promised not to pull such a stunt again.

Unfortunately, today's stunt had been pulled by Mr. Richards, leaving Henry in no position to refuse politely. But by now he certainly wished that he had.

The eldest of the Richards sisters had clearly been uninterested in joining Solomon's plan to make a real introduction with the younger Miss Richards. Henry had to admit that they had both been thrown into this uncomfortable position by her overly enthusiastic father.

Having met many men like Mr. Richards—with fortunes and fancy homes but no titles—Henry was positive that the gentleman saw potential for a match, possibly for both his daughters. And Henry was also positive that he would be disappointed on both counts.

But as he walked with Miss Richards on his arm and observed the other pair ahead of them, pointing out things or people they noticed and chatting amiably, Henry was once again struck by this unusual excursion.

Of course, Solomon was not without his pick of interested high-born ladies. And unlike Henry, he made sure to politely entertain each one at least for a time. A dance there or a carriage ride here, and then Solomon would withdraw quietly, leaving some other gentleman to finish his work and make a wife out of an eager young woman.

While Solomon enjoyed the temporary company, Henry never followed up with any ladies who may have taken a fancy to him, or at least his title. And Society's knowledge of his preference toward a shut-in lifestyle certainly helped to keep most acquaintances, man or woman, at bay. Everyone except Solomon, of course, who managed to bring Henry out to their club often enough to keep the public from speculating about his death.

Needless to say, Henry could hardly believe his ears when Solomon told him that he'd like to call upon a particular young lady. Though it was not quite what his friend had said, but how he'd said it, as well as his strange behavior following the masked ball.

In all their years of schooling and bachelorhood together —and knowing Solomon's unkind thoughts toward marriage —Henry had never seen such an earnest desire in his friend's eyes when he suggested they pay a visit to the Richards home. Nor had he ever seen Solomon so flustered as when they rushed out of Lord Henshell's ballroom. He hadn't said much about his dance, only that his partner had been such an uncommon woman that he had to remove himself from her presence as quickly as possible.

"Sissy! Look here!" Solomon's walking partner beckoned over her shoulder. She had broken away from Solomon's side and stood pressed against a shop window, excitedly peering in at whatever was on display.

Miss Richards suddenly came to life at her sister's call, a gleaming smile lighting up her countenance which had heretofore been quite downcast. She stepped forward to join Miss Juliet at the window.

Henry guessed that she must have felt badly about her accusation against him for she had been all but mute since. He knew he should say something to ease her mind, to assure her that he had not taken offense, to declare that he would never think such a well-mannered young lady would be uneducated or unintelligent.

But the fact of the matter was that he had taken some offense, though his wounded pride seemed to be recovering quickly as they walked together in silence. He would never have dared to question a lady's intellectual pursuits. Luckily Solomon had come to his rescue with a clever half-truth. It was true that his books were most popular among male readers. And he still found it rather unusual to hear of anyone reading his books, regardless of their sex—though if conversation turned to that subject, he merely pretended to be a fellow interested reader.

In any case, Henry did not appreciate being made out to be of such poor character. Yet even as the memory flared a fresh anger in his chest, he also knew that he had not been the most pleasant of companions thus far. And he had not planned on seeking another meeting with Miss Richards, even before their unpleasant exchange. He would much prefer to be reunited with his book, currently waiting for him on his desk.

"Though they may seem rather different in interest and temperament, the two make quite a pair of happy creatures," Solomon chuckled as Henry drew up beside him, his eyes fixed on the two young women. They seemed to have completely forgotten their companions, so enraptured by what Henry now saw was a beautiful dress in a modiste's window.

"You speak as if you know them well." Henry glanced at his friend, curious to see where Solomon's mind was.

"I do not." Solomon cleared his throat and lifted his chin up, a habit Henry learned long ago that meant he was trying to hide something. "It is a simple assessment. Miss Juliet is quite the conversationalist so I feel I have been given enough of the picture to make it."

Henry returned his attention to the Richards sisters and truly observed them. Though they were clearly from the same family, Solomon had been correct in saying that they were individuals unto themselves.

While Juliet Richards's flaxen hair sparkled, Cecilia Richards's honey gold hair glowed. The younger was shorter and wound like a spring, and the older was taller and carried herself with grace. One preferred open-air activities and the other enjoyed dinners with music. But they both shared a bubbling enthusiasm and sometimes surprising frankness. The sisters both eagerly admired the dress, but Henry could see that only one pair of eyes followed every detail of the stitching, embroidery, and ruffles.

He admired such qualities, but they had no place in his life.

"Wouldn't Mama love to see one of us in this gown?" The younger sister cooed, her pale blue eyes skimming over the surface of the dress, admiring the grand view.

"Oh Juliet, you know such a fine dress would surely suit you better, especially for your first Season. Perhaps Mama would have considered it for me a couple years ago. And besides, I've already had my turn in beautiful gowns this year."

As her deep blue eyes followed the cascade of embroidered rosettes over the bodice of the dress, something about the statement struck Henry as odd. In a flash he realized that his walking partner must have been the same Miss Richards that Solomon had confirmed earlier, the accomplished pianoforte player.

But she was also the same Miss Richards whom he'd heard whispers of amongst the *ton*, the title-hungry gentleman's daughter who entertained a suitor for a few weeks before moving on to another, never allowing one man to get close enough to offer for her hand.

Since she remained unwed, some speculated that she—or her parents—held out for the highest bidder. Others suggested that she simply enjoyed the attention and clicked their tongues at this nearly indecorous behavior. Though Henry didn't keep up with such news, it hadn't escaped his attention. More than one man at Boodle's had attempted to court her but been kindly set aside.

A sting of shock ran through him as he focused his attention on Miss Richards again, not sure what to believe about this young lady he'd spent his day with. An equally uncomfortable realization followed quickly on the heels of this thought.

Why should it matter to him what her reputation said, or which story was the truth? Before Henry could get lost in his suddenly frenzied thoughts, Solomon distracted him.

"I do believe the only thing that could rival such a lovely gown would be the fresh blossoms just coming out in the garden." He flashed his winning smile and the two young women turned away from the window to return their own. Henry stiffly nodded his agreement and looked away as Miss Richards's eyes trailed to him.

Drat that Solomon. Such words came so easily to him in conversation, yet Henry could only produce the same line if he was at his writing desk, pen in hand. Still, he filed a variation of it away for potential future use.

Now that their attention was pulled away from the dress, the group continued the walk, making their way toward the garden. With the Season now in full swing and spring seeping into the London air with each passing day, the garden grew lush once more, attracting many noble visitors.

They walked along the perimeter of the garden, allowing the tall trees overhanging the fence to shade them. A slight breeze slipped around Henry, and he realized that despite the awkwardness, the day had an idyllic quality. He and Solomon walked side by side now while the women walked ahead, chatting happily with each other as if no one else—and certainly not these two unfamiliar men—existed.

"Do you hear that birdsong, Jules? How lovely! I do think I could transfer it to the pianoforte." Miss Richards gripped her younger sister's elbow, a dazzling smile lighting up her face.

The younger woman shook her head and chuckled. "Only you would notice such a thing, Sissy."

Miss Richards wrinkled her nose in response, bottom lip poking out slightly—quite an endearing expression. Henry sensed that, in addition to her artistic talent, this woman possessed both a sharp mind and a spirited sense of humor.

His suspicions were confirmed as they rounded a corner and Miss Richards spied something that had her nearly bouncing on her toes. Her gloved hand shot into the air for half a second before she remembered her manners and tucked it back near her torso, restricting her greeting to a polite wave. A quiet laugh escaped Henry at the sight. There was no doubt that she was a well-bred young lady, but it seemed her enthusiasm got the better of her at times. Henry certainly couldn't fault her for that.

"How lovely to see you, Mrs. Ashby!" Miss Richards exclaimed to a woman coming towards them from the opposite corner. Everything in Miss Richards's world seemed to be lovely.

She strolled forward, her pale blue walking dress swishing about her feet. Mrs. Ashby unlinked her arm from the older man in her company and met Miss Richards halfway. She was older than Miss Richards but still youthful, and the warm smile on her face showed that she held Miss Richards in high esteem.

Miss Juliet hung back until Solomon and Henry drew up beside her. "A good friend?" Solomon asked.

"Of Cecilia's, yes. She's made many close friends and acquaintances during her past few years in London. Despite the fact that she says she prefers being at home alone with her instrument, she is quite the social butterfly. She is always being called upon or invited out by some lady or other." She watched her sister catch up with her friend, giggling and animated, with admiration.

Whatever Miss Richards's reputation might have been in Society, those who knew her clearly adored and respected her.

But Henry noticed Miss Juliet's eyes dart to the gentleman accompanying Mrs. Ashby—most likely her husband. Her normally friendly pale blue eyes narrowed almost imperceptibly while her lips pursed. The expression only lasted a moment but Henry gathered that she possessed an unflattering opinion of him.

"And is that not the case for you?" Solomon pried, peering into the younger sister's doll-like face. Henry gagged and nearly kicked his friend in the ankle. Only Solomon would think it a perfectly acceptable topic of casual conversation to ask a lady about her social engagements and popularity.

Rather than take offense, she simply laughed, the sound drawing a few curious glances their way. "I'm just a few weeks into my first Season, but I find that I am making new connections. Having my sister's connections to draw upon helps immensely. I suspect by Season's end I will be drowning in invitations from all the best ladies in town." The girl tossed her head, chin thrust into the air for a moment before casting a mischievous glance to them.

Solomon smiled and lowered his voice. "I am sure you will have far more company than you know what to do with, my lady. I do feel sorry for those who must fight for your attention." This comment earned a demure smile but knowing gaze from the young Miss Richards, and a gruff cough from Henry.

Henry's discomfort was back in full force as some sort of strange energy passed between Solomon and his companion. He stepped beyond them, closer to Miss Richards and her friends though he did not wish to be drawn into their conversation either. But he cared not to be part of Solomon's coquetry.

"Ah, here is one of them now!" Miss Richards must have spotted Henry inching closer. "This is Lord Neil. He and his friend over there, the Earl of Overton, are kindly escorting Juliet and I about town today. Lord Neil, this is my friend Mrs. Tabitha Ashby and her husband Mr. Lionel Ashby." She looked back and forth eagerly between the parties as she made the introduction.

From his peripheral vision Henry could see that Solomon and his new friend were engaged in deep conversation. He was far better off here with Miss Richards and this couple. "A pleasure," he murmured, tipping his hat to them.

"Lord Neil..." Mr. Ashby's eyes narrowed as they scanned Henry up and down, his name rolling curiously out of the man's mouth. "Why, you must be Lord Overton's studious friend."

Henry's eyes darted to the ground and bounced from one pair of feet to the next. Would he ever become used to this? Being so closely linked to such a well-known figure as Solomon naturally brought Henry's name to attention more than he'd like. Others often recognized his name upon introduction merely because of his association with the Earl of Overton. Some even recognized him by sight if they happened to see him out in Solomon's company. But no matter how many times Henry found himself drawn into Solomon's orbit, he found himself wishing he could escape the attention and materialize back in the safety of his study or library.

"Indeed he is! I am very lucky to share his company today." Miss Richards flashed him a warm smile. At least, it probably seemed warm to the Ashbys. Henry, on the other hand, knew that it was likely nothing more than an obligation, especially considering their earlier misstep with each other.

"And I am honored to partake in this fine day with such gracious ladies." Henry returned the compliment, the words stumbling out as he tried to strike upon the best thing to say. Stringing words together on the spot verbally was not his forte. The raised eyebrows on Miss Richards's winsome face indicated that he'd done well.

With introductions out of the way, Miss Richards and Mrs. Ashby quickly returned to their conversation, filling each other in on the events they'd attended thus far, events they hoped to be invited to, who had called upon them, and of course blossoming courtships.

"I confess I am not much of a reading man myself," Mr.

Ashby's said, his deep voice rumbling through his rotund chest. Eyes still narrowed, he watched his young wife converse with Miss Richards.

"That's quite alright. I myself am not much of a hunting man. Or a gambling man. Or a drinking man."

Henry kept his gaze towards the two women but monitored Mr. Ashby's reaction from the corner of his eye. The man was markedly older than his wife—not an entirely uncommon sight. But his instinct told him that Mr. and Mrs. Ashby did not possess many shared interests or personality traits.

He could see it in the way the older man eyed his wife like a hawk, watching for any blunders. And he heard it in the way Mr. Ashby snorted in response to Henry's lack of interest in most manly pursuits.

"How can women possibly have so much to discuss when most of their time is spent in this drawing room or that drawing room, or at dinner parties or on walks?" His voice carried a scathing tone that made Henry decidedly uncomfortable.

He did not pretend to be an expert on female forms of entertainment and social life, but Henry knew there must be some value in the activities women occupied themselves with. And besides, Mrs. Ashby and Miss Richards seemed to be enjoying themselves plenty.

"Aren't you out on a walk yourself just now, sir?" The slightly snide question slipped out before Henry could think of something more appropriate to say.

Mr. Ashby's eyes finally tore away from his wife long enough to glower at Henry. "Walking is such a dull pastime. But my dear wife insists on it at least once a week. As newly-weds we are supposed to be seen out and about in each other's company, so she says." He snorted again, a growling emphasis on "dear wife."

Henry nearly snorted to himself at the idea of Mrs. Ashby being taken out for a walk around the Square once a week as if she were the household pet. "I suppose newlyweds are typically supposed to be fond of each other, or so I've heard."

He'd struck a sour chord with his new acquaintance. Mr. Ashby cleared his throat, his neckcloth appearing to choke him for a moment, and he crossed his arms in his nearly too short coat sleeves. Henry found that he didn't mind. This was not a connection he had any interest in fostering. He kept his circle small and for very good reason. Avoiding men like Mr. Ashby was one of them.

Instead, he watched Miss Richards as she excitedly shared news with her friend, her face alight with genuine interest and affection. Unlike Henry, she never seemed at a loss for spoken words. He wondered if she knew what lay behind the frail façade of her friend's recent marriage.

When Mr. Ashby barked to his wife that they should carry on to be back in time for dinner—and Miss Richards's expression fell into something nearing despair for a fraction of a moment before waving her friend off—Henry knew that she knew.

As Mr. Ashby quickly steered his wife past their group, Mrs. Ashby turned back to Miss Richards and called, "Do come by for dinner later this week!"

Miss Richards approached Henry but her eyes remained on her friend as the other woman was led away by her husband. He could see concern etched in the furrow of her brow.

"A charming couple," Henry mumbled, not trying to keep the tinge of sarcasm out of his voice.

Miss Richards pursed her lips and shrugged her slender shoulders. "It is unfortunately obvious, isn't it?"

"If I may ask, how did Mrs. Ashby find herself in such a...an interesting match?" Henry felt confident enough that

Miss Richards shared his opinion of the Ashbys's marriage to ask this slightly rude question.

"I met Mrs. Ashby in my first Season two years ago, when she was still Miss Dunn. She's several years my senior and had been out for several Seasons already by the time I made her acquaintance. Her father is quite a successful business-man, but even still, finding a worthy husband proved to be challenging. They held out as long as they could, but eventually Mr. Ashby came along and Mr. Dunn realized he would be as good as his daughter would find lest she become a spin-ster." Her voice was quiet and heavy with sadness, her eyes faraway in memory.

"That is quite unfortunate indeed."

"Unfortunate or not, it is the way of the world at present. At least for quite a few matches I've seen." The sharp bitter tone in Miss Richards's voice caught Henry off guard, but she hastily changed the subject. "Let's untangle those two, shall we?"

Miss Richards marched past Henry toward Solomon and her sister, calling out to them in her cheery voice. They both jumped at the intrusion. The younger woman's cheeks colored with an attractive rosy hue and Solomon cleared his throat and glanced around, anywhere but either sister.

Their excursion naturally seemed to be approaching its end. Henry and Solomon escorted their respective compan-ions back to the carriage. Solomon and Miss Juliet walked arm in arm, discussing anything and everything in the process.

Henry and Miss Richards walked arm in arm without conversation. But Henry could feel the slight vibration from Miss Richards's body as she hummed quietly to herself. He had to admit, she certainly was an interesting young woman. But she didn't seem particularly keen on him or his reserved, awkward demeanor.

Even if she had been keen—Henry quickly reminded himself—watching her floating through the world, gushing over a beautiful dress, smiling with her sister, striking up a conversation on the street, and hearing of her vibrant social life.... He knew that there was no place for such a woman in his home.

In fact, as soon as the Richards sisters were dropped off at their home, Henry planned to honor a highly important engagement with his manuscript, waiting patiently for him on his writing desk.

Dinners and dances and calls upon neighbors—everything that Miss Richards found so lovely—would never be part of Henry's life.

CHAPTER 5

"*U*gh!" Cecilia stood so quickly that the bench scraped harshly against the wood floor, her fingers crashing down onto the keys as she pushed herself away from the pianoforte. She pressed a hand to her forehead and glared at the instrument, allowing frustration to overtake her for a moment.

After taking a deep breath, Cecilia crossed the room and collapsed into the plush armchair situated by the window. Once again, she'd made a silly mistake on a simple piece. A player of her caliber should have been able to execute it flawlessly.

How disappointing, she lamented to herself, gazing out the window. With her elbow propped up on the armrest, Cecilia let her chin fall into her palm. She knew it wasn't a very ladylike pose, but she was alone in the study and she had no one to impress here.

At least, until her mother walked into the room.

"Ah, there you are. Cecilia dear, do take heed of your posture." Mrs. Richards's voice sounded weary, as if every moment her daughter continued to live in this house was a burden. Cecilia wrinkled her nose but sat up straight, back rigid and hands neatly folded in her lap. Satisfied, Mrs. Richards continued. "If you have any engagements tomorrow evening, cancel them."

"May I ask why?" Cecilia didn't have any engagements tomorrow evening as a matter of fact, but the sudden demand for cancellation surprised her. Something far better, in her mother's estimation, must have presented itself.

"We have been invited to dine with the Earl of Overton at his home." Though Mrs. Richards tried to pass off the statement as normal—nothing less than what their family deserved or expected—Cecilia could see the hopeful shimmer in her mother's eyes.

"Ah. Delightful." A few days had passed since their outing with Lord Overton and Lord Neil. She shouldn't have been surprised that they would receive such an invitation considering how taken the earl had seemed with Juliet.

Even still, Cecilia was not eager to run into the man again, and especially not his brooding friend. She was sure she had not left a favorable impression on either of them thanks to her untoward behavior regarding Lord Neil. Though Lord Neil had proven to be more complex than she'd originally imagined, he still clearly found her presence to be irksome at best.

"I will not tolerate any unpleasantness from you at this event, Cecilia," Mrs. Richards barked. "Your future grows bleaker by the day but your sister still has hope. If the earl favors her, we cannot allow anything to happen that might damage her chances."

Cecilia knew she was right, but the words still cut. She swallowed the lump forming in her throat. She wouldn't let her mother break her down. Of course she didn't want to end up in a loveless match like her friend Mrs. Ashby or her own parents, but Cecilia was not ready to give up on her

ideals just yet. Not while that masked gentleman was somewhere in London.

"And the earl has graciously requested that you perform a
piece on his pianoforte. I trust that you will be busy readying
yourself until then." Mrs. Richards let the words slam into
Cecilia while she strode out of the room, the sound of the
door clicking shut behind her sounding like an avalanche to
Cecilia.

The lump in her throat that she'd tried so hard to smother
earlier unraveled itself and her tears rushed forward.
Suddenly her body felt far too heavy to support the turmoil
inside her and she buried her face into her hands, the heat
from her breath suffocating her, the sound of her shaky sobs
deafening her.

Perfect. Not only did she have to suffer another meeting
with Lord Overton, and most likely Lord Neil, but she would
have to perform. Just a few weeks ago, the inevitable nerves
would have been accompanied by a healthy dose of excitement. Just a few weeks ago she had loved playing, whether
she was alone in the study or surrounded by elite guests in a
glittering drawing room.

Ever since the fancy dress ball, her skills had regressed by
years. At times she felt like a young girl again, stumbling
through a lesson with her music master, fingers stiff and
eyes unable to recognize simple phrases in the sheet music.
Juliet insisted that she still played better than most young
ladies who collected the skill merely to add it to their reper-
toire of accomplishments, that she was being far too hard on
herself.

But that was not enough for Cecilia. She simply didn't
understand why she should struggle so much now. Why was
sitting at the pianoforte a chore rather than a joy? What
could be blocking her mind from performing to her usual
standard? The thought that Cecilia might be losing her love

for the artistry she'd cultivated for much of her life was terrifying.

"Sissy? My goodness! Whatever is the matter, dear?" Juliet's sweet voice floated into the room but Cecilia didn't pick up her face from her hands. In an instant, her sister's arms cradled her about the shoulders, one hand patting her back and the other slowly stroking her hair.

Cecilia didn't respond, instead allowing herself to be comforted by Juliet.

"I ran into Miss Henshell in the foyer, she's here to pay you a visit. I had her brought to the drawing room and came to fetch you myself. Should I tell her you're indisposed?" Juliet asked, continuing her soft ministrations.

With a sniffle and a steadying breath, Cecilia sat up straight again. "No, we can go see her. I just need a moment to gather myself."

Cecilia took her moment and threaded her arm through Juliet's as they made their way to the drawing room.

"Oh my.... Perhaps now is not a good time?" Rosamund stood as Cecilia and Juliet entered the room. Her eyes immediately searched Cecilia's face, noticing the red eyes and nose and blotchy cheeks.

"No, that's quite alright Rosamund. You've come all this way to call on me and I appreciate that." Cecilia chuckled ruefully, taking a seat near her friend.

Rosamund smiled and resumed her seat, a small table between them.

"Shall I call for tea?" Juliet asked, patting Cecilia's knee. Cecilia nodded and her sister crossed the room to ring the service bell.

"Do tell us what causes you such grief," Rosamund ventured. Her usual vivacious and playful demeanor had disappeared, replaced by worry. Juliet returned and took her own seat near the other women.

"Well I've just had some...news. From Mama." Cecilia sniffled as a measure of calm returned to her, at least enough for her to string together some coherent thoughts.

"About the dinner invitation from Lord Overton?" Juliet tilted her head curiously.

"The Earl of Overton, you mean? We've been invited as well," Rosamund queried.

"Yes. Though that is not the whole of it I suppose..." Cecilia inhaled deeply several times. Her sister and friend remained silent, allowing Cecilia the time she needed to gather herself. "Mama informed me that Lord Overton has specifically requested that I play on his pianoforte at dinner."

"Well, isn't that a good thing? You're a marvelous player, Cecilia. It speaks to your skill that Lord Overton would ask you to play for himself and his guests," Rosamund offered, the confusion in her voice masked by an attempt at positivity and cheer.

Juliet glanced to Cecilia, the corner of her mouth turned down. Cecilia hadn't spoken of it much in the days following their outing with Lord Overton and his friend. She hated to admit the power this conundrum had over her. Perhaps Juliet figured that the problem had managed to work itself out. Unfortunately, this was far from the case.

A maid entered the room with a tray of tea and set it on the small table, quickly excusing herself amidst the heavy atmosphere in the room.

"My skill has not been...up to par for quite some time." Cecilia busied herself with preparing her cup, not wanting to meet the gazes of the other two women.

"What could you possibly mean? You played superbly at Mother's ball, the best I've ever heard from you." Rosamund's spoon halted mid-stir.

"Therein lies the problem, you see. Actually, I think the problem is twofold. I know my performance at the masked ball was quite miraculous. But ever since, I've struggled to come even close to that level. I think I'm afraid that I will never be able to achieve it again, that I've somehow lost my passion for the instrument, and the fear causes me to stiffen at the keys. That's why I refuse to allow my name to be connected to that night. If everyone knew it was me, I don't think I could ever play properly again. I simply don't think I could live up to the expectation.

"And the other problem is a bit more...intimate. I danced with the most incredible man after my performance. But he seemed reluctant to share his name and I didn't press him for it, and I didn't share my name either. In all honesty I was quite caught up in the moment and didn't notice the fact until I realized I had no way of finding him again.

"You all know how I feel about the matter of marriage. Mama and Papa would see me married to a man of fortune and title, without a thought to his character or our real feelings for each other. But I can't bring myself to accept this— though I feel I am getting closer to that point with each passing day if I wish to have any kind of comfortable life. I know Mama and Papa are on the verge of dragging me to the altar if I don't manage to sort it out myself.

"I want love. True love. I know it's possible, so why shouldn't it be possible for me? None of the men who have tried to court me in these past few years have been the right one. I can feel it in my bones. But this masked gentleman from the ball.... I truly feel that if only I could come to know more of him, he could be what I've been looking for. But it's been weeks since and I've come no closer in discovering his name, or even the slightest clue as to who he might be. He comes into my thoughts every time I try to play, and my heart seizes up with regret and fear."

Cecilia's shoulders slumped forward, as if the tension inside her had suddenly been let out with her speech.

"Oh Sissy, I'm so sorry. I had no idea these issues weighed so heavily on you. I'm afraid I haven't been a very attentive sister." Juliet gripped Cecilia's hand, her large pale blue eyes pained.

"Nonsense, you're busy enjoying your first Season, as you should be. And in any case, I haven't been very inclined to discuss it myself. You didn't know any better."

Cecilia squeezed her sister's hand and smiled through her heartache. She was glad just to have her near, to have someone she knew she could call upon if she needed it. And she vowed to call upon her more often lest she break under her silent suffering.

"I too must apologize for not visiting sooner," Rosamund chimed in. "But I can offer my assistance now!" She stuck a gloved finger in the air as an idea struck and her face transformed into its usual bright countenance. "Let me ask Father if he might have an idea. He's friendly with many men about town and could steer us in the right direction. You should certainly not have to settle for a man who will mistreat you. I should know. I promise I will do everything in my power to help you find this man!"

Cecilia's heart skipped a beat at the suggestion, but it quickly sank back down into the pit of her stomach. Nothing good could come of her getting her hopes up. "Thank you, Rosamund. I would very much appreciate that."

Juliet nodded vigorously and continued, keeping her fingers wrapped tightly about Cecilia's hand. "I'm not sure what I can say about your other dilemma. You know I'm no lover of pianoforte or any other music—except for when you play, of course, and when it's time to dance. But, sister, I truly hope you won't give up on it. It's your dearest passion, all skill aside. You've loved it since you were tall enough to sit on the bench. That's worth holding on to. Whatever this is, you'll overcome it. Just give yourself time. Even if you never achieve the same level as you did at the masked ball, that doesn't detract from your talent. You shouldn't hold yourself to that expectation either."

Tears sprung so quickly to Cecilia's eyes that she had no time to stop them from trickling down her cheeks. But these tears were far different than the ones she'd shed just a few minutes ago. Instead of her heart being gripped by paralyzing fear and her stomach in sickening knots, a sweet calm settled over her entire body. She truly was an incredibly lucky woman, regardless of what happened from here on out.

"Thank you, both of you. You are the best friends anyone could ask for. I'll do my best, for the masked gentleman and for the pianoforte." Cecilia smiled and swiped at her tears with the handkerchief.

"I so admire you, Sissy. I hope you know that." Juliet pulled Cecilia to her feet and wrapped her in a tight embrace and Rosamund joined in. Cecilia nuzzled her face into Juliet's neck and pulled Rosamund in close with an arm tightly about her friend's shoulders. The three women stood like this for some time, drawing support from each other as well as lending support in the privacy of the drawing room. By the time they broke away and sat back down to resume the normal course of the morning call, their tea had gone quite cold.

ANOTHER LOVELY GOWN sprawled out over Cecilia's bed. This one was pale blue crepe with delicately embroidered swirling patterns and small touches of ruffles here and there. She recognized the dress as one from last year, but new details had been added to refresh it for another Season. Cecilia allowed her fingers to slide over the fabric gently. It had turned out beautifully, though of course it could not compare to the dress she'd worn at the Henshell family's ball. Nothing could compare to that night.

"Shall we begin, Miss Richards?" Violet's quiet voice drew Cecilia's attention back to the task at hand. It was time to prepare for Lord Overton's dinner. She nodded, her head heavy with anxiety.

Tonight would be an important test of her perseverance. Despite her heartwarming conversation with Juliet and Rosamund yesterday, the nerves twisted in Cecilia's stomach yet again. She had practiced all day today, with varying degrees of success, leaving her unable to gauge how she might play when it mattered most. She would simply have to bear it as best she could and hope that she came out of the experience unscathed.

As Violet put the final touches on Cecilia's hair, carefully arranging every curl and ensuring her headpiece was secure, the maid's eyes grew thoughtful. "Pardon me for speaking so out of turn, Miss Richards, but is something troubling you?"

"It's nothing to worry about, Violet. I appreciate your concern." Cecilia gave a reassuring smile to the young woman, who smiled back shyly. "I am simply nervous about this dinner. I've been asked to play on pianoforte, and the instrument has proven challenging for me of late. And...I believe there will be a certain man in attendance."

Violet's eyebrows arched up, the only clue giving away her interest on her otherwise professionally neutral face. Suddenly Cecilia wondered what love must be like for a servant; her heart sank with guilt when she realized that she'd never considered the question before. Clearly the prospect intrigued Violet.

But would she ever be courted and marry? Was such a thing an option for a working woman? Violet had far fewer chances to meet potential matches than Cecilia, and the thought weighed heavily in Cecilia's chest. Here Cecilia was, lamenting over the many suitors she'd turned down in hopes of finding her perfect future husband, while Violet would likely spend her life in service with no time or opportunity for love.

Cecilia wasn't sure what she might be able to do about that situation, and unfortunately now wasn't the best time to solve it. But she vowed to consider it further as soon as she was able.

"Yes, a certain man," she continued. "Juliet and I went on a carriage ride and walk with him and his friend recently. I'm afraid I made a poor impression on him. And even had I not, he seems quite uninterested in having anything to do with me, or anyone for that matter. I have reason to believe that he will be in attendance tonight, and I would rather not make contact with him."

Everyone knew of the close friendship between the gregarious, flirtatious earl and the reclusive, somber baron. A seemingly unlikely duo, but for whatever reason they were fast friends.

Lord Overton loved his social gatherings and could often be seen in the company of other gentlemen or escorting some lady or other. But Lord Neil, on the other hand, was rarely seen out except for with Lord Overton. Cecilia had her suspicions that the only reason Lord Neil regularly left his home was *because* of Lord Overton. As such, Cecilia felt it was almost guaranteed that Lord Neil would be present at the first dinner Lord Overton hosted this Season.

Violet's brow furrowed this time, processing the situation. "Well, I hope for your sake you will be able to avoid him if that is your wish. And if not, I hope you will be able to be quit of his company as quickly as possible."

Cecilia laughed. "Thank you, Violet. That is very diplomatic of you. Are we about ready? Mama will barge in here any moment now to drag me out by my curls if I don't present myself to her soon."

The maid glanced over Cecilia once more and nodded. With that, they left the room together and Cecilia headed downstairs to await the carriage.

IT CAME as no surprise to Cecilia that Lord Overton had a large, ornate home in Half Moon Street. Even still, the outside of the building alone caused her breath to hitch in her throat. And the inside was just as beautiful. Whether it was Lord Overton's taste or simply inherited décor, the foyer was full of plush rugs, expertly crafted furniture pieces, and expensive artwork hung on the walls.

The butler led the Richards family into the drawing room, where about a dozen guests were already gathered. Cecilia glanced about for Rosamund and spied her in the back corner, staring at the back of her mother's head with a glazed look in her eyes, clearly bored by whatever the older women were discussing.

"Mama, I've found Miss Henshell. May Juliet and I chat with her?" Cecilia asked.

"Indeed. Please do give my regards to Lady Henshell and Miss Henshell." Mrs. Richards responded a touch too loudly, glancing around to see if any other guests may have heard. Mr. Richards made a beeline for the other end of the room, where several gentlemen had gathered with glasses of champagne in their hands.

Cecilia and Juliet made their way through the room as quickly as was appropriate, nodding and smiling to the other guests as they went but without stopping to make conversation.

"Good evening, Lady Henshell, Miss Henshell," Cecilia

said quietly as she approached the small group of women so as not to disrupt their meeting but still make their presence known.

"Ah, good evening Miss Richards, Miss Juliet. How very lovely to see you both here." Lady Henshell, the epitome of grace and excellent manners, bowed her head slightly to acknowledge Cecilia and Juliet. She quickly introduced the two young women to her companions before politely removing her attention from them to return to her conversation.

Rosamund glanced to the wall, signaling them to follow her.

"Mother, we'll find some refreshments," Rosamund stated politely in the hopes of excusing herself to a quiet moment with her friends.

Lady Henshell turned only her eyes to her daughter and nodded sedately, keeping her attention on her conversation.

"Thank goodness you're here. I thought I might drop dead at any moment from that dreadfully tedious chatter. Surely the inside of a coffin would have been more interesting," Rosamund sighed quietly once they were out of earshot of her mother and any other guests.

Cecilia tapped her friend on the arm. "You are too brash, Rosamund," she chided with a chuckle. She thoroughly enjoyed Rosamund's ability to speak whatever wild things came into her mind, at least within their friendly company.

With her back turned to the room, Rosamund pulled a comical face that clearly mocked the pretentious expressions of the ladies who spoke with her mother, mouthing along silently.

Cecilia managed to hide her grin behind her gloved hand and stifle her laugh. Juliet, on the other hand, let out a high-pitched gasp that she quickly cut short, clapping a hand over her mouth as several heads turned sharply in their direction.

Rosamund's eyes squeezed shut as a silent laugh rolled through her body, the tremble of her shoulders betraying her.

That was when Cecilia saw him. Lord Neil. He stood almost directly across the drawing room from their small party. He stood alone, a nearly full glass in his hand. When her eyes found his, the baron's head snapped to the side as if something immensely interesting had caught his attention. He quickly wandered off in his new direction.

If Cecilia wasn't mistaken, she could have sworn that he had been staring directly at her before she'd noticed. But why, and for how long? The questions sent a flutter through her chest and suddenly her dress felt far too tight. But she didn't have long to ponder them as Rosamund drew her attention away from that spot by the wall where Lord Neil had just stood.

"I'm afraid I have some unfortunate news." Gone were Rosamund's cheers and jests. Her dark brown eyes conveyed the seriousness of the situation and the strange sensation that had just been in Cecilia's chest was instantly replaced by dread.

"I'm sorry, Cecilia, but Father was of no use. I gave him the description of the gentleman just as you told it to me. I think I saw about ten seconds of serious thought pass through his mind before he waved me away and said there were far too many gentlemen dressed in exactly that manner, and that he had many friends who claimed a love for the arts." She recounted the incident with bitterness in her voice.

"If I may speak frankly and in complete confidence, I do believe he was likely too deep in his cups to even remember which of his friends had been at the ball or what they were wearing. I even asked Mother if she had any guesses, since she's the one who assembled the guest list and sent out the invitations. But all she had to say was that she simply invites whichever names Father gives her and has nothing more to do with them."

Rosamund rolled her eyes while Cecilia and Juliet glanced sadly at each other. Though their parents were far from perfect—with nearly nothing in common in personality or interest—their single-minded determination to officially enter into the *ton* by way of at least one of their daughters' marriages provided them with a common goal.

The same could not be said for Rosamund's parents. In fact, Rosamund had lamented many times to Cecilia about how much her parents loathed each other, and how her father handled life's ups, downs, and everything in between with a drink in his hand. Lady Henshell at least cared for her daughter, but to Lord Henshell Rosamund might as well have been a visiting guest of little consequence in his home.

"That's quite alright, dear. I truly appreciate your effort. I know it can't have been easy for you." Cecilia patted her friend on the shoulder. Rosamund tried to avoid her father as much as she could, even when they were in the same room. They were not quite on speaking terms, so Cecilia knew it must have taken much effort for Rosamund to break the silence.

"Don't lose hope yet, Sissy. Maybe something will turn up when we least expect it." Ever the optimist, Juliet beamed a smile at Cecilia and Rosamund to keep their spirits up.

Cecilia sighed. She had told herself not to get her hopes up, but she would have been lying if she said she'd been able to squash all of it. There had been a glimmer of hope in the deepest corner of her heart. But with this lead exhausted, that glimmer was all but snuffed out.

CHAPTER 6

*F*inally, the butler announced that it was time to enter the dining room. Henry didn't understand why dinners had to include a period of standing around before the actual meal. Of course, he knew it was to allow the guests a chance to get to know each other and converse beforehand. But Henry found there was no one here he wished to get to know or to converse with. Except for Solomon, who was busy playing host and gliding about the room greeting all his guests.

And her.

Henry had known that she would be in attendance tonight. But the sight of her still shocked him somehow. Miss Richards looked quite lovely in her evening dress, as he had suspected she would. To his great embarrassment, he'd been caught staring from across the room.

He shuddered at the memory, at the look of complete surprise on her face when she'd noticed him, and his less than graceful escape. He could have simply crossed the room and greeted her, as most probably would have done. Instead, it was as if she was one of the insurmountable obstacles facing the heroes he wrote about. Though he knew he had next to nothing in common with his heroes.

But as Henry silently observed her from afar, he could see that she and her sister and friend, Lord Henshell's daughter, were clearly having a spirited conversation and enjoying the evening. He hadn't felt right intruding upon her fun.

Suddenly Solomon appeared at his side as it came time to head downstairs to the dining room. "Everyone looks very handsome tonight," he mumbled, but Henry could see that his eyes flickered to a particular corner of the room, where the Richards sisters and Miss Henshell cloistered together. Without giving Henry a chance to respond, he hurried off to the front to begin escorting the party to dinner.

Henry gave his arm to a well-bred lady whom Solomon had quickly introduced him to and led her into the room. At least, due to the Richards family's station, he wouldn't have to sit near Miss Richards and likely embarrass himself further.

Solomon had chosen his guest list well, and Henry was able to sit next to Lord Henshell. Solomon knew that Henry felt more comfortable at these affairs if he had at least one person he knew to converse with.

He chatted with the other baron as the first course was served, but eventually Lord Henshell found a more talkative guest in the woman on his other side. Henry decided to keep to himself as much as he could for the rest of the meal, only stealing an occasional glance down the table to Miss Richards, conversing happily with a gentleman on one side and her sister on the other.

HENRY WAS surprised that Solomon had gone with so many courses for this dinner. There was no particular celebration or any other meaningful event to tie it to. Just three courses would have been enough for an average dinner party. But as the evening wore on, Henry certainly noticed that Solomon's eyes often wandered down the table to the Richards sisters. Just as Henry's had, he realized with a jolt.

With the last course cleared away, and everyone quite stuffed, the ladies retired to the drawing room and a footman brought out the port.

"Finally! The course we've all been waiting for!" Lord Henshell declared as the footman poured, several of the other men in the room laughing with him.

The gentlemen naturally found their places with each other, loitering here and there in small groups and floating in between to join other conversations. Henry noticed that Mr. Richards eagerly zipped from one cluster to another, trying desperately to be part of all groups and not miss a single word said by anyone. And naturally, Henry stood alone against the wall.

"What do you think so far? Not too shabby for a bachelor, eh?" Solomon waltzed over to Henry, his decidedly casual gait looking rather forced. Nervous was not a look Henry was used to seeing on his friend.

"Ah, it is clear to me now. You're trying to impress her, are you?" Henry kept his voice low, but the lighthearted jab was heard loud and clear by its intended.

"Impress who? I have no reason to impress anyone, least of all the daughter of a gentleman with no rank." Solomon huffed and took a quick sip of his port, his eyes shifting to the door through which the ladies had gone.

"You give yourself away, friend. I didn't provide a name, and though you tried to play dumb you ended up answering your own question." Henry shot a sly glance to Solomon, the corner of his mouth drawing up in a smirk.

Solomon's eyes widened as he realized his mistake. He

pursed his lips together and shook his head. "Drat it all. There's no use hiding it, from myself or from you. Despite all my dearly held beliefs, yes, I am interested."

Henry immediately felt guilty for poking fun at his friend. Solomon ran a hand through his auburn locks, the frustration clear on his face. When he stopped to think about it, this truly was a serious development for Solomon.

The man had vowed to put off marriage for as long as possible, despite being an earl and his family's desperate pleas for him to at least marry someone—almost anyone, now—and produce an heir. So the fact that his heart now betrayed him must have come as a shock to Solomon once he realized what was happening.

"Come now, Solomon. Could it really be so bad? She seems like a lovely young lady."

"Yes, it could really be so bad," Solomon snapped. "She's lovely enough now, but I promise you if we were to wed, she would show her true colors the instant the vows are completed. And I will tolerate no such thing." The earl glared bitterly into his glass of port, as if he watched a play of events past unfold in the dark liquid. "Though, if I am to find out what kind of character this woman has..." Solomon peeked at Henry from the corner of his eye.

"Go on..." Henry hesitated, recognizing the sound of a plan being hatched.

"If I am to test this woman and find out if she is real all the way through, then I must well and truly court her." Solomon nodded sharply, as if he were strategizing a crucial battle maneuver in the trenches of France.

"Well, that's wonderful news." Henry clapped Solomon on the shoulder, surprise giving way to happiness for his friend. He truly hoped that Miss Juliet would prove to be a worthy companion.

"But there is one thing..." Solomon peeked at Henry again, a look of faux innocence on his face.

Henry sighed. "Go on."

"I think I should have a far easier time of it if you accompanied me." Solomon rushed out the words and just as Henry opened his mouth to protest, he held up a hand, anticipating the forthcoming disagreement. "Hear me out, Henry. You know I typically have no issues making acquaintances or keeping engagements or conversing about this and that. But this time.... For some reason I can't explain, this is different.

"I find myself flustered around her, even just at the mere thought of her. If you are nearby you can observe our interactions and provide your opinion of her sincerity. You of all people know how to read and understand someone."

Despite the plea in his friend's voice, Henry balked at the idea. "Solomon, you know I can't spend so much time away from my work..." he mumbled, but the excuse sounded hollow even to him. "And besides, you wouldn't want some useless tagalong following behind you on your adventures."

"That's just the thing!" Solomon bounced on his toes as he grabbed Henry by the upper arms and gave him a little shake. "You wouldn't be a useless tagalong! Of course not. Do you assume I think so little of you as to saddle you with such an uncomfortable role? We'll simply ask her sister to join us so you will have a companion, too."

"Solomo—" Henry tried to protest again but he was quickly shushed once more, Solomon growing bolder and more frenzied as his plan came closer to fruition.

"And I promise that you will still have plenty of time to write! I won't be calling on her every day. How about once a week? Surely you can spare a few hours once a week." Solomon peered eagerly into Henry's face, searching for a chink in his resolve.

Henry had to admit that it was nice to see his friend back

to his usual mischievous, enthusiastic self. It was quite the turnaround from the angst that radiated from him just a few minutes ago. Solomon must have given this proposal—and its implication for his ideals—much thought, Henry realized.

Still, he hesitated. His brow furrowed as he considered the possibility of being shackled to Miss Richards once a week. Perhaps he could have tolerated the idea more if their acquaintance hadn't gotten off to such an uncomfortable start. But as it currently stood, he knew that Miss Richards would think herself to be suffering in his company, even if she went for her sister's sake.

"Don't tell me you haven't given Miss Richards any consideration, Henry. You've been ogling her all evening. I'm doing you a favor, really." Solomon slapped Henry's arm with the back of his hand and wiggled his eyebrows.

"Ogling?! I certainly have not been ogling! If you want to know what ogling looks like you should have seen yourself at the dinner table tonight, glancing to their end every other second." Henry, well and truly offended now, felt disinclined to give in to his friend's ridiculous request. It wasn't Henry's responsibility to court anyone for Solomon's benefit.

Henry expected a tirade in response, knowing that he'd injured the earl's pride—his most prized possession.

Instead, a rosy blush sprung into Solomon's cheeks and he lowered his head. "You're right, my good man." He stood straight again and looked Henry squarely in the eye. "I can't seem to keep my eyes or my mind off her, and I'm at a loss as to what I should do. This position is very unfamiliar to me. I confess that I am afraid. Afraid of ending up disappointed...again."

Henry was breathless for a moment, so rarely did he see such a pained, earnest expression in his friend's eyes, small wrinkles appearing at the outer corners and a deep groove between his brows. His voice had grown deep and quiet.

This truly must have been a serious situation. Henry would simply have to put his own feelings towards Miss Richards aside and work harder on his book at other times. He knew that he could not allow his best friend to fall into the same disastrous trap as he had years ago.

"Alright. I'll join you. But once a week only. If you desire to visit with her more than that, you will have to go on your own."

"Excellent!" Solomon nearly splashed his drink over both of them in his excitement. "I suppose I should go mingle with her father for a time before we join the ladies in the drawing room."

Henry chuckled as he watched his friend nearly glide across the room on feet that almost looked like they were dancing.

ONCE AGAIN, Henry minded his corner as the entire party gathered together in the drawing room for more conversation, this time with coffee and tea rather than champagne and wine. He sipped quietly from his cup of tea as he watched the guests and picked up on bits and pieces of conversation.

Solomon, ever the dutiful host, made his rounds about the room, ensuring that all his guests received equal attention. All, perhaps, except for Miss Juliet. The earl had done a superb job of avoiding that small table where she sat with her sister and Miss Henshell, their mother standing behind their chairs so she could maintain a clear view of the room and its guests.

Unable to stop himself, Henry gave in to his habit of observation. But having learned from his previous mistake, he turned his body to the side and watched from his peripheral vision, keeping his face low over his cup.

As always, Miss Richards was engrossed in whatever tale Miss Henshell shared, her eyes wide as she listened. When the story came to its climax, Miss Richards's face lit up and even from this angle Henry could see the shimmer of amusement in her eyes.

A gentleman Henry vaguely knew, Mr. Faxby or some other, must have overheard their conversation and approached the group to join in. Miss Richards greeted him with cheer and fell quickly into a companionable discussion with him, trading off with the other ladies with such ease. He wondered what it might be like to truly enjoy this type of activity as she did.

Another movement nearby caught his eye and Henry looked up to see Solomon making his way toward him from the opposite corner.

"I know you try to be inconspicuous, friend, but how is it that I always managed to find you instantly in a crowded room?"

"That's quite simple, Solomon, so don't get too ahead of yourself. You've known me for years and you've been to countless such events with me. You simply know by now exactly where I'll be."

Solomon laughed heartily. "Too right you are. Then in that case, why don't we shake things up a bit? I've neglected a certain little gathering over there. Why don't you join me in a little chat with them? You needn't speak if you don't want to. But I'd like to have you nearby when I ask Miss Juliet to join me at Hyde Park in a few days."

Henry could already feel his palms growing slick with sweat, but he'd promised to assist his friend in this endeavor. He would need to leave his comfortable corner sooner or later. He nodded and followed Solomon.

"Ladies, Mr. Faxby, I trust you are enjoying your evening thus far?" If Solomon was nervous, he managed to hide it well under his gleaming smile. Only Henry noticed the way his thumb brushed against his knuckles repeatedly.

The ladies simultaneously praised the extravagant dinner and the wonderful furnishings in the Earl's home. Mr. Faxby nodded in agreement.

"I am so very pleased to hear that." Solomon laid a hand over his chest and bowed his head to accept their compliments. "Miss Juliet..." He cleared his throat as he turned to the youngest member in the group. The eyes of the three young ladies and Mrs. Richards all turned to Solomon. "I have already had permission from your generous father, but I thought I should ask if you would be willing to join me for a carriage ride in Hyde Park a few days hence?" His normally confident smile faltered just slightly at the corner as he laid out his request for their whole party to hear.

The young woman nearly jumped as Mrs. Richards's hands came swiftly down on her shoulders and squeezed. No doubt a silent demand for her daughter to accept. The sudden hunger in her eyes as they fixed upon Solomon spoke loudly enough.

"That would be just fine, my lord," she answered with a tight smile, either from the pain of her mother's fingers digging into her or from a bashful excitement, Henry couldn't quite tell. Perhaps a mixture of both.

"Excellent. I shall write ahead with the precise date and time. Oh, and my friend Lord Neil would also like to join us, hopefully with your charming sister in attendance as well."

Henry could have sworn that Mrs. Richards looked fit to burst with joy as she moved one hand from her youngest daughter's shoulder to her oldest.

"Ah, Lord Neil come to the rescue like the hero in those

popular adventure novels," Cecilia chuckled, a hint of playful taunting in her voice. Her mother did not appreciate the humor and dug her fingers into her daughter's shoulder, a wince flashing over Miss Richards's face for a fraction of a second.

"A hero?" All eyes turned to Mr. Faxby. He had been quite forgotten. "Do not compare a man like Lord Neil to the heroes in those works, madam. You do him a disservice. They may seem dashing and gallant at first glance, but they are nothing more than arrogant fools who find themselves in contrived situations that they are too dimwitted to escape without endless pages of struggle. I find it sad that so many people have fallen under the spell of these mediocre stories. I almost feel an obligation to expose them for the nonsense they are."

Mr. Faxby smirked as he looked down his nose at the ladies before giving Henry a proud nod.

Henry was utterly bewildered as to why this gentleman would speak so negatively of his books, though the man seemed to think he'd done Henry a favor. He knew him by name and by face as a new frequent at Boodle's, fresh out of university. Henry knew his works were not perfect, but he'd never received such a scathing review.

Some of the ladies had covered their mouths with their hands while Solomon's mouth simply hung slightly ajar. Such a tirade had been completely unexpected.

But, reserved though he may be, Henry was not without his pride. "I beg your pardon, sir, but I do not believe such words are appropriate for pleasant company. Miss Richards simply meant to pay me a compliment. Since you appear not to be such pleasant company, I would ask our host to see you out at once." Henry drew himself to his full height, which was nothing to boast of but still an inch or two taller than the young man. His dark eyes sent the challenge to Mr. Faxby, and he seemed to quiver slightly under what Henry hoped to be a piercing gaze.

"How disappointing, Mr. Faxby." Miss Richards stood, her elegant bearing cold and intimidating. "I should think that a man of your immense knowledge, as you have made so clear to us in the minutes since you made your introduction, would know very well that heroes are not meant to be perfect. They learn and grow during their trials and adventures. That's what makes a hero's journey so worth reading."

Solomon seemed to finally snap back to his senses. "Lord Neil has the right of it. I will not tolerate any harsh language during what ought to be a cheerful evening—especially not when Miss Richards has offered such a kind compliment to my friend. Show yourself out, or I will have my footmen and butler show you out. The choice is yours." He took a heavy step toward Mr. Faxby, hand at the ready to beckon a servant forward.

The younger man's cheeks blotched bright red and his nose scrunched in anger, but just before Solomon flicked his fingers to call a footman, he turned on his heel and marched briskly out the door.

Solomon summoned one of the footmen anyway and commanded him to follow the gentleman out and ensure he left the premises.

"Ladies, I am so sorry you had to bear witness to such a boorish scene." Solomon bowed his head, and Henry could tell that he was genuinely embarrassed.

"Do not trouble yourself over it, my lord." Once again, Miss Richards came to the defense. "We cannot control the actions of others, but we can control how we respond. Let's not allow this to spoil our evening." She smiled at Solomon, a warm understanding in her eyes.

"Perhaps some music would provide a happy distraction,"

Miss Henshell chimed in cheerily, standing up next to her friend. "Miss Richards is so very talented on the pianoforte."

"Yes, that would be splendid. We would be honored, if you would be so gracious to play for us." Solomon relaxed, his shoulders sinking down slightly as the tension eased away.

Miss Richards nodded with a small smile and began to make her way to toward the other end of the room, where Solomon's pianoforte sat in neglect.

"We will eagerly await your letter, Lord Overton." Mrs. Richards fluttered her eyelashes before following her oldest daughter. It would appear that this embarrassing event had not deterred her from allowing her daughters to share in their company in the least. The other young women also trailed behind Miss Richards.

"Goodness, I hadn't realized I'd asked the whole of the Richards family and Miss Henshell to also play tonight," Solomon muttered in surprise as they watched the women walk together to the instrument.

But Henry noted the way Miss Richards's younger sister intertwined their fingers, the way Miss Henshell gently stroked her shoulder and whispered something in her ear. Miss Richards only nodded stiffly at these gestures.

Solomon turned to follow them so he could announce Miss Richards, but Henry gripped him by the forearm and spun him back around.

"Though Miss Richards has been kind enough to offer you an escape, I will not let you go so easily."

Henry's eyes bored into Solomon's face, his anger at being criticized so harshly in his best friend's own home, by one of his invited guests, swelling to the surface. Worst of all, he'd had to pretend as though Mr. Faxby's words had no personal effect on him. "Who on God's green earth was that man? Did you know he had such an open disdain for my work and yet you still asked him here?"

The earl hung his head, his eyes closed in a pained expression. "I am truly sorry, Henry. I invited Mr. Faxby against my better judgement. He's a new fellow at Boodle's and he'd spent much of his time at Cambridge writing stories of a similar nature to your work. He seemed quite eager to have them published, as he's fallen on hard times and hoped to make some money to pay his debts. Not long ago he mentioned leaving a package at the adventure novelist's publisher to forward to the anonymous man himself…"

"Ah, I see." Henry already had an idea of where this tale led. His jaw involuntarily tensed and he massaged it as he thought back to a recent letter he'd sent, minus a return address.

"Yes, you have already worked it out for yourself. He had it delivered to you under his own alias, but that manuscript you reviewed recently indeed belonged to Mr. Faxby. It seems you sent your response to his friend's address and he collected it from there.

"Yet he seemed not to care at all if the other gentlemen at the club knew it was he who implored upon the fashionable mystery writer, only so that he could besmirch you as arrogant, tactless, and entirely unhelpful to anyone who would listen. I do believe he had a rather inflated opinion of his own ability, so when he read your honest evaluation his poor ego could not stand it, and he sought to blame you rather than his own lack of skill. And you are so rarely at the club that you never heard him speak of it."

"It's true that I made no effort to spare his feelings in my letter, but it was only in the hopes that it would inspire him to reexamine his manuscript. I have certainly been on the receiving end of such feedback from my publisher." Henry sighed and shook his head. He'd had no idea of the repercussions that awaited his blunt but well-meaning letter.

"You don't need to defend yourself to me. I'm no reader, but even after the few pages you showed me even I could tell it was awful," Solomon laughed.

"In any case, we had become quite friendly before all this. I spoke with him about these foulmouthed rants to see if I could soothe his wounded pride and he suggested that I might be the anonymous author based on my defense of the works. Of course I dissuaded him from this line of thinking but I swear it took everything in me not to box his ears and set him straight," Solomon growled, his hand balling up into a fist and his eyes glaring at the door as if he had half a mind to march out after Mr. Faxby and box his ears after all.

"When he heard that I was having a small dinner, he begged me for an invitation and I nearly declined, but of course I didn't want to raise any further suspicions. But fear not, Henry. You shall see no more of him here, or at Boodle's if I can help it." Solomon grew serious again, his eyes cold with anger as he continued to glower at the door.

"It's alright now, Solomon. I should have known you wouldn't do something to purposely injure me. The ladies are surely growing restless. You'd best get up there."

Henry nodded over the cluster of women by the pianoforte. Miss Richards in particular seemed very eager to start. Her eyes darted through the small gathering of guests and to the instrument and back again, her gloved fingers picking at the embroidery on her dress. Although the longer Henry watched, the more he suspected that "eager" had not been the right word.

"Ah, right. You are in for a treat, my friend. She may not be quite as accomplished as the young lady you seemed to favor at the Henshell ball, but I swear she is the next best in all of London." Solomon winked, the corner of his mouth pulled up into a sly smirk.

Henry rolled his eyes in response. Why couldn't his friend let that incident go? The woman clearly had not been interested in furthering their acquaintance, else she would have shared her name or given him some token to discover her identity by.

But if he did know who she was, he had no intention of seeking her out. His next book was finally progressing to his satisfaction, and now he would be distracted once a week to call upon Miss Richards. He simply could not divert any more of his time than absolutely necessary, especially on a dead-end quest.

Nevertheless, as Solomon introduced Miss Richards, Henry found himself inching closer and closer to the instrument.

CHAPTER 7

*C*ecilia's ribs ached, her chest far too small to contain the thundering of her heart as she took her place on the bench. Beads of sweat dotted her temples and the air seemed to catch in her throat every time she tried to take a breath.

She glanced to her left to see Juliet and Rosamund smiling their bright encouraging smiles, and just behind them stood her parents, their eyes expectant and nearly wild with the anticipation of opportunity that this night had already produced.

Now all Cecilia had to do was uphold her reputation as a skilled musician, and therefore her family's pride in the process. What task could be simpler?

As she shuffled the sheet music on the stand and Lord Overton made his exuberant introduction amidst a round of quiet applause, Cecilia mentally chided herself for her foolishness.

Mr. Faxby had provided a perfect chance to let her promise to play slip out of the earl's mind. If only Rosamund hadn't offered her up as a distraction from that unpleasant business. Her friend had apologized while they waited for the earl to announce her. She'd simply been trying to find a way to ease the tension and Cecilia's lovely playing was the first thing to spring to her mind. Though Cecilia now had the spotlight she'd come to dread, she couldn't blame her friend. This had been expected, after all. Whatever words Juliet and Rosamund had whispered in order to rally her spirits as they approached the dreaded instrument had simply gone in one ear and out the other.

But, as she delicately placed her fingers over the keys, she knew that all she could do now was play.

And play she did, the notes coming easily to her as her eyes read the music and her hands responded in time. Slowly the nerves began to float away into the air with the elegant sounds of the instrument, just as they had always done in the past. Cecilia could feel the old excitement humming in her heart again. She hadn't realized until that moment how afraid she'd been that the feeling was lost to her forever.

Finally. This is how it was meant to be. For the first time in weeks, Cecilia felt back to her true self. Instead of antici-pating stumbles, she allowed herself to sink into the music. She couldn't help swaying slightly on the bench, feeling the melody dancing through her body. As she came to the final movement, Cecilia closed her eyes and her lips lifted into a smile. By God, she'd finally done it.

With the last few measures in her grasp, Cecilia opened her eyes. She knew immediately that she'd made a grave error.

Just beyond the corner of her eye to her right stood a figure she had not expected or wanted to see—Lord Neil.

It took a mere second for her to take in his stoic glare, and in that same second she utterly lost her concentration. Her fingers clattered against the keys, the sounds grating against each other and piercing her ears.

Cecilia ripped her attention away from him but it was too late. Her confidence faltered and the triumphant thump of her heart was replaced by an erratic beating that slammed against her ribs. Those dreadful nerves came back in full force as she fought through those last measures that were supposed to prove her talent to herself once again.

Try as she might, she could not regain control of her trembling hands or her unsteady eyes. Cecilia closed the song out with a pitiful discord, the ugly notes ringing loud through the entire room, but loudest of all in her own head.

"Well done!" Lord Overton cheered with a clap, encouraging his guests to do the same.

Hot tears pricked at the corners of Cecilia's eyes and she could not catch her breath for the life of her. Suddenly, one desire eclipsed all others in her mind—she must escape.

Cecilia stood abruptly from the bench and gathered up enough of her skirts to allow her to swiftly exit the room without tripping.

The sound of applause, of her mother and sister calling out her name, of servants trying to assist her, slipped into a deafening silence as she tore through the earl's home, straight out into the small garden. There was not nearly enough air in that building. Perhaps outside she would be able to breathe.

Thankfully, Cecilia found a small table with two chairs tucked away near the back corner. Abandoning all propriety, she ran towards it as if it were her oasis in a cruel desert.

She flung herself into the chair and slumped over the table, burying her face in her arms and giving way to sobs of mortification. She could not have cared less if anyone found her here in this wretched state. The Prince himself could storm into the garden. There was nothing that could humiliate her more than the performance she'd just given.

Cecilia had no idea how long she remained in the garden,

wallowing in her shame and disappointment. It wasn't just the fact that she had ruined the song at the last moment by allowing herself to be distracted. She had been so sure until that moment that she had finally overcome her mental blocks and would be able to love the pianoforte just as she had always done. But that fragile hope that had built up with the song's crescendos had been shattered in an instant.

"There you are. Are you alright, Miss Richards?"

Cecilia jumped up at the sudden voice that intruded upon the miserable whirlwind of her thoughts. It seemed as though years had passed, the entire world had fallen away, since she'd fled into the garden.

She looked up to see the Baron of Neil peering down at her intently. If she had thought she could not be more embarrassed, she had been very wrong. Cecilia supposed that someone must come looking for her at some point, but she had expected her parents or her sister or even Rosamund to be the one to discover her.

Not the baron, with his dark, penetrating gaze. Cecilia couldn't tell what she saw in his face. Pity, or revulsion. Perhaps both.

"I should think it obvious that I am not at all alright," she spat as she quickly wiped her sodden cheeks, turning her face away and hoping that the dim evening light would hide her bright red blush.

"My apologies.... That was a rather stupid question, wasn't it?" Lord Neil took a step back, his eyes rapidly searching the grass near his feet.

Cecilia's heart pulsed with guilt. He had come all this way to find her, and she had scorned his kindness. Would she ever stop making a fool of herself in front of this man? Apparently, according to their first confrontation in the carriage, her performance this evening, and her poor behavior just now, the answer was no.

"It is I who should apologize, Lord Neil. I've been too harsh with you. Thank you for coming to see to my safety." Her head seemed suddenly heavy and she let it hang low between her shoulders. Somehow all her manners and good breeding seemed to desert her when Lord Neil was present. He didn't seem to be an unkind man, yet her instant reaction was to shove him away at the slightest provocation.

"It's nothing to concern yourself over. Everyone is quite worried about you." He kept his hands clasped behind his back and his eyes anywhere but on Cecilia.

"Oh my. I fear I've started an even uglier scene than that dreadful Mr. Faxby." She wrung her hands in her lap and peered around Lord Neil towards the house, expecting a small mob to come pouring out into the garden at any moment.

"Don't worry, Lord Overton has sent all the other guests home. Just your family and Lady Henshell and Miss Henshell remain. And myself, obviously."

A thought suddenly struck Cecilia, and a different blush threatened to paint her cheeks. "But Lord Neil, how did you know I would be here?" She kept her eyes on her restless hands as she asked the question.

"This is not the first place I looked, I'll admit. But then I realized what I would have done if I were to find myself in an unbearable situation. When I become so anxious or embarrassed that I feel I might melt straight through the floor, I suddenly have a very difficult time breathing. Getting out of doors is the only solution to getting away from my situation and restoring air to my lungs."

He had finally refocused his eyes on her. Cecilia looked properly into his face, and for the first time in their short acquaintance, she felt that she saw a glimpse of the real Lord Neil.

What she had seen as pity and revulsion before now

transformed into an intense concern. Somehow, he had exactly understood her feelings and been able to guess her location. The guilt she'd felt earlier returned tenfold. She continued to misread this man when he had read her so clearly in a matter of minutes.

Cecilia knew she was staring, but she couldn't stop herself. That strange sensation that had filled her chest in the drawing room earlier when she'd caught him eyeing her returned. It puzzled and somewhat frightened her, though the warmth that accompanied it was not wholly unpleasant.

"Miss Richards?" Lord Neil's heavy brows furrowed closer together as he sat in the other chair and leaned across the table to get a better look at Cecilia's face, searching for signs of illness or an oncoming faint.

"My apologies again, my lord. I am just gathering my bearings," Cecilia stammered, her eyes still glued to the baron. "I greatly appreciate your concern, and I am truly embarrassed that you've had to see me in this state, especially after letting Lord Overton and all the guests down with my playing." Now she looked away, unwilling to see any criticism in those dark brown eyes.

"Let them down?" Lord Neil sounded genuinely confused. "You've done no such thing. And I know I am not the only one who holds that opinion. Your playing was graceful and impassioned. Unfortunately I find that many women who are accomplished with pianoforte or harp often play with technical proficiency but lack emotion. You manage to play with both." His voice was soft, nearly a whisper, and Cecilia found herself leaning towards him as if trying to get closer to its comforting source.

"As you can see, I do not lack for emotion." Cecilia chuckled, glad that she was starting to relax and find morsels of amusement in the situation. Years from now, likely even just days from now, she would probably find the debacle to be quite amusing.

Lord Neil let out a gruff laugh, the first Cecilia had ever heard. The sound was deeper than she expected, as if it had been buried in some dark corner of his chest. And his true smile was wide, white teeth gleaming despite the darkness in the garden.

Just as Cecilia found herself thinking that perhaps the new arrangement that had been proposed tonight might not be such a terrible idea, an unpleasant thought sent a tremor down her spine.

"Unfortunately, I think Lord Overton must wish to retract his earlier interest in courting my sister and having you and I accompany them."

Shame ignited anew in Cecilia, her stomach churning. Perhaps the performance hadn't ruined Juliet's chance at a very favorable potential match, but her childish behavior afterward certainly had. No man would wish to court a woman whose older sister, the one who should lead by example, would do such an uncouth thing. If Cecilia had merely damaged her own reputation, she would not feel so awful. But to spill a stain upon her sister's reputation was nigh on unforgivable.

Lord Neil laughed again and Cecilia's head snapped up in surprise. "Have no fear, Lord Overton is quite unaffected by such things. And it seems he is ardent as ever about furthering his relationship with your sister. You won't put him off so easily."

"Did he say that he will still call on Juliet later in the week?" Cecilia's eyes were round with surprise and hope.

"He certainly did. I daresay he already has a letter drafted in his desk, just waiting for him to choose the date and time." The baron shook his head gently, his eyes softening as he contemplated his friend's eagerness.

87

"That is truly wonderful news." Cecilia let out a breath she didn't realize she'd been holding, thanking every star that glowed in the fading night sky that she hadn't spoiled her sister's future. "But, surely you would not wish to be seen with me around town after the gossip that will circulate about my little outburst tonight."

The relief was short-lived, replaced by an unexpected gloom. Just a few days ago, she would have dreaded the thought of having to spend time with Lord Neil.

And in truth—despite his kind words and her growing realization that this incident was perhaps not as severe as she'd thought—the hint of gloom Cecilia felt was balanced by her lingering embarrassment that she had been found in such a state of disarray by him. The performance and running out of the room, she could overcome. But something about showing Lord Neil this side of her, the side that sobbed uncontrollably over an ultimately inconsequential matter.... The thought did not sit well with her.

"Again, I am afraid you are mistaken." The mirth that had momentarily overtaken Lord Neil was gone. He returned to his normal terse and quiet manner. "I do not object to accompanying you alongside Lord Overton and Miss Juliet. Enough is said about me in some circles of Society that I find I don't much care for their opinions anymore. And besides, I promised my friend that I would remain by his side to support him in this venture."

Cecilia pursed her lips. Lord Neil was a gentleman, the foundation of courtesy bred into his blood. He had searched for her and asked after her health as was his duty. And now, he chose to spend his time with her not because he so desired her company that he would turn a blind eye to Society's whispers. But simply because he already had no interest in such gossip, and for the sake of his friend.

She gave her head a small shake to banish those troublesome thoughts. They had no place in her mind. She had known that Lord Neil was not requesting to court her. And Lord Neil was not the man she wanted to accept courtship from for many reasons. Her mind was far too muddled by the intensity of her emotions to think clearly.

"Thank you, Lord Neil. That is very generous of you. I am glad that my presence won't bring shame upon you. And you are kind to so willingly sacrifice your time on a silly girl like me to help your friend." Cecilia knew that her words very nearly crossed the line of politeness, but she kept the tone of her voice light and demure. She didn't bother to spare a glance toward him to see if he'd caught her true meaning.

"Oh, there you are! Thank heaven!" An anxious voice pierced the cool night air as Juliet materialized in the doorway of the house.

She wasted no time, nearly flying across the small yard to Cecilia. In her eagerness, Juliet pulled Cecilia out of her seat and slid an arm around her waist. "Oh my darling, we were so worried about you!"

Juliet pulled Cecilia snug to her side, her fingers gripping the fabric at Cecilia's waist. She could feel a slight tremble emanating from the younger woman's body.

"Juliet, I'm quite alright now. I'm sorry I worried you so."

Juliet let her arm drop away, but she wrapped her hands firm around her sister's wrists, perhaps to keep her from running off again. "We've been in quite a state trying to find you. There was no telling where you might have gone or what harm could have befallen you. Papa is probably still out in the street calling for you."

Cecilia grimaced. She had fled from the drawing room in the heat of the moment, not thinking about how her disappearing act might affect her loved ones. In a large, unfamiliar home, she could have hidden anywhere. Or even left Lord Overton's home entirely.

"I'm so sorry, Jules. I didn't realize I've caused such a fuss. But I promise, I'm just fine now. A little embarrassed, to be sure, but I'm in one piece."

Cecilia removed her hands from her sister's grip and cupped her soft round face, the heat from her skin seeping through Cecilia's silk gloves. She'd done such a thing countless times throughout their childhood—whenever Juliet scraped a knee chasing after birds on the grounds of their country estate, or nearly broken her ankle after falling out of a tree, or been teased by the girls at their seminary for her untamed mouth.

She wondered briefly when had been the last time she'd done this. Probably several years, as Juliet needed her reassurances less and less over time. Oddly, it brought a small smile to Cecilia's face. She was glad to know that her little sister still relied on her sometimes.

"Please don't ever run off like that again. You've scared us all half to death, and I swear if another minute had passed I would have sent out the servants to search for you," Juliet huffed. Suddenly she sounded like the older sister chastising the reckless and foolish behavior of the younger. Cecilia couldn't help laughing at the role reversal.

"On the plus side, Mama's hair has turned a very becoming shade of silver. It quite suits her, I think," Juliet giggled, her face slipping back into its easy demeanor.

"We should go and deliver the good news," Cecilia said after catching her breath. "Oh, but first Lord Neil—"

Cecilia turned to her side to give the baron his due credit for finding her and helping her return to her senses. But the baron had performed a disappearing act of his own. Her heart sank just slightly, and she hated that irksome sensation.

"Lord Neil? He left in quite a hurry not long after I arrived. Perhaps he wanted to give us privacy to reunite." Juliet shrugged before turning to Cecilia to wipe away any stray tears and adjust the curls that had fallen out during her escape. She turned back toward the earl's home, keeping Cecilia's hand in her own.

Cecilia frowned, a twinge of guilt settling in her stomach. How could she not notice him leave? And why did she care whether she noticed or not? His work here was done, his obligation completed. At least for tonight.

CHAPTER 8

*H*enry jolted awake to the sound of the heavy door opening. His heart raced for a few seconds, until his eyes adjusted to the dim lighting and saw the large curtained window to his left, and the floor-to-ceiling wall-to-wall bookshelves in front of him. The familiar shapes of his study brought him comfort and eased his momentary panic.

"Apologies, my lord. I did not realize you were still here." The young footman bowed but did not otherwise seem surprised to find his employer asleep in the study. All the staff knew by now that Henry spent just as many nights asleep at his writing desk or in a chair in the library as he did in his own bed. This was not the first time they had found him in such a state, nor would it be the last.

"That's quite alright. It's about time I was up anyways. Carry on," Henry grumbled, his voice cracking from disuse.

The sun was just barely beginning to wind its way through the fabric of the curtains, the staff getting their start on the day. Henry could have slept for several more hours if he wished, as many of the gently born part-time residents of London were no doubt doing.

But they did not have books to write.

Henry dragged his hands over his face and gave his cheeks a light tap to rouse himself. Running a hand through his hair told him that there was no hope for that sorry mess and he would just have to leave it be for now.

He pulled the bell and, while he waited for the maid, reviewed last night's work. Thumbing through the handful of pages, all he saw were lines of disappointment. When he got to the last page he'd written last night—or rather early this morning—stuck in the middle of a sentence, he gripped the corner of the sheet tightly, tempted to crumple the whole thing.

But the maid arrived at that moment and Henry loosened his hand, smoothing out the creases he'd created. "I'll take breakfast and tea in here today, thank you," he instructed without looking up from his work.

"Drat it all..." he muttered, propping his elbows up on the desk and burying his hands in his already disheveled hair.

Henry's publisher had given him the grand news last week that the latest installment in his series was doing quite well, a marked improvement from the steady climb of his previous books. It was popular in both circulating libraries and home libraries.

This finally gave Henry some real hope that perhaps his talents were truly being noticed. Solomon insisted that his novels were gaining traction, but Henry couldn't help doubting the veracity of such statements. He didn't think his friend lied to him for the purpose of bolstering his confidence. Perhaps just stretching the truth.

But hearing this from Frye himself struck Henry differently. Maybe, just maybe, his dream of sharing his imagined worlds and expressing his opinions and feelings through his characters to a larger audience were coming true.

The more Henry wrote, the more he realized that he needed his work to be shared. He had thought that he would be happy simply getting his ideas on paper and reading them back to himself over time as a private hobby. And he likely would have been content with that, had Solomon not given him the push to publish.

Now that the idea that people read and even enjoyed his writing had been planted in Henry's mind, he wanted to keep sharing himself in this way—even if no one knew it was really him.

In truth, it was the only way he could share any of himself.

Yet somehow these past few days had proven unusually difficult. Of course Henry ran into occasional road blocks with his stories, perhaps unsure of where to take the adventure next or struggling to find the right words to convey a scene. It happened to any writer, or any artist for that matter.

But he'd always been able to overcome it fairly quickly. A solitary walk about the park, or a quiet carriage ride down the streets of London usually sparked some inspiration in him.

There was just something this time that truly had his imagination in a bind. His hero was stuck in a seemingly impossible predicament, and Henry couldn't see how to get him out yet.

"My apologies, dear friend," he muttered to the sheets of paper clutched in his hands, addressing the character that lived there within flourishes of ink. "I will try to rescue you as soon as I can."

It was also not uncommon for Henry to speak to his characters out loud on occasion. As the work progressed, he found that he started seeing them more and more as real people who simply took a two-dimensional form rather than a three-dimensional one. He felt as though through writing the tale, he got to know more about them, and though he often had an idea of how the story would progress, these imaginary people often surprised him and redirected themselves.

Of course, Henry didn't share this quirky habit with anyone. Not even Solomon. He even checked to make sure that any footmen or maids had left the room first.

To Henry, this was a sacred artistic intimacy shared only between himself and his work. Besides, he knew it would sound utterly daft to anyone else.

Henry knew all too well the ebbs and flows of inspiration and motivation. But he had not anticipated suffering a creative block that seemed to dry up his pen for days, barely managing a few lines every time he sat down at his writing desk. Henry hadn't left his home for days, yet all he'd managed to squeeze out were a few pages—and mediocre pages at that.

And he had certainly not anticipated being dragged about town by Solomon on his courtship quest, and their first outing was scheduled for later today.

That thought had loomed large in Henry's mind ever since Solomon's dinner. His encounter with Miss Richards in the garden had been...peculiar. He wasn't entirely sure how to describe it.

He'd felt immensely sorry for the young woman and felt partly responsible for what transpired during her performance. She played very well, though not quite like the masked lady at Lord Henshell's ball. Even still, Miss Richards clearly had an abundance of talent and passion for the instrument.

If only he'd had the good sense to keep his distance. Yet something propelled him forward, some invisible string that connected him to the pianoforte and wound itself tighter and tighter by some strange force until he'd found himself just a few yards away, watching her play with an intensity that arrested him.

She'd been doing a wonderful job. That is, until their eyes had met. Henry knew she did not have any warm feelings toward him, nothing more than a polite tolerance most likely. Seeing him so nearby must have shocked her into fumbling her notes, and she'd clunked through the rest of the piece.

Just as Henry had stepped forward to apologize for distracting her, she'd left the room as quickly as she could manage in her dress. But not before Henry had seen the tears pooling in her blue eyes.

He'd considered it a miracle that he found her in the garden, and he had been ill prepared to deal with such a distressed young woman. He couldn't even blame her for snapping as she had at his insensitive and obtuse question.

As they'd sat together in the garden, he could have sworn that the uncomfortable air that had surrounded them since their first meeting was finally dissipating. But Miss Richards's last remark, before her sister discovered them and he'd taken his leave, still puzzled him and gave him the impression that she was not overly fond of him after all.

She had said nothing outside of the bounds of politeness, but the undercurrent in her voice had told him that she wished to be rid of him. He simply couldn't figure out why.

He sighed as he thumbed through his papers again. Unfortunately, there seemed to be much that Henry could not figure out these days.

"Breakfast, my lord." The maid entered with a tray piled

high with eggs, sliced ham, and toast accompanied by a pot of steaming tea.

"Thank you. You may set it there." He poked his nose toward the small table by the window. "I'll pick at it throughout the morning." That is, if Henry remembered it at all. When he took his food in the study, Henry often ended up sitting down to a very cold meal after getting caught up in his work for hours on end.

"Please do, my lord." The maid nodded as she backed out of the room. It seemed his staff knew this as well.

"Well, I'm not getting anything done so might as well nibble a bit," Henry said to himself, taking a deep whiff of the surely delicious food.

Abandoning his writing desk, Henry sat by the window and poured a cup of tea. He looked down at the mostly empty street that passed by the front of his London home, his thoughts returning not to his book, but to the garden and Miss Richards.

WHY MUST I BE HERE? Henry lamented to himself for the dozenth time that afternoon. Everyone else in London seemed to be enamored with Hyde Park, but Henry swore he could live the rest of his life without setting foot here again, especially at this hour. The whole of the *ton* seemed to be here, clogging the otherwise beautiful park.

But it was not just this overly crowded place that bothered Henry, though it certainly didn't help.

Miss Richards walked beside him once again, her gloved hand placed gently on his arm. He had to admit, she looked rather in her element here in the park, wearing a lovely walking dress and nodding and smiling to many other people as they passed by. Was there anyone in this city she did not know? If Henry wasn't mistaken, he was sure she wished she did not know him right now.

Their conversation had been minimal. After all, they were not the ones courting. Their presence was a mere formality on behalf of Solomon and her younger sister.

Nothing need come of their participation, Henry reminded himself. Certainly nothing *should* come of it. Every moment he spent here was a moment he could have been in his study, breaking through his slump and forging ahead on his novel.

But a promise was a promise, and Henry was a man of his word. Besides, he found the barely tamed eagerness in Solomon's face to be quite charming. His features seemed to have aged backwards, the anticipation transforming him into a young boy again. Solomon tried to hide it, but thanks to Henry's extensive knowledge of his friend it was plain as day.

Solomon's companion seemed quite enthusiastic as well. She clung to Solomon's arm and gazed up at him with a nearly permanent smile on her face. Whatever they spoke of, both seemed to find the topic of conversation completely engrossing and entertaining.

"Lord Neil, you haven't had any more trouble with that awful Mr. Faxby have you?" Miss Richards finally broke the silence, with one of Henry's most dreaded questions.

"No. Solomon tells me he hasn't shown his face at our club since the dinner, though I haven't confirmed this myself yet since I've been quite locked up in my study these past few days." Henry muttered his reply, his throat drying up at the memory of that embarrassing incident. He could feel heat spreading over the back of his neck despite the cool evening breeze.

"Ah, right. And how goes everything in your study?" Miss Richards's voice was measured and polite.

Her eyes were trained straight ahead, flickering over the

scenery from the tall trees to the other walking couples to the carriages rolling by, her eyes seemingly absorbing every detail. Surely she could not know that she was asking all the wrong questions.

"Everything is going as usual," Henry lied, hoping his nerves remained hidden. "I think this is my first day properly out in the sunlight since Lord Overton's dinner. I have been quite engrossed in a book of late but though I enjoy it, I find myself struggling to get through it."

The words fell out of Henry's mouth almost without him realizing. It certainly wasn't a lie, though Henry rarely discussed the specifics of the goings on in his study lest he let any potentially revealing hints slip.

Why on earth was he treading so close to the truth with this woman who was barely an acquaintance and who likely cared little for his company, let alone his private thoughts? And Lord knew what she might do with that perilous information if he did divulge too much.

The heat that had crept over his neck intensified, and he could feel tiny beads of sweat forming under his hairline. The hand at his side curled into a tight fist and then opened again several times, and he could feel his pulse thudding against the thin skin of his palm.

Henry should not be troubling a lady with his hobbies— truth or not—especially one he didn't know very well. The few ladies he'd been seated with at dinners or cornered into walks with (either by Solomon or eager Boodle's club members with eligible daughters) had all seemed rather uninterested in the contents of his bookshelves or his current reading list.

But, Henry realized, if he bored Miss Richards enough, perhaps she would deem him an unworthy conversation partner and revert back to silence and the occasional verbal courtesy for the rest of their undetermined time together.

Henry certainly didn't see the need for constant chatter, and Miss Richards need not feel obligated to provide it.

Henry awaited her response, expecting her to change the subject or tell him to abandon the venture. But the young woman said nothing for several moments. Suddenly Henry found that the silence he had wished for just a moment ago was made even more uncomfortable by the anticipation of whatever dismissive reply she was sure to make.

Having the advantage of height, he craned his neck forward slightly to peek just beyond her bonnet to see if he could surmise anything from her expression. Her legs continued to carry her body forward, her walking dress swishing slightly against his trousers, but perhaps he had somehow put her mind to sleep.

What he saw instead surprised him. Her face had lowered, brows furrowed and blue eyes examining the gravel walkway. She seemed to be carefully considering his words, else some other urgent thought had chosen that moment to captivate her. Somehow, Henry found the expression to be quite endearing, with the way the corners of her mouth turned down just slightly to reveal small shallow dimples.

"Miss Richards? Does something trouble you?" He hazarded, not entirely sure if it was appropriate for him to pry into her thoughts, or why he should want to do so in the first place.

She still did not respond right away, but instead she lifted her head to look forward again, her lips pursing in a puzzled fashion. Suddenly Henry couldn't help wondering just what she could be thinking to cause such a look.

"It seems you and I are not so different, Lord Neil," she mumbled.

"How do you mean?"

"Would you say you are experiencing some sort of block that is hindering your enjoyment of your hobby?"

"I suppose that would be a good way of putting it, yes."

Miss Richards nodded solemnly, taking a few moments to think this over. Finally, just as Henry was growing antsy to understand her question, she gave a deep sigh and shook her head slightly.

Surprised by this reaction, Henry halted in the middle of the path and turned to face her fully. Truly, this woman was a mystery. Henry could not fathom what she might be thinking at this precise moment, or why she questioned him so. She unlaced her hand from his arm and faced him as well.

"Perhaps individuals such as us, with interests within the realm of the arts, have this problem in common." Her once serious expression gave way to a small smile as she looked up into his face, some sort of understanding in her eyes.

"I see." Henry nodded quickly, trying unsuccessfully to pull his gaze away from hers. His heart fluttered in his chest, a rather different sensation than the painful, constricting hammering he was used to when presented with an unfamiliar situation. He could feel that he stood on the verge of something important. Something in him was being answered, but he did not know what, or why.

"I too have been suffering from some blockage that restricts my ability at the pianoforte. I want to play, to enjoy playing, but I can't seem to manage it. Unfortunately, this has plagued me for weeks. Ever since Lady Henshell's masked ball."

"Oh, you attended that event? So did I." For some reason this knowledge caused Henry to examine Miss Richards more closely. He suddenly felt as if he should have seen her there. It was the same night, after all, that Solomon had met Miss Juliet.

Henry swore that he saw a hint of pink color his companion's cheeks just before she threaded her arm through his and started up their walking again. This time her hand rested heavier on his forearm, her fingers almost gripping his coat sleeve.

"Yes, I was. Just as a guest. I spent most of the night dancing until my feet nearly gave out. So did Juliet, as you know." Something about the way she answered seemed rushed, as if she did not like discussing it, and her eyes stared pointedly at the back of her sister's head, who was now several yards ahead of them beside Solomon.

"I do indeed." Henry's response was gruffer than he'd intended.

His chest tightened as she spoke so casually about her popularity on the dance floor. He shouldn't be surprised as he had seen for himself how her lively energy attracted others to her. What concerned him more was the unfamiliar sting that had pricked his heart at her words. But it evaporated just as quickly as it had come.

"I'm sorry to hear that your hobby seems to grow dull. I know it is an unpleasant sensation," he added quickly.

"Yes, it troubled me greatly for quite some time. In fact, I've often feared that I might never see the end of it.... That my ability has been permanently stunted, and my joy with it. I felt I must be the only person in the world who can't seem to get myself in order. Yet, somehow, knowing that I do not suffer alone has given me hope." A small smile graced her lips once more, and her eyes were soft when they met Henry's.

The look arrested his breath, and he coughed liberally before responding, careful to mask his real meaning. "I understand your predicament very well. I confess this time for me is quite unusual. I can normally read for hours upon hours, even if I find the subject matter at a hand a trifle tedious, and I pride myself on finishing every book I pick up. Yet for some reason I cannot explain, I struggle to turn the pages of this book. It certainly does not lack for interesting material. But hold on. You played quite admirably at Lord Overton's dinner just a few days ago."

The thought struck Henry suddenly. If Miss Richards considered that performance to be a struggle, he could only assume that her usual talent must be remarkable. His thoughts flitted back to the masked ball again for a fraction of a second.

"Oh goodness..." Miss Richards shook her head, an embarrassed smile matching the slight blush on her cheek-bones. "That was quite the incident wasn't it."

"M-my apologies," Henry quickly stammered. "I did not mean to bring up a painful memory for you. We need not discuss this, or anything, further."

He was certain that his cheeks must be red, too. How insensitive of him to bring up an embarrassing event for her, especially after the tense moment that had passed between them in the garden. If she'd warmed up to him at all in these past few minutes, surely she had just found another reason to dislike him.

Surprising him yet again, Miss Richards laughed, perhaps a touch louder than was proper for a young lady. A few other people walking nearby glanced their way, including Solomon and Miss Richards's younger sister. But Henry did not mind their looks.

Despite having been born into this world, Henry would never understand the many strange rules of the *ton*, from needing to attend as many events as possible to seem polite and well-respected to how loudly a lady could laugh. Why should such a lovely, musical laugh need to be stifled just for the sake of seeming modest and refined?

"Don't worry yourself over it, my lord." Her words still carried traces of humor in them and her eyes sparkled. "I have since found the whole ordeal to be quite amusing. What good does it do to dwell on and groan over life's little dramas?

"In truth, I know I should be very pleased with my performance. Most of it, anyway." Her eyebrows twitched up as she remembered her fumbles. "And I should be doubly proud, considering how poorly I'd been playing on my instrument at home for quite some time before that. It just seemed as though every time I sat down my fingers would refuse to obey me, and my eyes no longer recognized the notes on the sheet music.

"I've never encountered such a problem, and the more I agonized over it the worse it seemed to become. Needless to say, I was very nervous when my mother told me that Lord Overton had asked me to play. I know I've played at other dinners where he had also been a guest, but I had no idea I'd left such an impression that he would personally ask for me to play at his own event.

"That performance was the best I'd played since this obstruction began. I finally felt as if I could enjoy my dear hobby again. I do wish I had been able to finish the piece successfully..."

Henry could hear the pain in her voice, and a heavy wave of guilt swept over him. If he had not distracted her at the last moment, she would have performed the piece flawlessly.

"I feel I must apologize for that, Miss Richards. I know I must have broken your concentration by coming too close. If it is any consolation, I still think you carried the performance off very well." Henry kept his eyes to the ground shamefully, unable to look at his walking partner.

"Of course that is not the case," Miss Richards rebutted quickly. "The only person responsible for the performance is the one who sits on the bench."

Henry didn't entirely trust her words. While they were technically true, he knew he had been the cause, and something in Miss Richards's voice told him that she knew this as well. That look of shock in her large blue eyes when they'd met his on the other side of the pianoforte had replayed in his mind an untold number of times since that night, often while his pen scribbled across the page.

But he didn't press the matter further, returning to their previous subject. "Have you had any luck in overcoming your obstacle?" Henry feared he knew the answer to this question already, and he knew it was his fault.

"Unfortunately, I do believe my performance at the earl's dinner was something of a fluke. My pianoforte skills remain much reduced." She gave a slight shrug of her shoulders as if the matter were of little consequence. But from the corner of his eye Henry could see a look of resignation pass over her face under her bonnet.

"I am truly very sorry to hear that. I do hope you will find joy in it again. That is the most important aspect, after all."

Henry's heart sank to a depth he didn't know possible as he realized that he could very well have ruined her chance at breaking whatever troublesome spell had been cast over her.

"There's no need to apologize." An unexpected cheer emanated from Miss Richards's voice and she smiled encouragingly at Henry.

Somehow the golden hair under her bonnet glowed under the evening sun, and the leaves rustled in their tall trees, and birds cooed their greetings to each other, and the air swam with the sound of lighthearted conversation between friends and couples. Henry's spirits lifted slightly as he took in the moment, allowing each different sensation to strike a chord within him, creating a harmonious melody.

"I know you are right," she continued. "I shouldn't be so worried about impressing anyone. I love the instrument, and I love music. That should be enough. I think—no, I know—

that we will both find joy in our hobbies again, even if we must go more slowly than we once did before."

The words bolstered Henry, a new determination igniting within him. He had no idea how inspiring it could be to have someone else who understood the artistic process, both the triumphs and the disappointments, to share his thoughts and struggles with—though of course Miss Richards had no idea how deeply her words could be applied. He felt sure that when he returned home tonight, the words would flow easily over his paper again just as they had before.

"Very well put, Miss Richards. Are you sure you are not a writer?"

"Oh Heavens, no. My skills can at least be confined to drawing rooms and balls. I don't think I could stand the thought of hundreds of people all over London—all over England, even—reading into my imagination. I still need to be able to dance and read and embroider and make calls, live a life away from my pianoforte." She giggled at her own casual statement.

But in an instant that radiant warmth and courage that had flooded Henry just moments before turned to ash.

Of course, Miss Richards need not worry about impressing anyone as she'd said before. At least not anyone too far removed from her family, close friends, and Society acquaintances.

Henry, on the other hand, had far more people to impress than he'd realized. He could always write for pleasure, but he must continually improve his abilities if he wished to continue sharing his created world with others.

He had thought for a few glorious minutes that he just may have found a kindred soul with whom he could share his experiences as a creative. And while Miss Richards may appreciate some aspects of it, Henry quickly realized with a sinking feeling that he could never share his identity with her, that she could never truly understand his situation—his need for dedicated time away from the world to work and unravel himself, partially driven by his own desire to do so and partially driven by the pressure he faced from the public's expectations.

In this, Henry knew he was entirely alone.

CHAPTER 9

"Unfortunately it seems we differ there," Lord Neil mumbled, his lips suddenly drawn tight.

Had Cecilia said something wrong? Surely they were finally connecting over their shared interest in art. Based on the reasoning he'd given for agreeing to these outings in Lord Overton's garden a few nights ago, Cecilia had all but given up any expectation that she would feel like anything other than some awkward and unwanted tagalong to her sister's meetings with the earl. Lord Neil seemed to see her company as an obligation and nothing more.

But here she had a glimmer of hope that they had something in common which could make their time together at least a bit more bearable. Perhaps even friendly.

Hearing that he too struggled at times with enjoying his hobby to the fullest had sympathized her to the baron. No one else she knew had such a fascination for the arts, whether it be music or painting or fine works of writing. Juliet could draw a decent likeness, but it was only a hobby to be enjoyed when she couldn't find something else to occupy her time or if the weather was too cold or dreary to allow her outside. Rosamund had quite a lovely voice, and Cecilia had provided accompaniment for her on a few occasions. But again, Cecilia knew that her friend primarily took pleasure in the praises that came after the song.

As such, Cecilia had had no indication that her current predicament was shared by anyone else in the world. For most, if a hobby no longer pleased them they would simply drop it from their life and pick up a new one. But for Cecilia, music was her passion. She had felt like an oddity in these past several weeks, unable to will herself back to her usual state.

It was a lonely feeling. She hadn't realized just how lonely until Lord Neil had confessed his own similar situation. If Lord Neil had a passion, Cecilia knew it must be collecting and reading books.

"How so?" She prodded. Something in the air about Lord Neil had changed.

"My interest is nearly all consuming. It may seem peculiar to others, but I have almost no need of the outside world when I have access to so many ideas and perspectives and histories in my library." His brow furrowed and his eyes stared ahead, not really seeing his surroundings.

Heat flared in Cecilia's chest. She had thought a few moments ago that they might be able to form a friendship over their passions. Yet every time she seemed to see a way through to him, he closed it off.

"Well then, I must thank you for tearing yourself away from your library to parade around the park with me."

Her good mood had quickly turned sour. Not just because of Lord Neil's words and her new conclusion about his world view. She found that, against her own wishes, her heart suddenly felt hollow at this development. She had hoped, more than she'd admitted to herself, that she could turn Lord Neil's favor to her.

"On the contrary, Miss Richards. I must thank you for accompanying me on this walk. I believe it has done me some good. Perhaps after some time away from my books I will return to them with a new appreciation."

His smile looked closer to a grimace, and while Cecilia sensed some sincerity in his words she also felt that he was simply trying to salvage the situation. Another nicety.

Cecilia should have taken the baron's words at face value and been happy with that. Yet her mind pushed back with an unexpected hunger.

Even if he did gain something positive from their walk today, the tug in Cecilia's heart told her that she wanted to be more than the baron's reminder of how taxing the outside world could be, driving him gratefully back into the solitude of his library.

The thought startled her, flipping her stomach upside down. An image of the masked gentleman floated into her mind's eye for just a moment. He was a man who truly understood love for the arts, including discussions of art. Yet still he evaded her.

Perhaps in the very deepest corner of her mind, Cecilia realized, this conversation had sparked the tiniest hope that Lord Neil could have been such a man.

But she saw now that he was not. He secluded himself to his library, just as much for pleasure as to keep himself protected from the world.

A strong breeze rattled through the park, the tree branches overhead clicking against each other.

"Oh!" Cecilia gasped as she felt her handkerchief take flight out of her slippery gloved fingers. She tried to catch it with as much ladylike grace as she could manage, but the breeze carried it off down the walking path.

Almost as surprising, Cecilia felt the warmth of Lord Neil's body disappear from her side. She had to clench her jaw to keep her mouth from falling open as she watched the baron trot forward and catch the mischievous handkerchief just before it touched the ground. The dainty square of fabric seemed tiny in Lord Neil's large hand.

"Saved it just in time." Lord Neil smiled shyly, a lock of hair knocked loose across his forehead during his dash to rescue the rogue handkerchief.

Dumbfounded, Cecilia retrieved her lost item from the baron and hid it away in her reticule, her eyes never leaving his.

"Miss Richards?" Lord Neil peered down at her, the dark brown lock falling further into his face. For one wild moment Cecilia desperately wished she could tuck it back into place, could feel her gloves slide against his forehead.

She forced a breath into her lungs. "Thank you, Lord Neil. Though I must confess, I never expected to see you running about the park." The last part slipped out with a slight chuckle, though she hoped her sincerity hadn't been lost in the jest.

Lord Neil offered his arm once more and Cecilia took it. "I wouldn't quite call that a run, but I do know how, yes. I only employ that skill on special occasions."

Cecilia smiled at the touch of humor in his voice and she glanced up at him from under her bonnet. Though the baron looked ahead at the path before them, she didn't miss the slight upward curve of his mouth.

Cecilia's head felt as though it was loose on her shoulders. Her estimation of Lord Neil seemed to change by the minute, but her own conflicting feelings were suddenly of far, far greater concern.

She needed to swim out of this whirlpool before it sucked her in any deeper.

$\approx$

THE NEXT SEVERAL weeks contained more of the same. A letter, wax sealed with Lord Overton's family crest, arrived once a week to ask for both Juliet's and Cecilia's company. And both girls dutifully attended whatever carriage ride or walk or picnic the earl had planned.

Mr. and Mrs. Richards were of course thrilled by this development. By their estimation, both their daughters could very well be married off by the end of the Season—to a baron and an earl, no less.

Cecilia should have been grateful. Their mother was in a far better mood than she'd ever seen, praising both her daughters endlessly and fussing over their every need. And their father, always the gentler of the two, suddenly seemed less interested in going to his club or playing cards when they attended dances, instead choosing to linger by his daughters' sides and introduce himself as a great friend of Lord Overton and Lord Neil.

Unfortunately, Cecilia also knew the truth. At least as far as her own prospects were concerned.

Every outing in which she had to cling to Lord Neil's arm only stoked her irritation. But she found that the source of her irritation wasn't really the baron himself. At least, not entirely.

After their clash of opinions on art during their first walk about Hyde Park, trailing after the real lovebirds, Cecilia had vowed to stop pressing the baron for conversation, to stop attempting to forge a friendship out of their provisional situation. They clearly would not see eye to eye on this most important matter, despite how desperately she'd wanted to.

Yet somehow, Cecilia could not stop herself from admiring his strong side profile, or the curl of his dark hair over his ears, or the gentle way in which his fingers gripped hers as he helped her down from the carriage.

And she certainly couldn't forget the way he gallantly

chased her handkerchief without a second thought. Though it was such a simple act, Cecilia couldn't help being reminded of those chivalrous heroes she read about.

These thoughts, vexing though they might be, did not worry her as much as certain other, far more galling thoughts. It was the latter that caused her so much annoyance when out and about with her sister and their companions, or when the next letter was received, or even when the baron seemed to barge into her mind at any inconvenient moment.

Despite the callous way with which he'd discussed his aversion to the world during their first walk—an impression Cecilia had tried to cling to in order to justify distancing herself from him—Cecilia found herself unable to shake a wretched desire in her heart to close that very same distance.

After all, he almost always spoke so tenderly, with an air of deep thought about him—if he spoke at all. And Cecilia often had her own observations about their surroundings, and life as a whole, mirrored in Lord Neil's words. Though they seemed to have reached an unspoken agreement to avoid topics relating to music, books, and art in general.

Cecilia squeezed her eyes shut for a moment and let her fingers brush against the leather cover of the book in her lap which happened to be latest installment from the popular adventure novelist. When she opened her eyes, she realized that she'd been reading the same few sentences repeatedly, one finger tucked under the corner of the page, ready to flip to the next.

She'd been lost in thought and had finally come back to earth, her senses grounding her with the feeling of the book in her hands and her back against the soft chair, rain gently knocking on the window. Cecilia's stomach turned as she realized the path her thoughts had taken once again.

"You foolish girl," she muttered under her breath,

scolding herself for getting lost in this fantasy world. No matter how often Cecilia's mind tried to transform Lord Neil into the hero in those books, she knew he could not be the hero she hoped for. Her hero, after all, wore a mask and danced elegantly and faced the world head on and understood that art could only be kept alive by sharing it.

She closed the book, slipping a piece of paper between the pages to mark her spot, and walked across the room to the window. The dreary sky seemed as gray her heart.

If only she could reduce Lord Neil to another one of her unsuccessful suitors. But she was tied to him for now, at least until Lord Overton asked for Juliet's hand, or one or both of them grew tired of the other and put an end to the courtship.

Or until she could finally discover who her masked gentleman was.

But as the weeks floated by in the warming London air, Cecilia knew in her heart that her chance had slipped past her. He very well might not even be in London anymore. Perhaps he had only been in London for that one beautiful night. The more she mulled it over, the more she felt that he must have been some kind of mirage, appearing only once in her lifetime for some mysterious purpose and never to be seen again.

Part of her irritation with Lord Neil, she guiltily admitted to herself, had to do with just how close he seemed at times to that man she'd shared that glorious dance with. Some of the things he said, even the way he said them, struck her as just the types of things the masked gentleman would have said. Of course, she knew she had no way of knowing if she might be correct.

What she did know was that she was chasing yet another unreachable dream. If finding a man she could love with all her heart and feel his love in return had been difficult, finding the one man who had finally sparked that possibility in her was completely out of the question.

Cecilia let her forehead press against the cool glass for a moment as she gazed into the soggy sky. The rain wasn't heavy, but it had been steady all day. The longer it rained the darker her mood had grown.

Today was not an ideal day for a ball. And besides, she'd just seen Lord Neil yesterday. He and Lord Overton had enjoyed a quiet dinner at the Richards home for the first time. Needless to say, their parents were absolutely thrilled by this development. They hadn't said anything outright, but their eyes had sparkled with the hopes of an impending engagement ever since the dinner plans had been set.

They had gone all out with dinner, overworking the poor cook and kitchen maids to produce several top-notch courses. Lord Overton and Mr. Richards never lacked for topics of conversation, with Juliet chiming in as she pleased, and even Cecilia offered her remarks from time to time.

Mrs. Richards had been content to quietly watch the evening unfold, shooting hungry glances between Lord Overton and Juliet. She seemed not to notice Lord Neil and Cecilia nearly as much, as Lord Neil had eaten mostly in silence. Clearly, their parents' hopes were pinned firmly on a match between the Earl and their youngest daughter.

Knowing that Lord Neil would be in attendance tonight, Cecilia's excitement at the prospect of another ball had dwindled significantly. Perhaps he would not ask to dance with her or even attempt to speak with her at all, since this event fell outside the window of his allotted time with her.

Cecilia glanced at the clock above the fireplace. She still had quite some time before getting ready for the ball. She needed to try something else to occupy her mind, since this book had been unable to do so. Even a poor session at the pianoforte would be better than agonizing over this for another moment.

~

"Mama, is it possible that I might stay home from this ball tonight?" Cecilia whispered the question. Her mother had been in exceptionally high spirits these past few weeks, but she did not trust the mood to last if she pushed her luck too far. Yet she had to ask, knowing that she risked fire and brimstone. That was how badly she wished to avoid Lord Neil.

Mrs. Richards's hands stilled over the dress sprawled out on the bed, another one of her favorites on Cecilia. She turned slowly to face her daughter, eyes narrow.

"And why might that be? Are you ill? Injured?" Such questions usually conveyed care and concern, but coming from her mother now, they sounded cold and harsh.

"No, I'm well. I just find myself disagreeable to the idea of a ball tonight. I've been out plenty so far this Season, and there will be more dances to come. Could it really hurt if I were to sit this one out? We're not even particularly close to the hosts. And besides, this is Juliet's Season. All eyes should be on her."

The justifications spilled out of Cecilia quickly, as if she were trying to address her mother's arguments before she could make them. But she knew in an instant that she had made a mistake. The air seemed to drain from the room. Violet found something to fuss with in the far corner, glancing over her shoulder furtively at her mistresses.

"Cecilia. Are you really such a fool?"

"Mama…" Cecilia's mouth gaped open. Her mother could be unforgiving and demanding, but she had rarely been so bluntly cruel.

"All eyes are already on your sister. It is you we are concerned with. Every man that has shown an interest in you has been turned away. And for what? Your silly ideals? True love? I knew you were naïve but I had no idea it ran this deeply.

"You will attend this ball. If you think the tension between you and Lord Neil has gone unnoticed, you are sorely mistaken. Whatever has happened between the two of you, put it to rest and dance with him tonight. Restore his favor to you or else your father and I will begin choosing gentlemen. We will choose a husband on your behalf, if need be. Consider this your last warning."

The pure shock froze Cecilia in place. She stared at her mother, who simply stared back with a look of contempt that Cecilia had never seen before. She'd had no idea until now how little her parents truly cared for her. They had been lenient, yes, but they had already decided how her life would play out in the end, whether she liked that ending or not. Her brave hero would not come to her rescue.

The realization hit her with such force that it knocked the breath out of her, tears flowing hot and fast. Cecilia staggered to the bedpost and wrapped her arms around it, but her legs could not support her weight any longer and she slowly sunk to the ground, her petticoat pooling up around her and making her feel like a pitiful child playing dress up.

"Clean yourself up. I expect to see you downstairs at the appointed time." Mrs. Richards left the room, no warmth in her voice.

Suddenly, a pair of small hands gripped Cecilia's upper arms, gentle but firm. Cecilia looked up, eyes blurred by tears but she could still make out the outline of Violet's face. The maid had gotten down on her knees so as to be eye level with Cecilia.

"Come now, Miss Richards. Let's get you up and ready for

the ball. You'll be the loveliest girl there by the time I'm done with you." Violet spoke quietly and slowly, as if comforting a child.

Cecilia was grateful for it. She could barely string a single thought together, the only words that swirled in her mind the ones that had just been uttered with such cold-hearted disdain.

Cecilia allowed Violet to help her up and attend to her appearance for the ball, but she was only half aware of anything the girl did. She had no idea how she would survive this evening. Her heart and all her dreams had been crushed, but she must converse and dance as if the course of her future hadn't been thrown off its rails.

FOR ONCE, the glitter and activity of the ball did nothing to entice Cecilia into a convivial mood. One of her favorite moments at such events had always been the arrival—the butterflies of excitement converging in her stomach as she stepped out of the carriage and took in the house ablaze with candles in every window, the footmen passing platters of refreshments, the scores of ladies and gentlemen wearing their finest in an array of beautiful colors.

But tonight, the butterflies had been replaced by rolling waves of nausea. The home their carriage pulled up to looked like an ugly mismatch of architectural tastes. The footmen seemed like a swarm buzzing about the front steps and the foyer without purpose. And worst of all, the ladies and gentlemen turned out in their best looked garish and ostentatious.

Cecilia could hear the music of the musicians as they approached the ballroom and her heart twisted sharply. Heaven only knew how long she would have to endure this sickening show while she felt as though she would crumble at any moment.

"Sissy, whatever is the matter? You look as if you've just been told your childhood pony has died."

Juliet sidled up next to Cecilia, breaking away from their parents in the general bustle of the ball. She'd chuckled as she spoke, but the look in Cecilia's eye silenced her into true concern.

"Mama knows I turn every man down because I'm trying to find someone I can genuinely love. She threatened that if I don't make more of an attempt to secure Lord Neil's favor, she and Papa will take matters into their own hands..." Cecilia choked back a whimper, the cry that was desperate to be unleashed scraping against her throat as she swallowed it back down.

Juliet blanched at this. "Take matters into their own hands in what way?"

Cecilia couldn't bear to look at her sister. She shook her head in defeat and closed her eyes, willing the tears to stay put for just a few hours. "They will make a match for me, whether I like the man or not."

"Oh no..." Juliet sighed. "Don't worry, darling. We'll figure something out. I promise. Let's just get through this wretched night."

Juliet squeezed her sister's hand lovingly. Cecilia heard the hesitation in Juliet's voice as she made a promise that might be impossible to keep. But she knew that if they could just survive the ball, they could at least console each other in the privacy of their home.

The two girls caught up with their mother, who was busy chatting with other mothers chaperoning their marriageable children.

"Ah, here they come now, my lovely daughters. Why, at dinner last night, the Earl of Overton commented to his friend Lord Neil that Juliet's eyes are just the same shade as the blue hyacinths grown in the garden at his estate," Mrs. Richards cooed, grabbing each daughter by the hand and dragging them into her circle of acquaintances.

Cecilia's mouth went dry and she thought she might be truly sick in the middle of the ballroom. Juliet looked about the same as Cecilia felt.

"Lord Overton and Lord Neil, you say. Their fortunes are certainly a catch, at least." One of the women said slyly, raising her eyebrows expectantly. She was clearly in the mood for gossip.

Mrs. Richards took the bait without hesitation. "Whatever could you mean, Mrs. Brace?"

The other woman shrugged a shoulder nonchalantly. "It's quite common knowledge that Lord Overton doesn't court for long. Not unlike..." She trailed off, but the pointed look at Cecilia finished her sentence. "What I mean to say is, most believe that Lord Overton is loath to settle down. He may remain wifeless and heirless for years yet.

"And Lord Neil. Some say that making a match with that man is a laughable quest. Any wife of his would wither away in that house. He never goes out if he can help it, except when Lord Overton bullies him into it. And he always seems so very bored and unimpressed when he does go out. That's another fortune that will likely go to waste."

Mrs. Brace sighed dramatically, expertly ignoring the way Mrs. Richards's jaw twitched.

"I can assure you that both the earl and the baron are gentlemen of the highest quality." Mrs. Richards smiled but spoke through gritted teeth.

Cecilia glanced down at her feet, the sick feeling in her stomach giving way to irritation.

She'd only heard a few mentions of Mrs. Brace in passing from her mother. The two were not close but Mrs. Richards nurtured any relationship that she thought might be advantageous for their family. Cecilia did not see this one lasting much longer given the several rude implications Mrs. Brace had made just now, not just against the gentlemen but against Cecilia as well.

A hot wave of anger surged through her breast, followed by an unexpected urge to defend Lord Neil.

Cecilia had just opened her mouth to state her opinions when Mrs. Richards tossed her head and jutted her chin into the air, looking down her nose at her acquaintance. "Come Cecilia, Juliet. I do believe refreshments are in order."

But as she turned to leave their company behind, the very subjects of their discussion approached through the crowd. Cecilia didn't try to conceal her glare at Mrs. Brace. She knew that if the woman dared open her mouth and speak such unkind things in their presence, Cecilia would not be able to conceal her contempt.

To Cecilia's great satisfaction, Mrs. Brace flushed. She scurried toward Lord Overton and Lord Neil.

"My lords, you are both looking very well tonight!" She simpered, curtseying with grand affectation.

Cecilia wrinkled her nose at the nauseating display of hypocrisy. She caught Lord Neil's eye and saw that he regarded her quizzically. She simply raised her eyebrows in exasperation, hoping that she answered his unspoken question. Based on his quickly suppressed chuckle, Cecilia knew that she had succeeded.

The quick, silent exchange sent an unbidden thrill through her heart. As Lord Overton asked their mother for the girls' dance cards, Cecilia's eyes remained locked on the baron's. She sensed that he somehow understood her vexation, and she realized that she was eager to discuss her thoughts with him.

"We shall be back shortly," Lord Overton announced,

beaming at the group of women before turning on his heel and disappearing back into the crowd. Lord Neil followed suit.

The Richards women quickly abandoned Mrs. Brace and found an open spot near a table with light finger foods to await the next dance set.

"A truly vile woman," Mrs. Richards scoffed as she bit into a morsel, her eyes sweeping over the crowded room with distaste.

"Oh really, Mother? As if you're any better? All you plan on doing is selling us off to the highest bidder. And for what? So you can walk around London bragging about your good family name and looking down on everyone else?"

Both Cecilia's and Mrs. Richards's heads whipped around to stare at Juliet. Of course, Cecilia had been thinking the exact same thing. But she'd had no plans of voicing those thoughts, at least not so bluntly and not during the middle of a ball.

Juliet, however, had no such reservations. Her anger was nearly palpable in the air about them, her chest heaving up and down and her eyes narrowed in a severe glare.

"How dare you speak to me in such an unladylike manner?" Mrs. Richards matched her younger daughter's gaze with her own nearly boiled over wrath.

"You speak as though you're so much better than Mrs. Brace, but I assure you you're cut from the very same cloth. All you care about is improving your own reputation, and you don't care who you hurt in the process. It's disgusting."

Juliet spat the words with such a fury that Cecilia had never seen or heard from her. She had greatly underestimated how this news would affect her sister, and she regretted sharing it at such an inappropriate time.

"Jules—" Cecilia put a hand upon the younger woman's

shoulder, but Juliet roughly brushed it off. She spun around and marched away into the throng of guests.

"What an insufferable girl!" Cecilia heard Mrs. Richards exclaim as she quickly followed behind her sister.

Cecilia caught up to Juliet's shorter steps and overtook her, clasping one of her hands and redirecting her towards a quiet corner with some chairs. Juliet sat in one of the chairs, still trembling with anger, and Cecilia sank into the other.

"I hate that they're doing this to us," Juliet growled before Cecilia could speak.

"I know. But as you said earlier, we'll figure something out. This is simply not the best time to do it." Cecilia kept her hand around her sister's, rubbing small circles with her thumb against the fabric of her glove.

Juliet fell silent for several moments, and Cecilia wondered if she were hatching some sort of grand plan right then and there. But a closer examination of her sister's face indicated that her mind wasn't working out a solution, but rather that it was fixated on some singular point.

Cecilia looked in the direction of Juliet's gaze, and immediately understood what had her so transfixed. Lord Overton stood almost directly across from them on the other side of the room. He was wrapped up in a rather humorous looking conversation with several other gentlemen. As always, Lord Neil stood nearby, just a touch too far away to truly be part of the group.

"Jules, are you sure that such a thing as marriage is still so disagreeable to you?" Cecilia asked softly, careful to make sure her voice carried no judgement. She had struggled to understand Juliet's viewpoint in the past, but she didn't need to understand it to know how important this matter was to her sister.

Juliet snapped back to the present moment. She almost seemed startled that Cecilia sat next to her.

"Don't get any ideas now. I won't say that I fancy Lord Overton...yet I won't deny that I enjoy his company."

Cecilia only raised an eyebrow in response. It sounded an awful lot to her like Juliet did indeed fancy the earl.

"I said don't get any ideas!" Juliet pouted for a moment, before a dark expression overtook her. "You think I haven't heard the whispers about him around town? About all the ladies he showers with his favor before casting them off? How he uses them for entertainment, for show?"

"But you've spent quite a good amount of time with him these past couple months. Do you really think he is that type of man?"

"Of course I don't. But didn't all his other favored ladies think the same?" The pain in Juliet's voice was clear, and her brows turned up with worry.

"I don't know, Juliet. The two of you seem to get on so well when we're all together."

Suddenly Juliet's head snapped up, a defiant look in her eye. "As I said before, don't get any ideas. I enjoy his friendship. But that is not the issue. Not the whole issue, anyway. If Lord Overton doesn't ask for my hand, or if he does and I don't wish to accept, Mama and Papa will either force me or find someone else to thrust upon me. I can't bear the thought of living such a lie, of having my freedom stripped away so completely."

"Yes.... I quite agree with you there." Cecilia frowned, picking at the fingertips of her gloves.

"But what of you and Lord Neil? I'm sure they would love for you to make a match with him. I know you've had your misunderstandings, but surely you can't find him that disagreeable. You have been staring at him all night. Couldn't he be a fine substitute for your masked gentleman?" Juliet nudged Cecilia in the ribs with her elbow.

Cecilia glared at her sister and was just about to retort when the subjects of conversation once again approached.

"Ladies, may we collect our dances?" Lord Overton bowed and though he addressed them both, his eyes were fixed squarely upon Juliet.

Juliet took his hand and stood to follow him onto the floor, but not before throwing a knowing glance over her shoulder to Cecilia.

Lord Neil didn't speak, but simply offered his hand to Cecilia. She took it, noticing the strength in his fingers as they gripped hers, despite the glove that acted as a buffer between them.

"You look very well this evening," he murmured as they took their places.

"As do you, my lord."

"I am sorry you had to suffer even a second in Mrs. Brace's company," Lord Neil apologized, beginning the steps of the dance.

"You know her?" Cecilia was surprised that the baron, who admitted freely that he kept his acquaintance list as short as possible, knew of Mrs. Brace.

"Certainly. She is quite the chatterbox. I fear she rather dislikes both Lord Overton and myself. Lord Overton had taken her daughter out on a few carriage rides several Seasons ago, but quit calling upon her after realizing her company was not to his liking.

"Then Mrs. Brace tried to encourage me to court her daughter." He coughed, as if the very idea of courting someone was impure and embarrassing. "I managed to avoid her, and ever since she has said a number of unkind things about both of us, despite the fact that her daughter secured a good match later that same Season."

Cecilia realized that she'd been gripping the baron's hand too tightly as he shared his story. The poor man seemed misunderstood by nearly everyone in the *ton,* yet he sounded rather unaffected by it all. "I'm very sorry you've had deal with such spiteful behavior."

The baron gave a small shrug. "I am more sorry you had to endure her vapid conversation. But such comments don't affect me overmuch. Our world is full of small people with small minds. They don't yet realize how little it costs to broaden one's perspective. Perhaps one day they will. I hope they will. Miss Richards? Are you alright?"

Cecilia nearly stumbled, forgetting her steps as Lord Neil's words rang in her ears.

"Yes! Quite alright! M-my dress must be a tad too long in the front." She hurried the words out and glanced down at her feet as if examining her gown's hemline for defects.

But what she really wanted to do was ensure that the baron did not see the rosy blush that surely must have flamed across her cheeks in an instant.

Lord Neil said something or other about hoping she would take care not to hurt herself but Cecilia paid little attention. His previous words rang a thousand chimes in her ears.

Our world is full of small people with small minds. They don't yet realize how little it costs to broaden one's perspective.

Her heart hammered in her chest and suddenly her hand in his felt far too hot. Her eyes wandered about his countenance, everywhere but his pensive dark brown eyes.

Had not her masked gentleman said something nearly to that exact same effect? Cecilia's mind flew back to that memory, willing herself to remember what the man had said. If her mind wasn't playing tricks on her, Lord Neil had phrased his astute statement word for word to the mystery man she'd danced with all those weeks ago.

Suddenly, Cecilia couldn't prevent her senses from honing in on everything Lord Neil did, analyzing the way he danced, the way he held her hand and lead her about the floor, how each step landed. Her mind was working at a breakneck pace to match Lord Neil to the memory of her much longed for dance partner.

Something in Cecilia desperately wanted the answer to be Lord Neil. Even just for the sake of having an answer.

But the longer she found herself swept about the floor, encircled in his arms, the more she realized that she enjoyed the sensation. She felt comfortable. She was intrigued by the workings of his mind.

Yet no matter how hard her memory worked, Cecilia could not verify with absolute certainty that Lord Neil and the masked gentleman were a match. Too much time had passed, and despite how often she'd replayed that dance in her mind, the finer details had slipped away as they were bound to do.

"Perhaps it is not appropriate of me to ask this..."

Lord Neil's low voice jolted Cecilia back to the present ballroom. "Yes?" She heard the breathlessness in her own voice and hoped beyond hope that he hadn't heard it as well.

"Have you had any improvement with your pianoforte troubles?"

The question sounded sheepish, and when Cecilia finally looked up into his eyes, she saw genuine concern and curiosity. Her chest tightened with a strange, but not unpleasant sensation.

"I didn't realize you remembered that," she admitted.

"How could I forget it? It seemed to trouble you so deeply. In fact, I had hoped to inquire about your progress on several occasions, but I feared the topic might be too sensitive." A rueful smile tugged at Lord Neil's lips and his eyes darted away from hers.

"I appreciate your concern, and I would be happy to discuss my difficulties with you." The truth of her own words stunned Cecilia. But the warmth that flooded the baron's face told her that she'd said just the right thing. "Unfortunately, my situation is not much improved."

Lord Neil nodded solemnly. "Nor is mine, I'm afraid. It seems books have lost their splendor. We appear to be companions in the same boat for a while longer."

Cecilia wished she could comfort the baron and immediately blushed at the brazen thought. But just then their dance came to an end. They exchanged bows and curtsies but neither of them left their spots just yet. Cecilia hoped that he would ask her for another dance.

"Cecilia! There you are!"

The spell over Cecilia shattered as the sound of her mother's hawkish voice pierced her ears, and surely everyone else's in the vicinity. Cecilia swore she saw Lord Neil wince ever so slightly.

"Our gracious hosts have heard about your accomplishments with the pianoforte, and they'd like you to play a piece while the musicians take refreshments."

Mrs. Richards nearly clawed at Cecilia's arm in her excitement and hurry to get her daughter over to the instrument.

"Mama—!" Cecilia attempted to argue but it was no use. She stumbled along behind her mother, but Cecilia managed to glance back over her shoulder to the baron.

He hadn't walked away yet. Instead, his gaze was fixed on her, and when their eyes met he gave a wide smile and quick nod. *Good luck*, he mouthed.

In that moment, Cecilia knew that her struggles with the pianoforte had been put to rest.

CHAPTER 10

Drat it all, Henry cursed to himself as Mrs. Richards dragged her daughter away. He'd just been about to ask for a second dance—something he had never done before.

But the look of hope that lit up her face as he'd wished her luck would suffice.

He followed behind Miss Richards and her mother toward the front of the ballroom, where the pianoforte and the musicians' instruments had been set up.

This time he was careful to keep his distance and remain out of view. He dared not risk a repeat of Solomon's dinner, especially since tonight's crowd was far larger. He chose a spot nearby but facing her back so that she would not be thrown by him again and lose her confidence.

The Master of Ceremonies called the guests' attention and introduced Miss Richards. She took her seat on the bench and adjusted the sheet music, finding the piece she wanted. But before she began, Miss Richards turned slightly to look over her shoulder, her eyes scanning the room for something or someone.

Henry hoped that she wouldn't turn far enough to notice him. Just as he was about to slip further back, Miss Richards found him.

Those ocean blue eyes locked onto his, and the corners of her lips curled up into a shy smile. Perhaps, Henry realized with a shock, Miss Richards had been looking for him after all.

He nearly brushed the thought away as absurd. Their dance had been pleasant, and they seemed to have overcome the awkwardness that had settled between them and worried him into a state of near silence at the dinner in the Richards home last night.

Certainly, Henry found that he had enjoyed the dance far more than he'd thought possible. Despite their numerous meetings over the course of the last two months, conversation had been limited. Henry blamed that on himself, as conversation had never been his strong suit. But the few glimpses he caught into Miss Richards's character and thoughts intrigued him.

Even from what little Miss Richards had said during their outings, Henry could see that she had a unique way of viewing the world. In her eyes, everything was lovely and charming and funny. Every person was a friend, until they proved otherwise as Mr. Faxby had done.

And yes, he had certainly noticed the way her eyes softened when they passed by young courting couples or newlyweds in the park. But there was always a hint of something else in her expression. Longing, perhaps.

He wished to speak with her and learn more, but he felt that he'd made the impression that he would rather be in his library or study than spending time in her company. And that had been true initially.

Henry knew he should have done more to prompt friendliness between them. Goodness knew he'd had plenty of opportunities. They weren't unfriendly, but any time they were together Henry could feel the weight of some wordless unease between them.

But the more time passed, the more Henry found it difficult to speak up. Every time she entered the room, or he helped her into the carriage, or she walked by his side with her hand upon his arm, Henry's voice failed him. He'd had too few close relationships to understand how to mend something that he wasn't sure was wrong.

Henry had resolved to finally break that barrier somehow tonight. Even if he didn't know what to say or how to say it. As his own struggles with writing continued Henry had been increasingly curious about Miss Richards's progress. But he didn't wish to upset her if the subject remained a sore one.

Tonight had almost been a failure in regards to Henry's secret self-imposed mission. Henry had been certain that he would never gain Miss Richards's good graces when he saw Mrs. Brace prattling on to the Richards women, and saw the troublesome woman's panicked look as he and Solomon had approached. He'd known without a doubt that Mrs. Brace had been gossiping about them.

But, as she was wont to do, Miss Richards surprised him. Her expression told him in no uncertain terms, almost as if she had spoken aloud, exactly what she thought of Mrs. Brace and her meddling gossip. He had been glad to learn that they were of the same mind when it came to those types.

The dance itself, however, was another challenge. Henry was aware of every second that slipped by, their feet completing the patterns with barely a thought, her gloved hand smooth in his.

Henry couldn't pinpoint it, but as they'd spoken and spun about the room, something in Miss Richards's entire aura changed. She suddenly felt soft in his arms, and her eyes had contained an expression he wasn't sure he'd ever seen directed at himself before. He wasn't sure yet what to call it.

Whatever it was, it had been enough to give him courage and finally ask what was on his mind. He was saddened to hear that she also continued to fight against her invisible foe, as he himself secretly did. Henry wished he could share his own struggles with her, that they could comfort each other through the trials of artistic interests.

A small victory—in a battle Henry didn't know why he felt the need to fight—but a victory nonetheless. He looked forward to more amiable outings, and perhaps a new friend with whom he could one day discuss his private writing woes.

Yet despite this victory, Henry was quite surprised to realize that—unless he was a far bigger fool than he'd thought—Miss Richards had indeed been looking for him in the crowd as she readied herself to perform.

The realization sent a chill down Henry's spine. His eyes had not deceived him. Miss Richards's eyes quickly darted to the side and then back to Henry. He somehow seemed to understand once again exactly what she meant. No words needed, even from across a room full of people.

Henry weaseled his way through the other guests until he found an empty spot near the side of the small stage set up for musical entertainment. Henry now had an unobstructed view of Miss Richards's side profile. His eyes quickly took her in, from the gentle slope of her neck as she looked over the sheet music, to the way her shoulders dropped down with grace, to the tall and proud bridge of her nose, to the puffy pout of her lips.

Miss Richards placed her hands upon the keys, ready to begin. She took a deep breath and as she did so, she glanced to Henry again out of the corner of her eye. He gave her a quick nod of encouragement. The young woman smiled and began playing.

DESPITE HER EARLIER CONFESSION THAT she continued to suffer mental blocks at the pianoforte, Henry was convinced within moments that she had not just overcome them, but leapt past them on sparkling wings.

The melody of the song was slow and dramatic, and Henry's heartbeat matched its pace with the deep chords. Every thump reverberated through his whole chest and Henry wondered why his heart had never beat with such force and impact before. And he wondered why it was doing so at this moment.

The beautiful music floated in the air and mesmerized the entire room—Henry most of all. He found it utterly fascinating that these sounds were being produced by every precise placement of Miss Richards's fingers, that she could coax such magic out of an otherwise lifeless object.

And better still, Henry enjoyed watching her perform. He'd noticed it at Solomon's dinner as well—the way she swayed in time with the music, the way her face shifted through a myriad of emotions as the song progressed. It was as if the piece told its story through her entire body.

Then it struck Henry, a hidden memory that he'd carefully filed away and buried beneath all his ideas for his new novel and most recently with his predicament as Solomon's courtship advisor.

Miss Richards reminded him of someone.

Something about her countenance and bearing had seemed familiar to him before, especially when she'd performed at Solomon's dinner several weeks ago. But he'd quickly banished the thought. Though he'd known even then that Miss Richards was very talented despite her mistakes at the end, Henry had been able to dismiss any similarities he'd drawn between them.

But listening to her play now, executing the piece perfectly and with such passion and love for the instrument as he'd never seen before, Henry's mind suddenly recalled that night at the Henshell ball. That heavenly pianoforte performance.

Of course, that lady had been wearing a mask, so Henry hadn't been able to obtain an accurate picture of her face. Yet certain moments of that memory were being superimposed over the present moment and over Miss Richards.

Her golden hair in the candlelight, the way her lips parted ever so slightly, the passion and precision with which she played—could Miss Richards be that very same lady?

But they had in fact brought up that very performance on their first carriage ride together, and Miss Richards had given no indication whatsoever that she had been the woman behind the mask. This would be an even stranger coincidence than some of the events spun in his own tales.

Just as suddenly as it had begun, the music came to an end, the last notes trailing away softly into the distance.

Miss Richards breathed deeply and smiled down at the instrument, her fingers brushing against the keys as though they were a dear friend she had been missing. She turned slightly to face Henry, and her bright face lit something deep within his chest. He couldn't stop himself from returning her exuberant smile.

The applause was polite but hearty, and Henry proudly added his own echoing claps to the mix. Proud. He hadn't realized he could be so proud of someone else's accomplishment and joy. But he loved seeing her triumphantly stand to accept her applause. It took Henry a moment to realize that it meant so much to him because he knew how long she'd struggled to get to this moment, and how painful the ache of wanting to create but being unable could be.

And dare he admit it? Yes, Henry decided that he would admit. It was nothing less than she deserved. Henry found himself truly inspired by Miss Richards. Not just her resounding performance, but her victory over her internal battles.

"She is something else, isn't she?"

Though the voice was soft and quiet, its sudden appearance next to Henry startled him. Tilting his head down slightly, he saw Miss Juliet Richards standing next to him. And beside her was Solomon. Her pale blue eyes searched his with a gentle knowing.

"Yes, of course. She is rather remarkable." Henry found himself agreeing without hesitation or embarrassment.

Miss Cecilia Richards deserved all the praise in the world, and he would give as much of it as he could as often as he could.

SLEEP evaded Henry for several nights. He could not even fall asleep at his writing desk. His words remained buried deep within his mind and he had to claw each one out onto the page. A few pages a day was the best he could hope for. He'd told his publisher that he'd hit a rut, but that he was sure to break out of it very shortly. Henry wondered how many times he had to say it for it to become reality.

But seeing Miss Richards's perseverance had indeed inspired him. He sat at his desk every day and scribbled out whatever lines he could manage. It wasn't much, and he was sure it wasn't very good, but they were better than nothing. If Miss Richards could apply herself to her craft every day to improve herself and overcome her mental barriers, then so could he. Though he ardently wished that that moment would come sooner rather than later.

Henry suspected that his lack of sleep did not help matters.

He wished, if his mind insisted on keeping him awake until morning, that it would occupy his time with figuring out how he could move his book forward.

Instead, his thoughts dwelled on Miss Richards, replaying their dance, her performance, and their many meetings, over and over. Henry dared not guess what clues his mind hoped to reveal in those memories.

These endless circles ran him ragged as he tossed and turned in bed. And last night had been particularly difficult. He hadn't been able to secure another dance with Miss Richards at their last ball. Her mother had filled out the young woman's dance card with every gentleman that approached. And there were many men eager to dance with such a talented lady, so many that by the time Henry edged his way over, all of Miss Richards's remaining sets had been spoken for.

But he couldn't let go of the remorseful look on her face as the first gentleman took her out to the floor. Or the way he'd caught her eye more than once as she twirled about the room in another man's arms.

And so Henry did something he would have never expected of himself, and having sent the necessary letters he found himself quite unprepared for the task he'd undertaken.

The day after the ball, he'd written to the Richards family, inviting them to his home for dinner. He had invited Solomon as well, of course. And he'd agreed that this would not count as one of their weekly agreed upon meetings. This event fell outside those bounds, marking it as something of a special occasion.

Indeed, it was very special, as Henry had never hosted

anything more than the very occasional casual drop-in from gentlemen he knew from Boodle's. Solomon was over near every other day, so his presence in the house hardly counted as a visit.

He had never considered that he might wish to host a family for dinner and amicable conversation. In fact, he hardly remembered writing and sending the letter. He had been in such a daze from the previous evening's events, and the first of his string of sleepless nights. When Solomon waltzed into his study and clapped him on the shoulder, beaming from ear to ear, Henry had thought his best friend had gone mad.

But it seemed that Henry himself had gone mad. Solomon had wrestled the blank sheet of paper from Henry's hands and thrown his pen across the room so that he could not draft a second letter to renounce his invitation.

That would appear very ill-mannered, Solomon had scolded him. But true to his nature, Henry's friend had not left him in the lurch. If Henry was a complete novice at organizing such events, Solomon was an expert.

He'd given Henry detailed instructions on what to prepare and when, and then repeated those same instructions to the staff, not trusting Henry to see to it properly himself. In fact, the staff positively buzzed with excitement as the event drew nearer. Surely they too had never thought that they would have an opportunity to see anyone else in the house but their master and the Earl of Overton.

Now the appointed day had arrived. Henry couldn't calculate how many hours of sleep he'd gotten the previous night, but he suspected that in total it couldn't be more than a handful, and the sleep had been light and broken.

Even still, the nerves managed to keep him from falling over in exhaustion and he bustled about the house, adjusting frames and turning vases that had already been adjusted and turned. He was nervous about hosting guests for the first time, yes. But his thoughts always returned to Miss Richards and what they would speak about and if she would find his home to be comfortable and pleasing. This, he surmised, was the true source of his anxiety.

Henry was pacing about the dining room, ensuring that every centerpiece and fork was in its designated place, when Solomon strode in with a confident smile on his face, arms open wide in an overly grand gesture.

"Here he is, London's finest baron and most gracious host!"

Henry merely shook his head at his friend's proclamation and continued tending to items that didn't need his tending.

"Aren't you even a little excited?" Solomon pouted, sliding between Henry and the sideboard he fussed over that would soon be laden with food.

"Surely this was a mistake, Solomon," Henry groaned, covering his face with his large hands. Every second that brought him closer to having the entire Richards family in his dining room was agony.

"Tell me, what are you so afraid of? That the food won't be cooked to perfection? It always is when I'm here. That the décor won't be pleasing enough? Every piece here was chosen with your keen eye, an eye that I would trust to furnish my entire home."

Solomon leaned back against the sideboard and crossed his arms. His voice was firm but understanding, and his brows furrowed together with concern. He might not always understand Henry's eccentricities, but he always tried to.

"It's not any of that. At least not mostly. But the real problem is that I don't know these people, do I? How could I ask near strangers to dine with me here? What do we have in common that we can discuss?" Henry let the exasperation and fatigue spill out of him and propped himself up next to Solomon on the sideboard.

"Well, how did you expect to get to know someone? You call on them, talk of whatever comes to mind, and learn about them that way. Mr. and Mrs. Richards might be pretentious, and they are not nearly as subtle about their social aspirations as they might think, but they are not scary people. They can't harm you. And the girls of course are both as kind as they come."

Solomon's words carried a sense of truth. Henry knew that he didn't take the time to cultivate relationships. It had always seemed to be an awkward endeavor, and therefore not worth the effort. Especially now that he wished to devote his life to writing. Solomon was the only person he knew with any depth, being an only child and with both parents passed away. But he hadn't needed to get to know Solomon. They'd been young boys when they met, and Solomon had done most of the getting to know bits.

But if he wanted to become closer to Miss Richards, to learn more about her dreams and plans, to hear about her childhood adventures, to understand what she thought of the world, he would need to embrace the transition period, awkward though it may be at times. And he would need to make a good impression with her family, if he wished to occupy more of her time.

"Yes, you're right. I only wish I could have half your confidence." Henry smiled ruefully.

"Confidence isn't the only thing that matters. And besides, everyone gets nervous. Yes, even me." Solomon dramatically waved a hand over his handsome face.

Henry laughed. "That is true. I've seen you become nervous more in these past two months than in our entire lifetime of friendship."

Solomon blanched at having his jest turned against him,

but Henry didn't press him and instead changed the subject. "Would you mind assessing my closet and help me choose a charming coat for this afternoon? I need a true dandy's eye if I am to make a decent impression."

⁓

SURPRISED AND VERY RELIEVED, Henry announced that his guests might join him in the drawing room or library for more relaxed conversation. He had indeed made it through the dinner with not so much as a hiccup.

Solomon gladly took the reins of the conversation, speaking equally to everyone at the table since their party was so few. He sat to Solomon's left while Mrs. Richards sat on his right, with the two young women on her side of the table and their father across from them.

On the one hand, Henry would have liked to be seated next to Miss Richards so they could speak more easily. But the seating arrangement had worked out for the best, as he might have ended up a bit too overwhelmed with her right next to him. But now that the meal was over, he hoped to find an opportunity to engage her quietly.

"I should very much like to see your library," Miss Richards offered. No one else objected, so Henry led the way down the hall, Mrs. Richards giving many flattering compliments to Henry's home the whole way.

"Good Heavens..." Miss Juliet gasped as they entered the room, her mouth ajar ever so slightly and her eyes darting all over the room.

Miss Richards also showed surprise in her wide eyes, but the surprise quickly gave way to wonder. She gazed about the large library slowly, taking in the floor-to-ceiling and wall-to-wall shelves that took up nearly every inch of the room's perimeter.

Henry thought very little about his library, having become so accustomed to it over the years, but as he watched Miss Richards's expression, he too appreciated just how magnificent the room really was.

Every shelf was filled to capacity with books of all heights and widths and subjects, carefully organized by topic and author. Henry liked to think that he had something of everything in his library. And no, he had not read them all, but he had little self-control when it came to the bookshop. His collection grew, but he did not mind that he likely would never read them all. Many of them were very well loved, with cracked pages and softened spines. Something about their presence brought him comfort.

Henry greatly enjoyed the sparkle in Miss Richards's eyes as she turned about in a slow circle.

"This is a very fine library you have, my lord. I daresay it could rival the Palace's library." She sounded nearly breathless with awe.

"Oh I highly doubt that, though that is one library I would love to browse," Henry laughed. "You're more than welcome to borrow anything that catches your eye."

Miss Richards only nodded quietly and walked to the far wall, eyes glued to the rows and rows of books. His other guests settled in wherever they wished. Mr. And Mrs. Richards seated themselves at a small round table while Solomon and Miss Juliet stood before the wide window and looked out at the street below.

Henry stood near the door of his library, watching the scene unfold. It truly was a strange feeling, seeing this room inhabited by other people. They all seemed engaged in their own thoughts and conversations, comfortable and companionable. Perhaps having people in his life wasn't as difficult as he'd thought.

He rang the bell for refreshments before crossing the

room to join Miss Richards at the back bookshelves, only vaguely aware of Mrs. Richards eyes upon him as he made his way toward her daughter.

"Have you found anything of interest yet?" He asked as he took his place next to her, keeping his voice low so as not to startle her out of her fixation.

"That's just the problem, you see," she responded without taking her eyes off the many titles before her.

"How's that?"

"Everything is of interest. How am I to choose just one?" She smiled, gently stroking the hard leather spine of one of the books, her fingers just barely brushing against the indented lettering.

"That is a predicament I understand very well. I dare say that's how I ended up with all these books in the first place. Each one looked so tempting that I had to have it. There are some that have been here for years that I haven't yet read as I keep accumulating more."

Miss Richards finally turned to look at him with a smile. "In that case, why don't I read the ones you haven't yet and I'll just give you a summary?"

He knew she meant it as a jest, but suddenly the idea sounded quite appealing to Henry. "Yes, perhaps I might take you up on that someday."

They continued to make their way along the bookshelves slowly in an amicable silence. Henry allowed her to take her time observing the books, while he observed her in turn, enjoying the curiosity in her eyes when she came across an interesting title or the sharp intake of breath when she pulled out a book to see a surprisingly intricate design on its cover. He gladly answered her questions as best he could, telling her what he knew of each book or what he'd liked most about this or that.

Solomon and Miss Juliet remained by the window,

discussing whatever they saw in the outside world, but Henry caught Solomon's pointed glance at Miss Richards on more than one occasion. Henry's neck burned and he hoped his companion remained oblivious.

Indeed she was so engrossed in looking over every shelf that she barely seemed to register that there was anyone else in the room. She seemed so perfectly comfortable in his library browsing through his collection. She seemed at home.

The tea and coffee came and went while the small group conversed about many idle topics. Mr. Richards loved to stealthily ask for Solomon's thoughts on the latest sporting news when the young ladies were engaged in their own discussion, often accompanied by soft laughter and smiles.

Mrs. Richards had selected a book of poetry and read while silently sipping her tea. But Henry could see the way her eyes roved over the page far too rapidly to take in any of the words. She wasn't reading but rather listening intently to all that went on in the room.

"You know what would be just lovely right about now? There's just something about a hot cup of coffee that makes me want to take a long leisurely turn about the drawing room. Lord Neil here has a such a spacious drawing room that it would feel as though we were walking through Hyde Park. Who would like to join me?" Solomon stretched his arms out to his sides, showing off his broad chest and shoulders.

"Yes let's do just that!" Miss Juliet happily gave her consent to Solomon's plan.

The rest of the Richards family agreed and their small group left the library behind. Solomon remarked on various features in the house as they walked through, playing the gracious host even in someone else's home. But Henry certainly didn't mind having less pressure to speak.

Solomon led the way, followed by Mr. And Mrs. Richards

and Miss Juliet while Henry and Miss Richards brought up the rear. He didn't remove his eyes from her, noticing how she took in every aspect of his home with interest, lingering especially over the artwork that adorned his walls.

Once again, Miss Richards gazed about the drawing room with that same look of wonder in her eyes as she had in the library. Henry smiled to himself. He found this quality more and more endearing every time he saw it. What a blessing it must be, to see even such simple everyday things as a library or drawing room or bird on a branch or gown in a window with such awe.

Just as Solomon had suggested, each couple looped arms and began walking through the rooms. Mr. and Mrs. Richards preferred going around the center of the room while the younger couples took to the outskirts in different directions.

"My, this must be one of the loveliest drawing rooms I've ever seen." Miss Richards sighed as she took in the fine furnishings and artwork. "But what's this?" Her eyebrows shot up as something in the far opposite corner caught her eye. "You never mentioned you owned a pianoforte, Lord Neil."

"Ah, yes. It belonged to my late mother. She enjoyed the instrument quite a bit and I couldn't bear to part with it. Unfortunately it has not seen much use in quite a number of years now." Henry coughed, feeling ashamed that he let his mother's pianoforte fall into disuse—though he still had it regularly maintained in her honor.

"I'm very sorry to hear that," Miss Richards offered quickly, her eyes turning down to the carpet under their feet.

"There is nothing to be sorry for. It happened some years ago. Her health had always been fragile, and after Father passed unexpectedly…. I believe she missed him so dearly that she followed not a year later. It is a shame, but perhaps soon the instrument will find someone to play it again."

The words came out of Henry faster than he could stop them. He rarely spoke of his parents—not for lack of love, but simply because he preferred quiet contemplation of their memories.

And of course only one person came to mind when he thought of someone playing his mother's pianoforte.

"I hope you will. I find that a little music can go a long way toward increasing the brightness in a home. But I'm sure you won't be surprised by my saying so," Miss Richards said with a gentle smile as she gazed at the instrument from afar.

"Indeed I am not," Henry chuckled. "But your singular enthusiasm for music is quite inspiring."

"Inspiring?" Miss Richards tilted her head to look up at him, her eyes narrowed with curiosity.

A flame of nerves flashed through Henry's body. He swallowed hard to drag down the lump that sprung into his throat.

"Yes, I simply mean I admire your passion for your craft. It inspires me to cherish my books all the more." He pulled his shoulders even straighter and gave a sharp nod, hoping to add earnestness to his awkward explanation.

Miss Richards giggled quietly. "Everyone needs something to cherish. I'm happy I could help in some fashion."

Henry felt himself relax as she easily accepted his half-truth. No, Henry realized—it was the truth.

They continued on their slow path, Henry contentedly answering Miss Richards's questions about the décor or listening to her keen observations on all manner of subjects. Henry had never pictured himself escorting a lady about his drawing room, but he felt surprisingly comfortable given his nerves earlier in the day.

But Henry's peace was soon disturbed as they approached

an unassuming end table that contained an unfortunately revealing bit of evidence. He had been so enamored with Miss Richards's conversation that he entirely forgot that the letter he'd received from his publisher this morning still sat open for anyone to see on the end table.

He may have missed it himself if it hadn't been for Miss Richards's dress brushing against the table and catching the corner of the letter, knocking it to the ground. Henry's eyes fell on the logo at the top of the letter and his heart leapt into his throat.

"My apologies!" She removed her arm from his and hastily bent her knees to reach for the fallen letter.

"Allow me!" Henry cried out and nearly fell to his knee as he grasped the letter now in Miss Richards's hand, his fingers brushing over hers. She quickly relinquished it to him.

Henry clutched the page to his chest and attempted to stand but his head knocked against something hard, forcing him to fall back onto his rear. The pain pulsed through Henry's forehead and he squeezed his eyes shut, willing it to dissipate quickly.

"Cecilia! What are you doing on the floor?! You ungraceful girl!" Mrs. Richards's sharp voice cut through the room and Henry opened an eye to assess the situation.

Miss Richards sat before him on the rug, her skirts pooled up around her and a hand pressed to her temple. She glanced over at him, her pained grimace giving way to a quiet laugh.

Henry quickly pushed himself up to his feet and held a hand out to Miss Richards. "I'm terribly sorry! Mrs. Richards, this was my fault. I accidentally bumped Miss Richards as I retrieved something that had fallen to the ground."

Miss Richards stifled a giggle as she accepted Henry's helping hand. A soft blush spread across her high cheek-bones. Over her shoulder, Henry could see Mrs. Richards eyeing them carefully but her small smile seemed to indicate that she accepted Henry's explanation.

"Do be more careful next time, Cecilia dear," Mrs. Richards huffed.

"Yes, Mama." Miss Richards smiled sheepishly at Henry. "Thank you for your assistance, my lord. I apologize for causing such a ruckus."

"It's nothing to worry about, I assure you."

Now that everyone had regained their feet, Henry remembered the damning letter in his hand. He shot a glance to Solomon, who stood still along the opposite wall with Miss Juliet on his arm, watching the scene unfold.

"My goodness, I could talk for hours about all the pieces in Lord Neil's home. There are so many beautiful and unique items here with rich histories. As a matter of fact, I think I could use some refreshments. If you will excuse me, Miss Juliet." Without missing a beat, Solomon picked up on Henry's silent plea for help.

He gave a faux cough to indicate his supposedly hoarse voice and the Richardses all laughed at his joke. He led Miss Juliet to the center of the room to her parents and Henry did the same with Miss Richards. The two men went together to the service bell and awaited the footman.

"Thank you for rescuing me," Henry whispered breathlessly.

"And what am I supposed to have rescued you from?" Solomon arched a curious eyebrow.

Henry had folded the letter into a small square and kept it tucked securely in the palm of his hand. He turned his hand up just enough for Solomon to catch a glimpse of it.

"Miss Richards accidentally brushed this off my end table as we walked by. We both went to pick it up and bumped heads. It's a letter from my publisher that I received this morning. I must have forgotten it on the table in my anxiety to oversee the preparations for this dinner."

"Goodness. You don't think she saw any revealing information, did she?"

"I hope to God she did not…" Henry groaned quietly, fear spiking in his heart again. "A pot of tea, please," he commanded when the footman arrived, hoping his voice did not give away the fact that he felt his knees would buckle at any moment.

Henry and Solomon made their way back to the rest of their party. "She doesn't appear to have any suspicions," Solomon whispered as they approached the Richards family now seated on plush chairs around the center of the drawing room.

Despite Henry's desire to avoid looking at Miss Richards entirely lest he see any questions in her eyes, he forced himself to observe her. To his great relief, she simply sat next to her sister with an attentive expression as Miss Juliet shared some tale with her. When the two men approached, she glanced up to Henry with a gentle smile. Henry returned it, glad that she seemed unaffected by any new knowledge of her dinner host's secret life.

The tea arrived quickly and the small party chatted happily while sipping their warm beverages.

Eventually Mr. Richards stifled a yawn, which earned him a disapproving glance from his wife. "My goodness, it has grown quite late," he mumbled, not caring to hide his drowsiness or his interest in finishing the night.

"Come now, my dear, our hosts are so kind to share their evening with us. Shouldn't we make the most of it?" Mrs. Richards gently chided, barely caring to hide her annoyance at her husband and her interest in extending the night as long as possible.

Henry glanced to Miss Richards and saw that the

moment had not escaped her notice. Her jaw twitched and her normally pleasant smile now seemed strained.

"Indeed it is quite late…" Henry agreed, unsure of how to go about ending these events. Though he had enjoyed having Miss Richards in his home more than he'd expected—the letter incident excluded—Henry found that his capacity to enjoy conversation or company had depleted significantly.

"Oh Sissy, why don't you play something for us before we leave? Just a short piece. I know how much Lord Overton and Lord Neil both admire your talent," Miss Juliet suggested with a twinkle of excitement in her eyes.

Miss Richards giggled shyly at the request, looking back to Henry for approval.

"I would love to hear you play, only if you are willing," he responded to her unspoken question.

Her form relaxed and she smiled appreciatively, smoothing her skirts over the bench and trilling her fingers over the keys before gently placing them on the instrument.

Everyone else found seats throughout the room as Miss Richards prepared herself. Henry didn't want to take the chair closest to the pianoforte lest one of his guests desired it. But Mr. And Mrs. Richards found a pair of chairs in the far opposite corner of the room, and Solomon and Miss Juliet Richards both nodded for Henry to take the close chair while they situated themselves in the middle of the room.

Henry swallowed and seated himself, adjusting the chair slightly so he could have a better view of Miss Richards's face while she played. She smiled when she saw him settled in.

The melody started light and fanciful and Henry struggled to place the name of the song.

Whatever the piece was called, Henry enjoyed it immensely. Not just because Miss Richards played it, though her skill handled the piece well and she seemed to travel through its peaks and valleys with practiced dexterity. The song itself was simple, but its simplicity was its advantage. Every note and chord and phrase rang clearly, spilling into the next with gentle ease.

When the last few notes lingered in the air as Miss Richards's hands stilled, Henry finally found fault in it. It was far too short.

"Sissy... That was beautiful. Wherever did you learn such a song? I don't pretend to have great interest in learning music, but I may have to ask you to teach me this when we get home." Miss Juliet sounded just as awestruck as Henry felt. Her eyes were wide and eyebrows raised, the expression stuck as she appeared to process the music.

Miss Richards turned around on the bench and smiled at her sister, clearly pleased with a slight hint of a blush on her cheeks. "I'd be happy to teach you, but let me write out the sheet music first. This was just a small piece I figured out myself."

More than one gasp could be heard within the room, including one from Henry. "Miss Richards, you wrote that song yourself?"

She glanced shyly down at her hands, as if she too were surprised that such a lovely creation came from her own fingertips.

"That was beautiful. You should be immensely proud. And I hope you continue creating your own original pieces." Henry, unused to expressing such sentiments, felt stiff as he offered his praise, but hoped Miss Richards would understand.

Miss Richards met his eyes with a strange look that Henry couldn't identify, but it sent a tremor down his spine. "Thank you, Lord Neil. I must admit you inspired me a good deal."

Henry found himself winded and almost lightheaded. Miss Richards's song had been too short, because Henry wanted to hear it here in his home for hours upon hours, wanted to watch her sway gently on the bench and run her fingers over his books.

He suddenly had a vision of himself in his study, sitting at his writing desk with pages sprawled out before him and his hands smudged with ink. And when he looked up in his imagination he saw Miss Richards nestled into a chair in the opposite corner, a book in her hands, and she too looked up at him with a soft smile before returning to her own devices.

And when the Richards family left, with Solomon following shortly after, Henry felt the heavy air of emptiness that filled his home. No matter how hard he tried to return to normalcy, he saw imprints of Miss Richards everywhere he looked.

CHAPTER 11

*F*rye Publishing.

The name and logo had become fixed in Cecilia's mind. She hadn't meant to read the baron's private correspondence but she couldn't help seeing it as it fell from the table. She hadn't gleaned anything other than the name of the publishing company and its logo.

She'd done her best to act ignorant and carry on the evening as usual. In fact, Cecilia wished she'd never seen it at all. Now she could not banish it from her mind. She knew there must be some explanation as to why Lord Neil would receive a letter from the same publisher who put out those anonymous adventure novels. Even still, that knowledge sparked an interest in her.

She also could not ignore the sense that an immense but deeply buried shift had occurred between them during the last ball they'd attended together nearly a week ago. As she sat up in her bed, with one of those adventure tales in her lap yet again, Cecilia's mind pulled away from the vivid fictional world and instead roamed back to those memories. They were even more vivid than the story, because she had lived them.

From the way they seemed able to communicate without speaking, using only their eyes and subtle expressions to ask and answer each other, to the sublime dance, to the way he watched her while she performed and the total ease she felt while his eyes were on her—something had changed in the midst of all that. Certainly something had changed in Cecilia, and she felt that there was a good chance that the baron experienced it as well.

The time she'd spent in his home today indicated as much, at least. His home had been beautiful, and Lord Overton had made a point to inform them that much of the decoration and furniture had been chosen by Lord Neil himself. The dinner itself had been mostly uneventful, but she couldn't shake that current of air that seemed to connect them even though he sat at the head of the table. He hadn't spoken much, but Cecilia did not think she flattered herself to claim that his eyes never strayed far from her.

And of course, she adored Lord Neil's library. She'd always thought her father kept a distinguished collection of books, but never had she seen such a vast library in anyone's home. It shouldn't have surprised her, considering all she'd heard of the baron's hobby, but her breath had still been taken away the instant she stepped through the door.

Cecilia could have spent many an hour simply allowing her eyes to slide up and down the hundreds of leather spines, some worn and cracked and some still pristine. Even if he hadn't read each book himself, Lord Neil still knew enough of each one to tell her about its author or subject matter. But best of all was the pride in his eyes as he patiently answered her questions. She sensed that Lord Neil did not often have the opportunity to discuss his treasures with anyone, so their shine had dulled over the years as they became commonplace to him.

She couldn't help shivering slightly as her memory wandered back to their walk around the drawing room. Though her room was warm and a tepid cup of tea still gave off small trails of steam on her bedside table, Cecilia snuggled a little deeper into her blanket. She carefully marked her place in her book. It wasn't likely that she would be able to concentrate on it any more tonight, not with the baron looming large in her mind.

She had been surprised that he'd spoken about his late parents and to hear that she inspired him. She saw it as a sign that perhaps he viewed her as an intellectual equal.

And because he'd shared such personal thoughts with her, Cecilia felt it only natural to return the favor in his drawing room by playing an original composition. She'd only been tinkering with it for a few days, and much of it sprouted up naturally as she played on the baron's pianoforte. At one time, such a notion would have been appalling to her. But somehow her conversation with Lord Neil, and seeing him sitting nearby with an eager expression, gave her the courage to perform her first self-written song.

Lying in bed now, Cecilia couldn't believe that she'd done such a bold thing. She threw the covers over her head, a wave of heat washing over her. The courage she'd had at that moment had fled to the furthest corners of the Earth and she was now left with the inevitable embarrassment of how close she'd come to making a fool of herself if she had made a mistake or if her song hadn't been well received.

But the baron's uplifting words in the drawing room echoed in her ears, and Cecilia vowed to sit at her pianoforte first thing in the morning to polish this song and then begin work on another.

Cecilia's bedroom door opened quietly, accompanied by a

small gasp. "Miss Richards? Is everything alright? Are you hurt? Ill?" Violet rushed to Cecilia's bedside, her shoes making small scuttling sounds over the wooden floor.

Cecilia laughed and threw the covers off her head. "I'm quite alright, Violet. In fact, I'm doing just lovely. I was simply...reminiscing."

Violet smiled knowingly as she collected the tea tray. "You seem to have been in very good spirits these past several days."

A strange fluttering sensation started up in Cecilia's stomach. It wasn't uncomfortable or painful, more like receiving a tickle of whispered touches, barely there but just enough to set her skin tingling.

"Yes indeed. I believe my luck in a certain department may be finally turning. I'm not entirely sure yet, but I can't help hoping..." Cecilia's voice trailed away wistfully as she rubbed her palm over the rough cover of the adventure novel.

She had just been in his company a few hours ago, yet time stretched out endlessly. Cecilia wanted to know more of him, and of the place that was so precious to him that he rarely let anyone inside. She had felt so comfortable and welcome there.

"I am very glad for you, Miss Richards. I do hope all your wishes will come true. You are most deserving of a life of happiness. Good night."

Violet spoke softly as she always did, but her eloquent words did not mask the hint of longing that lingered in her voice. She lowered her head respectfully as she took the tea tray away, closing the door behind her.

"What a sweet girl. I swear she could compose quite fancy poetry." Cecilia vowed that when her mind was not so occupied with other matters, she would find a way to encourage her maid to take up writing when her time allowed.

~

CECILIA WASN'T sure how long she laid awake in her dark room with only a sliver of moonlight teasing through the curtain for company. At least an hour, possibly two, if she had to guess. No matter how she turned and flipped, nothing was comfortable. But it wasn't her bed or her pillows or her blanket or her nightgown that were the problem. Her body was perfectly snug. It was her mind that refused to be still.

Snippets from the ball and the dinner—the baron's eyes reading her unspoken thoughts, the way he felt so familiar when they danced and said words that she felt so sure belonged to her masked gentleman, the adoration in his voice as he spoke about his books, and of course the praises he had given her song—flashed through her mind's eye in rapid succession.

As Cecilia's mind flickered over these scenes, her heartbeat thumped irregularly. One moment it was calm and content as she recalled Lord Neil's soothing presence by her side in the library, and the next it hammered away when she envisioned his awestruck expression after she played her piece.

"Ugh!" She groaned, kicking her feet under her covers in agitation. She had been reduced to a child throwing a tantrum, unable to express herself due to sheer overwhelm.

Cecilia wallowed for a few more moments before finally giving up. Lying in bed alone with her swirling thoughts was getting her nowhere. She ripped the blanket off her body and planted her feet on the cool floor, wondering what she could possibly do at such an hour.

But before she could wonder too long, Cecilia's body seemed to guide her across the room to her bedroom door. She opened it as quietly as she could and peered out into the hallway, glancing back and forth several times before embarking into the dark.

Cecilia prided herself on her light feet, perfectly suited to dancing with ease and grace. But tonight, when she needed them to float as she did during a quadrille or cotillion, Cecilia's feet felt sticky and cumbersome. Her breath stilled as she slowly picked her way down the hall in the dark, hoping that no servants were up and about so late at night.

Finally, after a few agonizing moments, Cecilia reached her destination. She didn't bother knocking lest she alert anyone to her midnight wanderings.

This room was even darker than her own and Cecilia had to blink into the black surroundings for some time before her eyes finally adjusted. The door clicked quietly behind her. Nothing in the room stirred.

She tiptoed to the bed and sat on its edge, cringing as it creaked with her weight. But the slumbering form remained undisturbed, a light snore hitching slightly before returning to its normal rhythm.

"Jules? Are you awake?" Cecilia whispered as loudly as she could, leaning down into her sister's ear. When Juliet failed to respond, Cecilia realized the foolishness of her question.

"Jules. Wake up!" Changing tactics, Cecilia gripped one of Juliet's shoulders and shook it lightly. The sleeping beauty merely wrinkled her nose and gurgled some incomprehensible sound.

Cecilia rolled her eyes, remembering how much trouble Juliet had given their governess, and later their schoolteacher at their seminary, with waking up. If they had any appointments first thing in the morning, an extra ten minutes needed to be accounted for in the tiresome battle to rouse Juliet.

This time Cecilia dropped any pretense of being gentle and took her sister's limp shoulders in both hands, shaking her roughly. Juliet startled awake and cried out more nonsense.

"Shh!" Cecilia clapped a hand over Juliet's mouth, leaping over her body to the other side of the bed and squirming under the covers, prepared to duck should anyone decide to check in on the room.

"Sis...what are you doing here? Is it time to call on someone? Is breakfast ready?" Juliet scooted herself into a seated position, rubbing her eyes with both hands.

Since a few moments passed and no one burst into the room looking for a disturbance, Cecilia also propped herself up against a pillow.

"I'm sorry for waking you. It's just that my mind is in turmoil. Perhaps turmoil is too negative a word. In any case, it is restless and keeping me from sleep." Cecilia dropped her head back against the headboard, allowing resignation to sweep through her body and soften her into the plush bed.

Juliet yawned and then chuckled. "I figured you might be sneaking in here sometime soon."

"Why's that?" Cecilia demanded.

"You're my sister. You've been my best friend my entire life. I know when something troubles you, even if I don't know exactly what it is. But this time, I think I could wager a pretty sum with complete confidence."

"Jules, you know gambling isn't an appropriate topic for us." Cecilia couldn't stop herself chiding her younger sister and her sometimes unorthodox statements.

"I know, Sissy. That's why I only say such things with you. I know my place, for the most part. In any case, I suspect that a certain baron has been pacing through your thoughts tonight."

Cecilia shouldn't have been surprised that her sister guessed correctly right away, but a wave of heat still swept over her entire body. She hid herself under the covers again.

"I see I have the right of it," Juliet laughed. "You two did look so very sweet together at the last ball and tonight during the dinner. The sight almost made me nauseous, it was so sweet."

The younger woman grimaced and Cecilia sprung up from beneath the blanket to box her sister on the ear.

"Ow!" Juliet cried out in a whisper, ducking from another blow. "You've been in such a daze ever since that ball, and I just knew you were thinking of Lord Neil the whole time. Your behavior at the dinner proved me right."

"Don't mock me!" Cecilia grumbled through gritted teeth, trying to wrap her arms around her sister so she could give her a proper punishment.

Juliet squirmed, nearly falling out of bed in the process, breathless giggles from both girls filling up the once silent room. But their energy quickly ebbed as arms and legs ceased flailing, the blanket tangled up around them in a dreadful mess.

Cecilia caught her breath and smiled wearily. It had been quite a long time since they'd been able to tussle with each other without restraint. Most likely not since they were little girls, and even then their governess or their mother would break up their playfights with clicking tongues and harsh reminders of ladylike conduct.

But alone in the darkness of Juliet's room, they could be honest with each other, uninhibited. And Cecilia knew it was high time for a heart-to-heart.

"You are right. You've seen right through me. Or was I just that obvious?" Cecilia asked sheepishly, her mind recalling every instance with Lord Neil and wondering if everyone else in the world had seen what she'd been blind to.

Juliet rolled onto her side to face her older sister. "You didn't make a fool of yourself if that's what you're asking. Some girls will cling to a man's arm even as he tries to shake her off or bat her eyelashes so rapidly she could take flight the next second." A tinge of distaste colored her voice.

"Come now, Juliet. That's a bit harsh, don't you think? It's what women have to do if they hope to catch the affection of a well-bred man and make a good match to secure their future," Cecilia reasoned, though such affectations looked silly to her as well.

But she couldn't blame ladies, especially young debutantes with hopes of falling in love, securing a good match, and marrying all in their first Season, for trying so hard. In fact, she had likely done just the same when she made her debut. But she'd settled into more comfortable behavior after failing to find the man she dreamed of in her first year.

Of course Cecilia still minded all the rules of proper etiquette and conduct, but no longer did she simper and sigh at any man she danced or walked with only to find him shallow or uncaring. But she knew her discerning attitude was gossiped about here and there in the Society circles they frequented.

Juliet groaned. "I know it is not their fault. Still, it all feels so disingenuous. How can you know that the person you court is really the person you will end up marrying? Is anyone in this city a real, honest person?"

"I still have hope that there are some who act as their true selves, yes."

"Of course you mean to say Lord Neil."

"And Lord Overton, as well. I know what they say about him, but he always seems so charming and pleasant. And besides, he looks utterly taken with you whenever he's in your presence." Cecilia nudged Juliet in the ribs with her elbow playfully, trying to break her sister out of the dark turn her thoughts had taken.

"Let's not talk about him for now, shall we? You came here to talk about your baron after all." Juliet quickly changed the subject and continued before Cecilia could protest. "You know what they say. A girl in love can hardly sleep because her reality is finally better than her dreams."

"In love?!" Cecilia shot upright, ignoring Juliet's shushes. "Jules, I think it is far too early to be speaking of love."

"Is it? I know you weren't terribly fond of him at the start and, despite the fact that you haven't engaged in a lot of conversation even when you have been out together, I always see that silent current of curiosity between you. You look as though you want to speak with him, yet you don't know what to say or how to say it so you remain silent, and he looks as though he suffers the same struggle.

"And I've seen the way you look at him, and the way he looks at you, even if no words are said. But don't tell me. Are you still caught up with that man from the masquerade? Is that why you haven't been able to converse with Lord Neil as comfortably?"

Cecilia squirmed under the blanket as her sister read her mind.

"No.... Well, at least not so much anymore. I did indeed hold back at first because I didn't believe Lord Neil to be the gentleman I sought. And at times I felt that my company was a burden upon him. Perhaps I have misread that aspect of him. But Jules, after recent events I believe that Lord Neil and the masked gentleman may just very well be one and the same."

"Truly?" Juliet gasped, gripping the blanket tightly under her chin, eyes round as if Cecilia had told her a ghost story. Although perhaps the likelihood of Cecilia's speculation being correct was as farfetched as any ghost.

"Truly. He said something to me at the last ball during our dance that almost exactly mirrored something that gentleman told me during the masquerade. Then suddenly everything about the way he moved seemed so familiar. And

PENNY FAIRBANKS

earlier today at his home...everything just felt like it was falling into place. I only wish there was some way I could find out for certain." Cecilia trailed off forlornly.

"Would it be so horrible to simply ask him directly?"

Cecilia blanched at the idea and shook her head vigorously.

"I know it seems like the easy solution, and I could have done so long ago. But now that my heart is warming toward him, I fear that if he is not the masked man, I'll always wonder what could have been."

"Ah, so you admit your heart is warming toward him." Juliet eyed Cecilia with a mischievous smile and Cecilia blushed in response.

"You have missed the point of what I said. But yes. If you must have it in precise wording, I do believe I am becoming attached to the baron. I can't yet go so far as to say I am in love. But the possibility that my feelings could grow in that direction is there."

Cecilia didn't look at her sister as she finally spoke what had been weighing heavily on her heart and mind these past several days. She fiddled with the edge of the blanket to give her nerves something to do.

"I don't see anything wrong with that. In fact, it seems like a wonderful thing to me," Juliet whispered warmly.

She took one of Cecilia's hands in her own and squeezed it gently. Cecilia looked up to see her sister gazing at her with nothing but happiness.

"Now that you have the baron in your life, do you really need to find the identity of the masked gentleman? Whether he and Lord Neil are indeed the same person or not, that night led you to a fortuitous meeting. Perhaps it is now time to focus on what you have before you.

"I know your ideals, sister. You want someone you can be a true companion to, someone you can love for their mind and spirit. And you want someone who sees the same in you. If I may be so bold, I think there is a great chance that Lord Neil could finally be the one to match you."

Juliet smiled encouragingly as she spoke, keeping her hand firmly around Cecilia's. Cecilia paused to consider the words. They echoed what she herself had been feeling, though she hadn't been able to put it into words. Hearing them said so eloquently from Juliet confirmed for Cecilia that this was correct.

"My goodness. When did you become so wise and mature?"

"I am only this way because I've been watching my big sister for my entire life. I've learned so much from you. Especially what it means to stick to one's beliefs. But I've also watched your worry grow as you've gone through multiple Seasons without making a match. I'm simply happy that it seems your patience and perseverance will pay off in the best way possible."

Juliet dropped her head onto Cecilia's shoulder and clung to her arm. Cecilia realized that she must be quite tired.

"Thank you, Jules. I'm still not sure how all this will unfold. I know our parents would be thrilled if I did secure a proposal from a baron. And if I do fall in love with him, Mama's threat will come to nothing. But for the first time in a long time, I feel hopeful. Perhaps there can be a happy ending for all of us."

The younger woman stiffened slightly. "For some of us. Mama's threat still applies to me. But if you can maintain your beliefs, then so can I. For now, I'd rather focus on seeing you happily wedded in short order."

Cecilia chuckled, but not without a slight flicker of guilt in her stomach. It seemed that her troubles in the marriage mart might come to an end soon, but Juliet's battle was far from over.

But Cecilia did ardently hope that Juliet's situation could be resolved peacefully soon. Especially considering how friendly she and the Earl of Overton seemed to be. As things progressed with Lord Neil—if they continued to progress— some attention would be taken off Juliet for the time being. But if Juliet did not wish to talk about that matter yet, Cecilia wouldn't press her too hard. After all, there was not much to be done at this late hour.

"We can sort Mama out another time. You should go back to sleep. Thank you for hearing me out and easing the burden in my mind. You're more than welcome to sneak into my room and do the same, if you wish."

Cecilia climbed slowly out of the bed to keep any wayward creaks at bay and Juliet slipped back down into a comfortable position. She already looked half asleep.

"I will, Sissy. I promise," she mumbled, snuggling deeper under the covers. Her breathing steadied in an instant.

Cecilia made to leave the room, but she turned back to her sister's already sleeping form. At this moment, Juliet looked so much like the innocent, untroubled child she'd grown up beside. Cecilia leaned down to give her younger sister a quick peck on the forehead. She smiled as she left Juliet's room and tiptoed down the hallway back to her own. When had Juliet grown up so much?

Her heart dropped slightly as she closed the door on her bedroom. She'd left out only one small detail of her troubled thoughts: Lord Neil's letter from Frye Publishing.

CHAPTER 12

Several agonizing days passed after Henry's dinner before the next scheduled outing with the Richards sisters. He missed her. He admitted it to himself openly now. Miss Richards had only been in his home for a few hours, yet her ghost lingered in every corner. If he became too lost in thought, he could swear that he felt her presence by his side.

Perhaps it was this hollow feeling that finally broke Henry's mental barriers surrounding his book. Whenever Miss Richards took over his mind, Henry rushed to his writing desk and scribbled away at the page, spilling out word after word.

The world and its many pointless obligations had always distracted Henry from writing, and now writing distracted him from the world—specifically from one particular inhabitant of the world, the one with golden hair and deep blue eyes and a melodic laugh.

The light drained out of the sky as he peered over the side of Solomon's carriage, watching London bleed by as the driver steered the horses toward Covent Garden.

Crowds gathered in the street as Society's most elite

members filed out of their carriages and into the theater. Families with young daughters and sons eyed the other guests, looking for acquaintances or potential matches to be introduced to. Lords and ladies greeted each other eagerly with handshakes, bows, and curtsies. The women fawned over each other's dresses while the men heartily complimented each other on their superbly cut coats and shining boots.

The entire display looked like an unspoken competition to Henry. Who was being courted by the most eligible bachelors and which young lady had the finest dowry? Who wore the latest fashions and who exhibited the most grace and sparkling manners? Who had the most connections among the *ton*, proving their worth through a collection of shallow relationships?

Henry felt himself growing stiff as he and Solomon alighted from the carriage. He rarely came to the theater. In fact, he'd only gone once last Season and none at all this Season, until tonight. At times Henry regretted not participating more as he loved the drama and farce. Watching words from a page come to life through acting was, in Henry's opinion, a very special form of art.

Unfortunately for the rest of Society, the masterful storytelling seemed to come second to the opportunity to show off their clothing, their marriageable children, and their acquaintances in high places. As a result, Henry typically avoided the theater at all costs.

Yet when Solomon had suggested inviting the Richards family to watch a Shakespeare play at Covent Garden, Henry accepted without a second thought. He eagerly anticipated spending time with Miss Richards again.

That feeling held firm in Henry's heart as they entered the theater to wait for the rest of their party, despite his uncomfortable awareness of the hundreds of people gathered here and their boisterous chatter. His desire to spend time with Miss Richards eclipsed even that which would normally have sent him into a dizzying cloud of nerves. The image of the smile he hoped to receive steadied him.

Solomon, who had never had any such qualms, strolled through the room, greeting friends from his various clubs and bowing low over the hands of ladies who hoped to be courted by him.

Of course, Solomon was turned out in his finest, a fact which did not go unnoticed. Solomon enjoyed the grand display of such events but, unlike everyone else, Henry knew that he did not dress out to compete or prove his status. Rather, he loved fashion and discussing trends with his like-minded friends.

Being left momentarily to his own devices, Henry found a spot by the wall with a view of the door so that he might spot the Richards family when they entered, for Solomon was not likely to notice with his current engagements.

If time had felt torturously slow these past few days since he last saw her, it moved excruciatingly slow now. Henry knew that she must be arriving at any moment, but every moment that slipped by without her silhouette appearing in the doorway seemed like a cruel and unfair punishment.

Henry's foot bounced with anxiety; he wondered if the Richards had decided to cancel at the last moment. But finally he saw her enter the crowded theater.

As always, Miss Richards was a sight to behold. But rather than trying to repress his interest, as Henry had done so many times in the past, he allowed his eyes to take in her face and figure, enjoying the deep warmth that flooded his chest.

Despite the many ladies in the room, all dressed up in their most beautiful gowns, Henry considered Miss Richards to be in a league all her own. The dress she wore was exquisite, even to his untrained eye, but her face captured him the most.

As soon as she stepped through the doors, Miss Richards's expression transformed into wonderment, her eyes scanning the room's resplendent décor and the many well-dressed theatergoers. A smile spread across her face and she said something to her sister with glowing excitement in her eyes.

She craned her head to peer around the throng of people waiting for the play to start and Henry's heart leapt at the realization that she was likely looking for him.

Several attendees greeted the family as they walked in. Miss Richards took it all in stride, as Henry had observed before. She smiled graciously and laughed politely, and when one lady or gentleman walked away another replaced them.

Watching her self-assured interactions and clear enjoyment of the company, Henry couldn't help contrasting his own unsettled stomach and uneven breathing.

A sudden flurry of gloved arms and silk skirts temporarily obstructed Henry's view as Miss Henshell approached Miss Richards, taking her friends hands in hers with an animated smile. Solomon had also invited the Henshell family to share his booth, knowing that their daughter was very friendly with the Richards daughters.

Lord Henshell already appeared disinterested while Lady Henshell looked nearly fit to burst as she said something sharply to her daughter. Miss Richards gently took Miss Henshell by the arm and steered her further into the room.

He watched for a few moments, noticing again how at home she seemed in a place like this. Something deep in his mind gave an uncomfortable tug, but he couldn't quite place it. And he didn't have time to, as Miss Richards finally saw him in his corner. Just as he'd so ardently hoped, she smiled with enthusiasm and her eyes blazed for a moment as they connected with his.

Henry's knees seemed to unlock and he made his way through the crowd toward her.

"Good evening, Miss Richards. I hope you are well." He took her outstretched hand and bowed low over it, his lips barely brushing the smooth fabric of her gloved knuckle.

"I am far better now that I am here in your company," she replied with a curtsey.

Not knowing what else to do, they simply stood in the middle of the room while others filtered around them, taking in each other's faces as if they hadn't seen each other just a few days ago.

"Ahem." A quiet cough jolted them both back to their senses, and Henry flushed at the sly glint in Miss Juliet's eye as she caught up with them. "We should find Lord Overton and make our way to the booth, don't you think?"

They did just that, collecting Solomon away from a small crowd of dandy acquaintances. The theater itself was just as magnificent, with its rows upon rows of seats and booths and of course the grand stage. Even Henry could put aside his anxiety to appreciate the architecture.

Solomon led them to his private box. The view perfectly captured the stage and much of the seated audience. Henry knew he had secured this particular box for that very reason. After all, Solomon enjoyed the show both on the stage and in the crowd.

The ladies took the front row of seats while the men sat behind, with Mr. Richards and Lord Henshell directly behind their wives. Henry and Solomon sat behind the Richards sisters.

Latecomers filtered in, the buzz of activity humming through the theater.

"I am so thrilled to be here tonight," Miss Richards

commented, turning to Henry. "I actually haven't been to the theater yet this Season, but I enjoy it so! Theater is such an incredible work of art, don't you think?"

Her eyes shimmered with delight as she looked from him to the beautifully built room to the hundreds of people anticipating the play.

"I absolutely agree." Despite the opulent setting, Henry found he couldn't remove his eyes from Miss Richards's charming face.

"I thought you would." Her attention returned to him with a bright smile. "Although I must confess that I enjoy coming out not just for the story and acting. It's a great opportunity to encounter acquaintances I don't often see, and to admire all these well-dressed people."

As if to emphasize her point, Miss Richards's eyes darted back out to the audience and she waved to several people as they took their seats.

Try as he might, Henry found it nearly impossible to focus on the play. He always enjoyed Shakespeare's works, but certain thoughts nagged his attention away every few minutes.

First and foremost, of course, was Miss Richards's proximity. Though she sat directly before him, Henry had an excellent view of her animated reactions as she turned her face from side to side with the actors' movement.

Henry marveled at the way she seemed to have a new expression for every feeling. He wondered if a lifetime would be long enough to see each one. And he found that he did not care if he missed the entire play, preferring to watch it unfold through Miss Richards.

If those were the only thoughts that occupied Henry's mind, he would have considered the evening a success. Below the surface of his fixation on Miss Richards, something else prodded at a deep corner of his mind.

They were nearly through the second act when it somehow became clear to Henry. How could he imagine a future with Miss Richards, when she clearly loved these lively social events and he did not? He had only come tonight for the chance to see her. If he asked for Miss Richards's hand, would he be forced to spend all his nights at operas or dinners instead of writing?

"This acting is superb. I've so missed coming to the theater but I've been so busy with other engagements," she whispered to him over her shoulder. If she noticed the way his jaw clenched as her words confirmed his misgivings, she didn't indicate it.

He needed a world lived inside, where he could write in peace and quiet. She needed a world lived outside, amongst the people she enjoyed doing the things she loved.

Who was he to take that charming vitality from her?

THE PAGES in Henry's hands felt stiff and coarse. He should have been happy to have a completed manuscript after how long he'd struggled to write it. But holding the draft in his hands now, Henry felt nothing but disappointment and shame.

He'd just finished reading the draft, hopeful that it had turned out better than expected. Unfortunately, the opposite proved true.

He threw the pages onto his desk and dropped his face into his hands. The manuscript was a complete failure. Though he'd given his best effort, Henry fell far short of his usual ability to bring his world and characters to life. The words existed on the page in his handwriting, but they were dull and uninspired and foreign.

Henry groaned, the frustration swelling into a pulsing

headache. Suddenly Henry stood, pushing his chair back with such force that it nearly fell backwards. An urge to do something, anything, seized Henry's body and he snatched the draft from his desk. The pages crumpled in his fingers as he stormed across the study to the fireplace. He watched the red and orange flames dance. This seemed the only fitting home for his defective manuscript.

As Henry lifted his hand to throw the pages into the fire-place, something stilled him. He had no other copies or record of this work. If he did this, he could not recreate it save for whatever remained in his memories. But he only needed to recall a few subpar sentences and scenes to decide his course.

The flames clung eagerly to Henry's offering and the paper curled and blackened obligingly under their influence. Henry watched for a moment as the fire transformed his words into ash.

He suddenly could not bear to be in his study any longer. He turned on his heel and marched out of the room and up the stairs to the drawing room. He could have retreated to his library but Henry wanted nothing to do with any books at the moment.

Once in the drawing room, Henry lowered himself into the plushest armchair he could find and allowed himself to sink back into the soft fabric. Sunlight from the large window gleamed against the highly polished furnishings and bathed Henry in warmth. He leaned his head back and closed his weary eyes. Perhaps he could have a brief rest. Lord knew Henry had barely slept these past several nights while he studied his manuscript.

But the headache thundered through Henry's skull, pulsing and coiling beneath his skin. He sat forward with his head drooping between his shoulders and propped his elbows up on his knees. With a heavy sigh, Henry brought his head up and opened his eyes.

The pianoforte in the opposite corner immediately caught Henry's attention. Thoughts tumbled through his mind as he gazed at the instrument. His mother. Miss Richards. The masked lady.

As if by magic, Henry's headache lifted away and his eyes grew wide with a bold new idea. In truth, the idea was not new. Nor was it Henry's.

"Of course..." he whispered to himself, the pieces of his plan clicking into place. He'd been such a fool. The key to enriching his writing had been handed to him on a platter months ago at Lord Henshell's ball.

Just as the mysterious pianoforte player had said, Henry needed female characters in his stories to add variety and depth and new perspectives.

And he knew just the woman who inspired all those qualities.

In a frenzy, Henry rushed back to his study and spread fresh pages across his desk, his pen nearly slipping through his fingers in his haste. Henry had always believed far more in the importance of discipline over inspiration. But he thanked the heavens for this miraculous inspiration. With pen at the ready, Henry vowed to devote himself to his work like never before.

"BUT SOMETHING IS NOT RIGHT! I know my friend, and he does not avoid me like this for no reason. Allow me to see him at once!"

Henry felt a sharp stab of guilt as he heard Solomon's pleading voice in the foyer. Henry had instructed all his staff to refuse anyone admittance to the house until further notice. Even Solomon. It would appear that his friend had stopped believing their excuses of Henry's illness.

"I am sorry, Lord Overton, truly. But Lord Neil is in no condition to entertain—"

"It's quite alright. Let him by." Henry stepped out from around the corner and interrupted his butler.

"Henry!" Solomon called out with surprise.

"It's nice to see you, Solomon. Let's go to the library." Henry asked the butler to see that tea was prepared and brought to the library.

The door had barely clicked into place behind them when Solomon rounded on Henry and his frustrations burst forth.

"What in the world is going on with you, Henry? I've been turned away from your home for two weeks. All your letters say is that you are suffering from some sort of persistent sickness. Good Heaven, I feared you might be on your deathbed. But I knew something felt amiss. And here you stand, fine as day. Why have you refused to see me or write with any actual information?"

The exasperation in Solomon's voice took Henry by surprise. He had indeed missed his friend, but Henry couldn't bring himself to leave his desk aside from the bare necessities of human nature. The words flew out from his pen with incredible speed and he dared not break his concentration.

Solomon stared at him with anger and a hint of hurt in his perceptive brown eyes. The guilt weighed heavily on Henry. Pride had gotten in the way of the one true relation-ship he had in this world.

"I'm sorry, Solomon. It's nothing you did, I can assure you of that. I finally finished that blasted draft two weeks ago but it was so terrible I threw it into the flames."

Henry sank into an armchair and Solomon followed suit, leaning forward to give his full attention to Henry. Henry gave an overview of the many faults he'd found in his manuscript.

"I'm terribly sorry to hear that, my friend." Solomon frowned, his voice low and grave. He sounded almost as if Henry had told him he'd contracted consumption and had but a few weeks to live.

"I'm rewriting it now after taking into consideration advice I received some time ago. It's going much better now and I think this will improve my entire approach. I was simply embarrassed that I failed so spectacularly with my previous attempt, and I didn't want to confess it."

Solomon sat in silence for a moment, peering at Henry with thoughtfully narrowed eyes. "But that doesn't fully explain why you lied to me."

Henry blanched at his friend's forthright assessment. He should not be surprised that Solomon could sense something deeper going on beneath the surface.

"You could have written and told me you were busy with work. I can always understand that. I know you promised to escort the Richards sisters with me, but I would never truly hold you so tightly to it if I knew you needed to focus. Why did you insist upon telling me that you were ill?"

Though Henry had gone pale just a moment before, his face now flared with a scarlet blush.

"Aha," Solomon chuckled dryly. "So it is something to do with Miss Richards."

Henry ran a hand through his already messy hair. "Yes. There is no point in denying it now. You know that Miss Richards had been weighing heavily on my mind. In a favorable way."

"And didn't you two have a grand time at the theater? Or did I miss something?"

"We did have a very nice time. I confess I was so focused

on her that I barely remember the play itself. It's like she was all the entertainment I needed..."

"Then I don't follow. What could be wrong with that? It sounds as though you admire her greatly. I would even go so far as to say that you seem quite attached to her. And from what I've observed, she's fond of you as well."

Henry shook his head in defeat, closing his eyes against reality. "That's just the problem, you see. I am fond of Miss Richards. Terribly fond. And I think she may harbor some similar feelings. At least until I disappeared after the night at the theater.

"But after thinking back over the past few months, I realized something. My writing slump began after I met Miss Richards. Any time I tried to write, I could not will myself to focus.

"You see, she was always there in my mind. I just didn't come to terms with it until recently. I allowed myself to be distracted. I lost all focus and sense of direction in my work.

"I do not blame her for this, of course. The failing and weakness is entirely on my shoulders. But if I cannot handle having her in my life while I write...I think it best if I retreat from her and finish this manuscript."

Henry sighed, a light feeling of relief washing over him as he finally expressed the inner turmoil he'd been trying to navigate on his own.

"Good Heaven, man." Solomon slapped his forehead dramatically. "You're just in love."

Henry blushed again at that word, the word he hadn't allowed himself to fully connect to Miss Richards. But he said nothing to correct Solomon.

"Henry, this is all new to you. You've never allowed yourself a chance to get to know a lady well enough to get close to feeling love for her. Somehow Miss Richards has bypassed all your careful precautions. And for that I tip my hat to her.

"But you don't yet know how to deal with these feelings so naturally they take over your mind and turn you into a bumbling fool. It happens to everyone when they fall in love —especially the first time. Give yourself a chance to incorporate this change into your life. Maybe you'll see that they can coexist. Your senses will come back to you in due time."

Solomon leaned over and laid a hand on Henry's shoulder. Henry turned his face away, biting his lip and glancing about the room to avoid meeting his best friend's eyes.

Solomon withdrew his hand and sat up straighter, eyes narrowing suspiciously. "What else aren't you telling me?"

"I wish it could be that simple, Solomon." Henry passed his hand over his face in exasperation. "You might be right. I might be able to reorient myself and find a balance, find a way to keep thoughts of Miss Richards at bay while I write so I can give my full attention to the thing I love and that I've devoted my life to.

"But it's worse than that. Even if Miss Richards felt the same, even if she accepted me if I asked for her hand...I'm not only asking for her hand, you see. I'm asking her to sign her life away to a man who can't give her the lifestyle she deserves. I'm asking her to wither away in this house while I write for hours on end.

"Or if she does go out and about in Society, she must go with someone else. She loves the Society life. Not all the artificial pandering and pretentious rules. But she loves being surrounded by excitement and activity and people. She loves experiencing opulent events and dancing and performing.

"I am not naturally inclined to any of those things. It would be entirely too selfish of me to ask her to give them up or find company with others while I remain at home in my study."

Up until that moment, these thoughts had remained as mostly vague feelings inside Henry. But giving voice to them now in the presence of another person, he felt their weight all the more. He simply didn't see how he could maintain Miss Richards's happiness and his own needs as an introverted writer.

Solomon sat in silence for several moments, pondering everything Henry had said. When he finally spoke, it was with the resignation Henry had feared he would hear. "I see. I suppose your points do make sense. The issue of compatibility in the future, not just the present, is important as well."

Henry nodded weakly. A small part of him had hoped that Solomon might have some clever solution up his sleeve.

"But I will say this." Solomon's voice grew louder and he fixed Henry with a firm stare. "I respect your love for writing and I respect your desire to share it with your readers. I would only suggest that you do not sell yourself, or Miss Richards, short.

"Take your time to sort this out, but I've seen the way she looks at me for news when I come by to escort her sister. She wishes to hear from you. Perhaps, between the two of you, you can find a way to have the best of both worlds."

Solomon's words sounded hollow to Henry's ears. He ignored the way his heart dipped in his chest when he imagined Miss Richards searching for him at Solomon's side. He knew his friend was right on one count. Miss Richards deserved some sort of explanation from him. But he did not agree with Solomon's other point. Henry had pondered the issue himself many times over, and he did not see a solution in which they could both be happy.

"I will certainly take that into consideration. In the meantime, I simply need to bear down on this manuscript and finish it out. I haven't experienced this level of focus in months. I would like for her to read it when it is finished. She's done a great deal to inspire this new work. Perhaps after that..." Henry glanced down at his hands as he trailed off, not yet wanting to confess to his friend that he'd already made his decision.

"Excellent!" Solomon clapped his large hands together in triumph. Henry flinched at the sound but his friend seemed not to notice. "I wish you the best of luck, my friend. You'd best get back to work, haven't you?"

Solomon stood as if to excuse himself, frowning at Henry.

Henry chuckled ruefully. "Strange. You are usually scolding me for working too much. But thank you for hearing me out today. It did me more good than I thought it would. I promise I won't put up boards on the door to keep you out anymore. But I will be quite busy until my manuscript is complete."

"Understood."

Solomon soon took his leave and Henry took his battered heart back to his study.

CHAPTER 13

*L*ord Overton appeared in their foyer once again to collect Juliet, this time for another trip to Gunter's. Cecilia peered behind the earl, hoping that Lord Neil would finally walk up behind him.

Again, she was disappointed. There had been no sight or sound from the baron in nearly two weeks. She had no idea what she'd done wrong to cause such an abrupt silence. Her heart sank as she thought back to the theater, the last time she'd seen Lord Neil. Everything had seemed to go so well. She'd loved the play, and most of all she'd loved having him nearby and whispering her thoughts and impressions to him in between acts.

Perhaps that had annoyed him. Though he had shown her his sense of humor numerous times in the past, Cecilia couldn't deny that he was largely a serious man, a deep thinker who admired all things artistic. Maybe sharing her opinions so frequently had been too distracting for him.

Her attention came back to the foyer as Lord Overton jovially greeted her parents. Cecilia looked to the front door once more, clinging to the tiny hope that perhaps Lord Neil was running late, that he would walk through the door at any moment.

Juliet glanced to Cecilia, her pale blue eyes conveying her regret on Cecilia's behalf. She slipped her hand into Cecilia's and gave it a quick squeeze before taking her place next to Lord Overton.

She smiled politely to hide her pain and bitterly wondered how she had come to be in this position. Just a few months ago, she had shrunk from the idea of attending these calls with Juliet because she found the baron's presence to be awkward and uncomfortable, even when she tried to forge a friendship.

But now, tears pricked at the corners of her eyes, barely held back from spilling in front of her family and the Earl of Overton. Lord Overton had visited Juliet several times last week, and this was their third visit this week. Each time, Lord Neil had been absent and all Lord Overton could tell her was that he was indisposed. Once again, Cecilia was left behind.

"My lord," she nearly whispered. She took a hesitant step toward the earl, her breath coming and going faster as her eyes desperately searched him for answers. "Please tell me…. Is Lord Neil well?" She hoped he would understand her real question beneath the polite query.

The way he swallowed and broke eye contact with her told Cecilia that he had interpreted her meaning correctly. "He is very well indeed. Exceedingly well. He has been terribly busy with some important matters."

A cold shiver swept through her stomach as she stared at the man before her. He was tall, taller than Lord Neil, and certainly very handsome. After having spent many days in his company, she did not wonder that so many ladies of the *ton* desired his attention, and ultimately ended up heart-broken when he withdrew it. His good looks were merely a bonus to his winsome personality, to say nothing of his wealth and status.

But even as the earl stood just a few feet away from her, his probing brown eyes examining her expression, his auburn hair perfectly styled to emphasize his youthful yet angular features...

Cecilia felt that he lacked the baron's calm, quiet, soothing presence that sometimes surprised her with its congenial and sharp-witted warmth. He lacked the ability to read her mind, for though he gazed into her eyes now she could see that they knew nothing of her mind. He lacked the deep-set eyes that understood her, and the handsome broad nose and square jaw and permanently ruffled dark hair. Simply put, he was not the baron.

"That is lovely to hear." Cecilia's lips pressed into a painful smile.

Suddenly everyone in the room felt very far away, as if Cecilia looked at them through a telescope. Her heart was torn in two as she stood in the foyer and watched Lord Overton escort her sister out into the bright London sunlight and their parents waved them off with gleeful anticipation.

As soon as the door shut, Mrs. Richards turned to her eldest daughter, the sparkle in her eye immediately dulling to a cold glint. "Cecilia, do you have any idea why the baron has stopped visiting with Lord Overton? What matters could be so important that he cannot find time to visit you?"

The questions felt like hot stabs in Cecilia's stomach. Her mother had no idea how deeply those words affected her. Even if she did know, perhaps she wouldn't have cared to spare Cecilia's crumbling heart.

But Cecilia did not have the energy or the mental fortitude to come up with some quaint excuse. She was moments away from breaking and holding herself together took all her willpower.

"If you must know, Mama, I believe Lord Overton simply concocted a gentle excuse for his friend's extinguished interest." Cecilia abruptly turned on her heel and rushed out of the room.

"Ceci—!" Mrs. Richards called out, but Cecilia was already halfway up the stairs.

The moment Cecilia's body hit her soft bed, the tears burst forth violently. She felt like the whole room must be shaking with her sobs. The worst feeling was not the fact that she missed Lord Neil deeply, but that she had been so blindsided by this sudden cold shoulder.

No matter how many times she analyzed their last meeting, the night at the theater, Cecilia could not for the life of her see where she had gone wrong.

Her best guess was that her chatter during the play had irritated him, but she'd saved any comments for the transitions between acts so as not to detract from the performance. But even when she considered that, she could discern no sense of irritation from him in her memories. In fact, Cecilia remembered very well the heat that crept up her neck as he sat behind her, aware of his eyes on her throughout the entire show. He had given no indication whatsoever that anything had been wrong.

Cecilia didn't know how long she laid on her bed in the exact same position, her face buried in the blanket, nearly suffocating herself.

The tears did not stop, but somewhere in their midst she fell into a fitful sleep plagued by fragmented dreams of Lord Neil.

~

PALE SUNLIGHT TICKLED Cecilia's eyelids open. She sat up in bed, rubbing her forehead as a pulsing headache made its presence known. Looking down at herself, she saw that she wore her nightgown. But her memory of the day before was so hazy that she couldn't be sure when she had changed. It must have still been early afternoon when she'd fallen asleep.

She rang the bell and Violet appeared in the doorway in almost no time at all. She must have been particularly mindful of Cecilia's call today.

"Good morning, Miss Richards." She curtsied quickly at the door before shuffling over to the side of the bed. "How are you feeling today?"

Cecilia melted slightly at the concern in her maid's voice. She must have been in an awful state yesterday, and it had been up to Violet to care for her during one of her lowest moments. Cecilia couldn't help giving the young woman a pained smile.

"I haven't been up long but so far I can tell that I have quite the headache. I'm afraid I don't remember much of what happened yesterday after I took my impromptu afternoon nap. Would you fill me in?"

Violet fussed about the tea tray on the bedside table while she spoke. "There's truthfully not much to fill in, Miss Richards. You slept for a long time, and it didn't seem right to disturb you so we left you in peace. I only woke you last night long enough to get you changed for bed, but you seemed rather in a fog so I'm not surprised you don't remember it."

Violet's words jogged very dim memories in Cecilia's mind and she realized how deeply this situation must be affecting her. And as if right on cue, Cecilia's stomach announced itself to the room with a loud groan.

The maid stifled a giggle as she settled the tea tray over

Cecilia's lap. "Just in time. I imagine you must be ravenous after you ate so little yesterday."

Cecilia's mouth was already stuffed with buttered rolls, rendering her unable to reply.

"Shall I tell the Mistress that you'll be joining them in the dining room shortly?"

A groan escaped from Cecilia in between bites of bread. She did not at all look forward to facing her parents after yesterday's events, and what they would have to say about the situation. But she knew she couldn't hide forever.

"Yes, I'll join them for breakfast," she said with a resigned sigh. "Mama will expect it."

"Ah yes well..." Violet fluttered around the room, collecting Cecilia's garments to ready her for the day.

Cecilia froze with a piece of toast halfway to her mouth. "What is it? What didn't you tell me?"

"I'm not sure if it's appropriate for me to say..." The maid glanced around the room nervously, her fingers worrying away at the edge of the petticoat still in her hands.

"You may speak to me freely, Violet. What happened?" A quiver of nerves rippled through Cecilia's stomach.

"Miss Juliet had something of a row with the Mistress. She did want to wake you and discuss whatever had happened earlier, but your sister refused to allow her near your room."

Violet looked nearly guilty as she told Cecilia the truth. The maid clearly cared for the family she'd served since she was a young girl, even if she wasn't directly involved in any of their lives beyond dressing and fixing hair and fetching tea. Even still, Violet and the other staff knew far more about the family than they let on.

"I appreciate your discretion, but I appreciate your honesty even more. I know it is not comfortable to discuss such matters. I'm ready to be dressed now." Cecilia hoped that Violet understood her sincerity.

In truth, Cecilia did consider Violet to be something of a friend, as close to a friend as a maid could be. She knew that Violet had only omitted the fight in order to protect her. But if Cecilia were to face her mother in a few minutes, she would rather know exactly what she would be dealing with.

∾

CECILIA IMMEDIATELY NOTICED that only two people occupied the dining room when she walked in.

"Good morning, Cecilia." Mrs. Richards's cold greeting indicated anything but a good morning.

"Morning, my girl." Mr. Richards at least tried to sound more cheerful, but even his usually robust voice seemed to quake in the midst of his wife's simmering anger.

Cecilia mumbled a response as she went to the sideboard and filled a plate with herring and eggs. The numerous rolls and slices of toast she'd already had in bed had only partially satisfied her hunger.

Neither of her parents addressed her again as she sat across from her mother, but their demeanors were markedly different. Mr. Richards bent over his plate and quickly forked food into his mouth to avoid conversation, his eyes darting anywhere but his wife and daughter. Mrs. Richards sat straight backed, her neck long and taut, her fork gently poking the steaming food on her plate and raising it to her lips with severe grace.

Suddenly Cecilia's appetite vanished as the uncomfortable air in the room surrounded her.

"Is Juliet down?" She finally broke the silence after struggling to swallow a dry bit of egg.

"I believe she has asked for a tray in her room." The frost

in Mrs. Richards's voice chilled Cecilia. "And have you recovered from your indisposition yesterday?"

"Yes, thank you. I'm feeling much better this morning."

"I'm most pleased to hear that. In that case, can you kindly explain your ill-bred outburst yesterday?" Mrs. Richards put her knife and fork down, the silverware gently clinking against the plate.

The color drained out of Cecilia's face and her fork slipped from her hand. She knew she would have to address this, but she hadn't anticipated it coming so abruptly.

"I don't know what you have done to displease Lord Neil so severely when everyone could see that you have been closing in on securing a proposal." Mrs. Richards launched into her right away, her eyes icy and her voice thick with scorn. "And it seems that his important matters are more important than you."

Cecilia flinched, her jaw twitching as her teeth clamped down against each other. She knew what her mother said was exactly what her tortured mind had been thinking, but hearing it come from another person in such a hateful sounding way.... It cut her deeper than she could have imagined.

"As I made clear to you not long ago, if the baron did not ask for your hand, or if you chose to refuse him, your father and I would take matters into our own hands.

"If the baron does not personally request your company or call here with Lord Overton by the end of the week, we will begin seeking other suitors for you and you will graciously accept whatever match we choose."

Cecilia had not thought that she could be made any lower than she already felt, but somehow her mother managed to slice through every trembling cord that barely held Cecilia's heart together.

"I understand, Mama." Cecilia's voice trembled as she

realized the hope she'd clung to for three years had finally come to an end.

Mrs. Richards stared at her daughter in silence for a few moments, her gaze calculating, determining her next course of action. Mr. Richards glanced furtively between the two women but kept his opinions to himself, as usual.

Cecilia had known her whole life that while Mr. Richards might be the head of the household in name, it was Mrs. Richards who was truly the force to be reckoned with.

"You have until the end of the week. If the baron does not seek you out in some way, you can expect to have a full schedule of engagements with other eligible gentlemen." With that, Mrs. Richards pushed herself away from the dining table and left the room.

"Papa?" Cecilia mumbled weakly as she wiped at her face with a napkin.

Mr. Richards coughed uncomfortably and he too stood from the table. "I'm sorry, my girl. We think this is the best route. I had hoped that Lord Neil would win out. You two seemed to get on very well recently.

"But...you will need to marry, and soon. Our options will only continue to dwindle as the Seasons go by. You don't really want to be a spinster, do you? I know many kind men who could provide a comfortable life for you, and finally bring our family into the finest circles. You'll make your mother so happy. Wouldn't that be nice, dear?"

He sounded resigned, pleading almost. Mr. Richards excused himself and left his daughter alone with those thoughts in the dining room.

Cecilia managed to stifle her tears long enough to make her way to Juliet's room. But when her knock received no answer Cecilia grew concerned. Surely Juliet could not still be asleep. She pushed the door open slowly and quietly but still no one greeted her.

"Jules?" Cecilia peered into the room but there was no sign of her sister. Truly puzzled now, Cecilia stepped in and noticed a folded letter on the bed. She rushed forward and grabbed the piece of paper.

Sissy, I've gone for a carriage ride. I can't bear to be in this house a moment longer. I shall be back in a few hours. If Mother cares to ask after me, inform her of my whereabouts.

The letter being directly addressed to her, Cecilia knew that Juliet didn't expect their mother to look for her. Indeed, Mrs. Richards had seemed quite indifferent to her youngest daughter during breakfast. The fight they'd had must have been even worse than Violet indicated. They acted as if they were strangers sharing the same roof.

Cecilia folded the letter and took it back with her to her own room. As soon as she closed the door a fresh wave of tears hit her body. This was all too overwhelming, everything her mother had said now sinking into her very bones. And she didn't have Juliet to comfort her when she needed her most. But her heart ached even more for the fact that Juliet was suffering through her own pain.

She could only hope now that whatever futures they faced, they would be able to endure them together.

As Cecilia had suspected, Lord Neil did not call upon her or invite her for an outing. Despite the cold attitude she'd adopted of late, Cecilia could see that her mother grew restless.

After her absence from breakfast and her spontaneous carriage ride a few days go, Juliet had put in her appearances during family meals and dutifully attended the dinner they'd already accepted an invitation to last night. But it was as if Juliet's body went through the motions, devoid of her vivid mind and spirit. She spoke to Cecilia when Cecilia made a comment or asked a question, but her answers were short and dull—lifeless. At home, Juliet kept to her room nearly all day and did not answer the door for anyone.

Cecilia knew her sister, and she knew that something was deeply, deeply wrong. Yet Juliet avoided her, and Cecilia could not get close enough to find out what troubled her so.

She sobbed quietly in her room every day as a whirlwind of pain caused a storm in her overburdened mind. Her only solace now could be found in the drawing room. Whiling away at the pianoforte provided a modicum of relief and distraction from her woes.

Cecilia awoke on the third day, Lord Neil's last chance to prove his intentions, with certainty in her stomach that the baron would continue his streak of silence, and tomorrow she would be whisked away by some other man of her parents' acquaintance.

Somehow Cecilia was glad to have reached this day. The uncertainty had been excruciating. Even if she knew that the likelihood of hearing from Lord Neil had decreased with each passing day since the theater, the weakest flicker of hope continued to burn in the very deepest corner of her heart.

Today, that flicker could be put out, and she could focus her attention on her new obligations. At least they would provide her with some distraction from the hundreds of thoughts of Lord Neil that passed through her mind each hour.

She'd written to Rosamund yesterday to see if she would like to join Cecilia at the Egyptian Hall, hoping that spending some time among beautiful artworks would bring momentary peace to her mind. And she was desperate to share her thoughts with someone. Of course she most wanted to speak with Juliet, but that seemed an impossible challenge at the moment.

And besides, it had been some time since she'd been able to have deeper conversation with Rosamund since she had been carted all around London with Lady Henshell on a full calendar of calls.

Violet helped Cecilia into one of her finer dresses, for the museum was a place of refinement and gentility, but she had some time before Rosamund arrived in the fine Henshell family carriage. Cecilia took the opportunity to practice on the pianoforte until her friend arrived, lest she be overcome with unwanted thoughts if her hands and mind remained idle.

A small gasp startled Cecilia as she entered the drawing room, causing Cecilia to gasp in response. The scene she saw surprised her into silence.

"Sissy..." Juliet mumbled from her seat on the pianoforte bench. Her cheeks were red, as if she'd been caught sneaking chocolates just before dinner.

"Jules, what are you doing here? Were you actually...playing?" Cecilia couldn't keep the incredulity out of her voice.

Juliet had never enjoyed practicing musical instruments of any kind and had avoided it with all her might during their younger years. More often than not their governess and their music master had had to chase her down the halls and nearly drag her to the instrument.

Juliet's blush deepened and her eyes remained downcast. "I was trying to. I wanted to learn that piece you wrote, but it's not coming together."

"You know all you have to do is ask and I can help you with it," Cecilia said softly, stepping forward carefully as if her sister were a wounded animal that might bolt at any moment. And judging by the way her eyes glanced to the door and window, Cecilia might not have been too far off in that assessment.

"I know. Maybe some other time." Juliet stood, smoothed out her skirts, and began inching towards the door—still without making direct eye contact with Cecilia.

But this was the first time Cecilia had been alone in a room with her sister and she was not about to squander the opportunity. She stepped directly in front of Juliet, blocking her escape path.

"Jules, what's been going on with you? You haven't been yourself since your fight with Mama. I can understand why that would weigh heavily on your mind. But I don't see why you should be avoiding me as well. Have I done something to offend you?"

"No, no. I've just been distracted by my own troubled thoughts. I'm terribly sorry I haven't been available to you recently." Juliet sighed and lowered her head.

"It seems we've been caught in a very tumultuous period and it's made a mess of us both. There's no need to apologize for dealing with your own struggle." Cecilia smiled weakly and took one of Juliet's hands in hers. She had missed her sister desperately of late, but above all she was glad that they could support each other now.

"But tell me," Juliet said with a sad smile, turning to Cecilia. "I'm afraid I haven't given you the chance to speak of what's happened between you and Lord Neil. I can only imagine how painful it must be, whatever it is."

"Actually, I invited Rosamund out today for a trip to the museum and I was going to speak with her about it all then. Why don't you join us?"

Juliet smiled with relief. "That would be very nice indeed. I haven't been out of the house in some time. It's starting to feel like a cage. I think a change of scenery will do me well.

And I'm in a better place now to hear you out and lend my support."

Cecilia returned the smile, thrilled to have her sister back on her side.

～

CECILIA HAD ONLY BEEN to the Egyptian Hall once before, during her first Season, but the place had left a deep impression on her. She'd thought about visiting again multiple times but her schedule had always been so filled with engagements.

She only wished she didn't have to carry such a heavy heart with her as she walked through the massive, ornate halls. But having her two dearest friends by her side helped ease the weight on her shoulders.

They had walked through the exhibits mostly in companionable silence, occasionally pointing out artifacts or works of interest. Juliet and Rosamund both seemed to hold back any questions they had, waiting for Cecilia to broach the subject.

Oddly, now that Cecilia was here, she wasn't sure where to start or what she wanted to say about the situation. After all, no amount of unburdening her heart through conversation would take away the heartache left behind.

Perhaps coming here had been a mistake after all, Cecilia realized. Everywhere she looked she saw Lord Neil. She would have loved to come to such a beautiful place with him and hear his thoughts on all these magnificent works of art and curiosities.

In fact, many of the depictions of faraway lands around the world, places that seemed almost fictional to Cecilia, reminded her of the fantastical world in those adventure novels. She could almost see the heroes galivanting about the pyramids in Egypt on their way to defeat some monster or corrupt foe. And since seeing that letter in Lord Neil's drawing room, Cecilia could not untangle the adventure novels and the baron in her mind.

"Cecilia?" A curious voice broke Cecilia's concentration and she jumped, turning to find Rosamund peering at her. "We didn't realize you'd lagged behind. You've been staring at that creature for quite some time."

Cecilia turned back to whatever had captured her attention and jumped again as she came face to face with a preserved rhino. Juliet, who had walked back to rejoin them, laughed a bit too loudly and the sound echoed through the large room. A few other visitors clicked their tongues at her but as always, Juliet paid them no mind.

"I'm sorry. I was lost in thought," Cecilia admitted as she put a hand over her heart to calm it.

"Is that so? And about what, might I ask?" Rosamund prodded with her wily voice, a brow arched over her curious eye.

"You look as though you already know the answer," Cecilia chuckled.

Rosamund and Juliet glanced to each other. "I'm sure we do, but you did invite us here to discuss what troubles you, did you not?" Rosamund pouted, getting more eager to hear the details now that Cecilia had alluded to the situation.

Cecilia sighed and resumed walking so they could continue to take in the museum. "Of course my mind is on Lord Neil, which you both know."

The other girls nodded quietly, allowing Cecilia to speak in her own time for which she was grateful as she sought to gather her scattered and foggy thoughts.

"I felt as though Lord Neil understood me, he appreciated my perspective and opinion. For the first time since making my debut, I felt that this man could really be the one I'd waited for for so long. And I thought everything was going very well. I even anticipated that he might have a more serious conversation with me about his intentions. But it seems I failed to give him enough encouragement and he's turned away from me."

Cecilia swallowed hard, a wobbly lump lodging itself in her throat.

Juliet looped an arm through Cecilia's and gently patted the back of her hand while Rosamund rubbed comforting circles on the small of Cecilia's back. Cecilia knew that Rosamund in particular must be dying to get to the meat of the story, but she appreciated their patience and support as she steadied herself to continue.

"I won't pretend to understand why he has cut contact with me so suddenly. I can't help but wonder if...maybe Lord Neil isn't so different from anyone else.

"And now Mama and Papa have already scheduled a series of engagements for me for this week, until I either indicate that I find one of the gentlemen suitable, or they choose one for me. I must have been a fool to think I could find true love. Maybe it is true that such a thing only happens miraculously, for the lucky ones in our world."

She couldn't stop her voice from breaking as she confessed the deepest, most painful feelings that had taken up residence in her heart over the past few weeks. Warm tears collected at the corners of her eyes and the dull ache in her chest flared into a sharp incessant stinging.

"Oh, dear," Rosamund cooed as she turned Cecilia toward her and swiped at her eyes with a gloved finger.

"Thank you for sharing with us, Sissy. I can't imagine how you must feel right now, or how much it hurts to give voice to your suffering." Juliet's voice was quiet and concerned, her hand wrapped tight around her older sister's.

"I should be thanking you for listening to my pitiful tale. I feel like I've been such a fool for holding onto these ideals when the end result would have always turned out this way." Cecilia continued to sniffle quietly as they made their way through the exhibit, the tears swimming in her eyes blurring her surroundings.

"Hush now, I won't hear any talk of pitiful this or foolish that," Rosamund clucked. "There is nothing wrong with your desires and they don't make you abnormal in any way. I'm sure many people feel the same, but it's difficult to find matches made in love because other factors take precedence at times. And I won't have you feeling less than the kind, wonderful, talented, smart woman you are. Any man would be lucky to have you as his wife and life companion.

"I have to admit that I'm also surprised by Lord Neil's behavior. I never knew him well, but he always seemed to be a genuine and pleasant gentleman to me. If a little shy. I can't fathom why he would do such a thing to you, and it angers me greatly. But I will say this. Your situation is far from ideal, but use this opportunity to your benefit. Take your mind off the baron with all your upcoming engagements. You never know, something unexpected just might happen. If any of us can have hope for that, it would be you, Cecilia."

Rosamund smiled warmly at her friend, the corners of her eyes wrinkling with the mirth that came so naturally to her.

"I agree," Juliet chimed in. "Lord Neil has just lost the greatest treasure in the world. But one of these gentlemen might just be the right one to recognize it. I know such a thing is far easier said than done, but keep an open mind. We may be at the point of having no choice but to accept the situation. But that doesn't mean some good can't still come of it."

Cecilia breathed in deeply, as if hoping to soak up her companions' words out of the air. Every beat of her heart still felt like a bruise being prodded, but she felt more centered. She didn't know if she would find love in any of these courtships set up by her parents. But, as Rosamund said, the unexpected was always a possibility.

If Cecilia had nothing else to cling to, she could at least hope for a pleasant match. A meaningful life could still be lived without love. But even as Cecilia said those words to herself, she felt something within her deepest core wither and crumble in on itself.

"Thank you, my dear friends. Your words have done much to fortify me. I can't say that it will be easy to convince my heart to let go of Lord Neil, but I can try my best. And some distraction will be good for me."

"There's my brave girl!" Rosamund cheered and numerous heads whipped around to glare at her. She seemed to remember that they were in a museum, but rather than shrinking under the annoyed gazes, she simply shrugged her shoulders at Cecilia and Juliet, wrinkling her nose playfully. "Why don't we hop in my carriage and make a quick stop at Gunter's?" She suggested, nearly skipping at her own tantalizing idea.

"Ah yes," Cecilia giggled. "Ice serves as a great distraction as well."

But as they finished in the exhibit, passing by the large works of art and preserved creatures and expansive murals, Cecilia's wounded heart continued to beat to the same broken drum—*if only I could be here sharing this beauty with Lord Neil...*

CHAPTER 14

*S*olomon paced about Henry's library, one arm folded behind his back and the other propping up his chin. His brows were creased with a deep line between them. He looked almost like a stage actor, playing up the drama before delivering a sobering and plaintive monologue. Not unlike the actors Henry had watched a few weeks ago, when Miss Richards had still been by his side.

"I do hope you know the rug you are abusing was quite expensive. Should I send the bill to your London home or your country estate?" Henry grumbled from his armchair, closing the philosophy book he'd been attempting to read.

His friend needed no further prompting. With a dramatic flair, the earl spun around on one heel and brought his hands to his hair.

"I simply do not understand what is happening," he cried out in exasperation, ignoring Henry's gibe. "Why would Miss Juliet say she cannot continue to see me? And without telling me what error I made to turn her away from me? It makes no sense, I tell you."

"Is that because you have never been refused in the past?

You were always the one to pull away first." Henry put his book on the small table beside his chair. He suspected no reading would be accomplished whilst Solomon was still in the room.

The other man groaned in frustration, returning to his pacing. "Yes, that is true and I am surprised by that. I haven't experienced rejection in a long, long time. But it is more than that, Henry."

Solomon halted in the middle of the room, turning to look at Henry with such a look of distress that Henry's blood froze for a moment. Despite his friend's seemingly silly and over the top antics, Henry realized that he was absolutely serious.

Henry sat forward in his chair, putting his full attention on Solomon. "In what way?"

"I just can't fathom why she would withdraw from me now. Why would she ask me to stop writing and asking for her company? I thought our friendship was progressing quite nicely. At first I wondered if it was because of your refusal to see her sister."

Henry bit his lip at this, guilt piercing his stomach both at the mention of Miss Richards and at the possibility of having ruined his friend's courtship. He certainly hadn't considered this outcome when he'd made his decision to quit Miss Richards's company.

"But something tells me it's not that. I could see it in her eyes. There was something deeply troubling her. She seemed quite unlike herself. Yet she refused to tell me, she refused all my offers of assistance."

Solomon rubbed his temple, his eyes racing over the rug as his feet had done not too many minutes ago, but Henry knew they didn't see anything in the room. They were searching for some answer, some solution that could rectify the situation.

Unfortunately, due to Henry's own current troubles, he wasn't inclined to be hopeful about any positive results.

"Thank you for delivering the manuscript to Miss Juliet this morning. I'm terribly sorry she used the opportunity to withdraw from you. But Solomon, I fear you are going to put a hole in my rug one way or another. Why don't we get some fresh air at Hyde Park? It's almost the promenade hour," Henry suggested.

Though he tended to avoid Hyde Park during this time of day due to the influx of people, he knew it to be a favorite pastime of Solomon's. Where Henry found comfort in solitude and silence, Solomon preferred the hustle and bustle of community to rejuvenate himself.

Solomon snapped his fingers together. "A fine idea, my friend. Let's take my carriage over and I'll return you here afterward."

HENRY SHUDDERED as soon as he stepped out of the carriage. Just as he'd suspected, the park was full to bursting with people of all ages and social standings walking about while leisurely chatting or driving their carriages slowly so as to be able to call out to acquaintances.

Solomon, on the other hand, already seemed spritelier and he inhaled deeply to soak in the energy of the atmosphere.

Henry let his friend pick their direction and they forged ahead through the throng of people and horses and carriages. Within moments Solomon was nodding to the ladies and gentlemen passing by, acquaintances or friends from some place or other. But he didn't stop to encourage any of them to strike up a conversation, which left Henry feeling immensely grateful.

But, Henry admitted to himself, being out during the promenade hour wasn't entirely insufferable. He and Solomon had come to Hyde Park with the Richards sisters on several occasions at this exact time. When he looked back on those memories—aside from the heavy ache in his chest that he'd become accustomed to when he thought of Miss Richards—he found that they lacked the stressful quality of his other excursions here.

He'd enjoyed it more because Miss Richards had been there. Something about her had been able to draw him out of his panicked thoughts so he could better observe her. But as he noticed everything about her, it was as though he were finally able to fully see his surroundings, to see the world she lived in. The world he had also shared for a time.

Unbidden, Henry noticed those things now. From the way the tree branches swayed over the crowds, dappling them in dancing shade, to the way the other park visitors walked and smiled and chatted together, happy and calm and enjoying their company.

Henry clenched his fists as that all too familiar rush of pain swept over him, starting from his chest and radiating to his very toes and the hairs atop his head. There was nothing here to ease his mind about being in this crowded park amongst dozens of strangers. He would never have that comforting presence near him again, never have a conversation that was both idle and profound all at once.

He regretted coming here, even if he knew it was for his friend's benefit. It was too overwhelming to see Miss Richards in every tiny blossom that lined the sidewalk, in the swishing folds of every colorful dress that she might have worn.

"Henry, I am in danger." Solomon's grave voice finally broke the silence that had fallen between them.

Henry jumped slightly at the interruption of his thoughts. "What threatens you?"

"What threatens me?" Solomon repeated with a rueful laugh. "The same thing that has always threatened me. Intimacy. After all these years of thinking I had abandoned any inclination toward such a vulnerable state, I seem to have found myself right back where I started.

"It was foolish of me to take up a serious courtship and develop such an interest in a woman. I should have been satisfied with flattering the various ladies of my acquaintance until they proved their interest only in my title and wealth. That made it easy for me to break things off and turn my attention to another. I could have carried on that way for years. I'm still young enough, after all. All this business about heirs can wait.

"Miss Juliet was the first woman to truly capture my attention in years. I assumed she would turn out like all the rest. In fact, I even sort of hoped she would, so I could set her aside before I became too attached, for I could feel it happening even from the very beginning."

Henry couldn't help smiling a little as he thought back on the early days of their acquaintance with the Richards sisters, and how flustered Solomon had been. It was a nice change for Henry to see a side of his friend he hadn't glimpsed in a long time, a side he had thought he would never see again.

"The anger and hurt and shock in me wants to claim that I've been tricked again like..." Solomon trailed off, but he didn't need to finish his sentence for Henry to know the event he now thought of. He glanced to his friend and saw a twitch in his jaw and a darkness in his eyes that only appeared when he thought back to that period.

"But it couldn't be that same situation again. That wouldn't make sense," Henry offered. "It was mere days after she broke off the engagement that the newspaper announced her impending wedding to that duke."

Solomon flinched at the reminder of one of his darkest moments, and Henry was loath to bring it up but he needed to make his point. "If Miss Juliet was being courted by someone else at the same time, wouldn't you have heard talk of it? She has been quite popular this Season, but I haven't heard that she's accepted anyone else's attentions as often as yours."

"Exactly." Solomon tilted his chin up, eyes gazing into the pale blue sky thoughtfully. "My initial reaction was to compare Miss Juliet to that previous horrid incident. But something in me tells me that whatever her reasons are for breaking off from me, they are vastly different. Yet I still cannot surmise what else could be the cause. I can't imagine that her parents don't find me favorable. They nearly throw themselves at me every time I call on them. Could it be that she simply...doesn't like me?"

Solomon's voice grew quiet and insecure, an occurrence so rare that it was jarring to Henry.

"Well I suppose that is a possibility. But my instinct tells me that is also not the case. When you asked me to accompany you on your calls, I also agreed to act as an unbiased observer.

"From what I've seen thus far, she seemed very taken with you. And not just with your charming behavior, and certainly not your title. Her eyes seemed to try to see you, truly see you. And you seemed to respond in kind."

"That's just the thing. Despite all this, I know you are right. I felt it, too. Yet somehow knowing that makes not knowing why she has forsaken me that much worse. Something has afflicted her, and I am powerless to help because I am being kept at arm's length. I cannot stand this feeling of helplessness. If only I could speak to her, I'm sure we could overcome whatever keeps her from me."

The frustration in Solomon's voice rang clear in the golden evening air. Henry rested a hand on his friend's shoulder and squeezed. "I am truly sorry, Solomon. I'm not sure I have any answers or suggest—"

Henry's hand slipped from Solomon's shoulder as his eyes locked on an unexpected sight. Time froze and Henry found himself trapped in this horrible, gut-wrenching moment.

"Henry?" Solomon's startled voice came to him as if through a thick wooden door. It reverberated hollowly in his ear before echoing back upon itself. Henry's eyes could only stare ahead at the scene before him. As far as Henry knew in that moment, Solomon and the whole of London could have been on another planet.

At first glance, Henry could have sworn that his eyes deceived him. But now, rooted to his spot, stuck in this agonizing loop, Henry had plenty of time to confirm the truth.

Across the walkway, perched in a small, slow moving curricle driven by a finely dressed groom, sat Miss Cecilia Richards. Next to her was a dashing young gentleman clad in what could only have been a brand-new outfit, perhaps made specifically for this outing.

Whatever he said must have been exceedingly witty or charming, for Miss Richards flashed her breathtaking smile and quickly hid behind her hand as she laughed in response.

Henry could just barely make out that sweet tinkling sound that he'd come to love. Or perhaps he only imagined he did. It was so easy for him to hear it in his own mind now, as he'd mentally recreated it dozens of times each day.

Of course, Henry knew that Miss Richards would inevitably continue searching for a match. It was foolish to think that his silence had rendered her too distressed to venture back into the marriage mart at the first opportunity.

In truth, she looked entirely at ease with her companion and her surroundings. She looked to be exactly where she belonged—out enjoying company on a bright day.

She looked happy.

"Oh no..." Solomon's muttered curse broke Henry's trance. "I think it's about time we head back, Henry."

Solomon gripped Henry's elbow and turned him around so sharply that Henry stumbled over his own feet. He hoped Miss Richards hadn't heard any commotion and turned to see him. Solomon marched him out of the park as quickly as possible, maintaining his firm hold on Henry's elbow.

The short carriage ride back to Henry's home consisted mostly of Solomon bombarding Henry with dozens of questions, asking every few seconds if he was alright. Too dazed to properly respond, Henry simply waved away each query, mumbling things he couldn't remember.

Though Solomon had initially planned on returning Henry and going straight home, the earl followed Henry into the town house. Despite Solomon's continuous jabbering about Henry's well-being trailing behind him through the foyer and down the hallway, Henry didn't pay it any mind. Everything else fell away into background noise.

"Henry, wait!" The shout stirred Henry out of his stupor long enough to realize that he'd made it to his study and was in the process of closing the door in Solomon's face.

"What are you still doing here?" Henry asked, his voice dry and monotone. He stared at his friend on the other side of the door without feeling. His closest friend since boyhood now seemed like a stranger somehow. Everything inside Henry had gone blank and numb.

"Henry, answer me for once. Are you quite well? I know seeing that can't have been—" Solomon slipped his muscular arm through the door, trying to worm his way in. But Henry held firm.

"Let's not speak of that. I'm fine. As fine as anyone might expect. I don't see why I shouldn't be."

"Come on, Henry. You are not yourself right now. Let me in, please." Solomon wriggled against the door in earnest but Henry continued to push against him.

"I'm as much myself as I've ever been. I really should get to work now. You can see yourself out, I trust. I'm no longer in the mood for company."

Henry could bring no life to his voice. He could hear how cold and hollow he sounded as he banished his friend, but he couldn't stop himself.

This surprised Solomon enough that he stood back from the door, his eyes round with shock and mouth slightly ajar. "Hen—"

But Henry had already closed the door. He waited there for several moments, long enough to hear Solomon's footsteps retreat down the hall.

When he was sure he was alone, Henry dragged himself to his desk and slowly sank into his chair. His own copy of the completed draft sprawled before him. It had only taken him another week to complete the book after his discussion with Solomon.

Henry stared at the pages now, crisp and fresh. But they all looked cold and empty and pointless now.

Miss Richards was well and truly gone from him. The hundreds of times he imagined turning up at her door and apologizing for his behavior now crumbled into ashes. She had seemed so happy at the park with that gentleman, so happy to be part of Society.

And why shouldn't she be happy? This room, these pages before him, were Henry's life. She couldn't be part of it. She belonged out there in eternal sunshine meeting friends and enjoying events.

He picked up the stack of pages and slipped them into a large folder, ready to be brought to Frye for publication.

This was the life he had chosen. He chose a life of solitude. He chose a life without Miss Richards. But she didn't need to make the same choice. Surely she would make a fine wife to a lucky gentleman someday soon.

But Henry Neil had never been a lucky gentleman.

CHAPTER 15

*C*ecilia curtsied to the gentleman outside her front door after she and her footman descended from his carriage. He tipped his hat to her as he instructed his driver to carry them away down the road.

She had barely stepped an inch into the foyer and her mother and father already assailed her with questions. She hadn't even had a chance to loosen her bonnet.

"Wasn't he quite charming, Cecilia?" Mrs. Richards prodded, the sharpness in her voice conveying not so much a question as a statement that she intended to sell to Cecilia.

"Did you learn more about his family? He's only a second son but he must have some sort of allowances." Mr. Richards pried, his eyes sparkling.

"Yes, he was very charming. And yes, he is on good terms with his older brother who assures him that when he inherits his title all the younger siblings will be provided for." Cecilia rattled off her answer almost as if she had rehearsed it.

Rather than embarking on these outings with these numerous gentlemen to learn about their interests, personalities, or perspectives, Cecilia had grown into the habit of filing away a different set of information. Every time she returned home or finished a dance with an eligible gentleman, her parents were sure to launch a dozen questions at her.

None of their questions had anything to do with how well she'd gotten along with the man, or what she thought of his ideals and hobbies. They only had to do with whether or not he was tolerable enough to potentially marry and what titles, estates, or other inheritances he could claim.

"Hmm." Mrs. Richards tapped her foot rapidly. "I think we might still be able to find a better suitor. A second son is never ideal. But perhaps I can arrange another meeting with that young heir you danced with a few days ago." She trailed off, lost in her plans, as she ambled through the foyer to the stairs, no doubt heading to her chambers where she could draft more letters on Cecilia's behalf.

"Don't listen to her," Mr. Richards chuckled. "A second son would do just fine, as long as he will have some sort of allowance." He also saw himself out of the foyer, leaving Cecilia alone with her thoughts.

She sighed as her father's words rang in her head. He'd rather missed the point. Cecilia wasn't concerned about who was a second or third or fourth son. At this point she simply wanted to find someone she could reasonably endure. Unfortunately her companion for today had proved rather vacuous, despite his beguiling smiles.

And of course there had been Lord Neil. The look in his eyes haunted her for the rest of her carriage ride about the park. She knew he had seen her, but his expression had been cold and empty.

With no other engagements scheduled for today, Cecilia was free to do as she wished. She made her way to the drawing room with the scene playing out over and over in her mind, her heart sinking further each time. She found

Juliet sitting at the pianoforte, a sight she'd grown more accustomed to over the past week.

"Practicing again? How diligently unlike you," she laughed as she approached her sister.

"Hush, you. I'm doing this for you, because you wrote such a lovely song that it would be a shame not to learn it and share it with others. And I need distraction." Juliet scrunched her nose up, her fingers fumbling over the keys at the interruption.

"There's nothing wrong with admitting you enjoy the process." Cecilia sat next to Juliet on the bench and flipped back to the previous page of sheet music. "You're still struggling with this passage here."

"I didn't think it would take me so long to learn it, but now the challenge has so irritated me that I feel the need to overcome it." Sticking her tongue out of the corner of her mouth, Juliet played through the section Cecilia pointed to. She furrowed her brows as the notes came out smoother, but still not perfectly.

"Well if you practiced regularly it wouldn't be so difficult. You're quite out of condition," Cecilia chided.

"That's strange, I didn't realize our governess had come back after all these years. She looks more like you than I remembered."

Cecilia only sighed and continued her instruction. "Play the passage again. I require utter perfection if you're going to play my piece," she demanded with faux arrogance.

But Juliet ignored Cecilia, turning the conversation away from her poor playing. "How was your trip today?"

Cecilia sighed and shrugged her shoulders in defeat. The deep melancholy that had shaken her when she'd seen the look on Lord Neil's face crept over her again.

"I saw him today. At the park. And I know he saw me chatting away with that gentleman in the curricle." She dropped her face into her hands, frustrated and wounded. Cecilia hated the fact that that look would forever be etched in her memory as the last time she saw the baron.

"Oh my. Did you speak with him?" Juliet took one of Cecilia's hands away from her face and clasped it tightly in her lap.

"No. He was too far away. And besides, I wouldn't know what to say to him if I had been able. I cannot tell if he despised me for being with another suitor or if he simply did not care."

"Sissy...maybe you should go and rest for a while," Juliet suggested softly. "As a matter of fact, you've had a delivery from Lord Neil himself. It's waiting for you on your bed."

Cecilia's head snapped around to look into her sister's face. Her heart hammered. "What?"

"I don't know the contents but when I was out with Lord Overton this morning he asked that I deliver it to you on behalf of the baron. But you'd already left for the day by the time I returned home."

Cecilia stood so fast she nearly tripped over the hem of her dress. Without another word, she left Juliet behind and flew to her room.

Once inside, Cecilia stood with her back against the closed door as she stared at the parcel on her bed. Her heart still pounded against her ribs and her breath came in sharp and shallow. By now she had given up hope of receiving even a simple "hello" from the baron, much less a package.

She placed a hand on her chest in an effort to soothe herself and crossed the room to her bed. The parcel, wrapped in plain brown paper tied with string, was entirely unassuming. Yet Cecilia could feel that it contained something highly important.

Lowering herself with weak knees to sit on her plush covers, Cecilia removed her gloves and set them aside. The package was large and heavy, the paper rough on her smooth palms. She tugged one end of the string and it fell away easily. With trembling fingers, she unfolded the stiff wrapping paper and pulled out a tall stack of pages and placed them carefully on her bed, as if they might crumble into ash at any moment.

At the top of the stack sat a neatly folded sheet. When she picked it up, Cecilia read the fancy flourishing writing on the page underneath.

The Hero's Companion.

Cecilia's brow furrowed. It appeared to be a title, something befitting the popular adventure novel series. Perhaps, for some reason, Lord Neil had received an early copy from his connection at Frye Publishing and thought to pass it along to Cecilia.

But first, the letter. Cecilia held her breath as she unfolded the sheet.

Dear Miss Richards,

I would like to extend my sincerest apologies for withdrawing my attentions so suddenly. I hope you enjoy this gift—if you choose to read it—and I hope you find happiness wherever life may take you.

Warmest regards,

Neil

Conflicting emotions battered against each other inside Cecilia's chest as she quickly read the short note. She felt as though she were being bruised from the inside out. She could not have guessed what would be in the letter, but she had hoped for something more personal than two simple sentences.

Perhaps he really hadn't cared for her any more than a note of less than a paragraph warranted. And his dark expression at the park suggested that his feelings for her were not entirely favorable.

With a heavy disappointment settling in her stomach, Cecilia turned her attention to the rest of the package. She read the title again and flipped through a few pages. Elegant handwriting covered each sheet. It did indeed appear to be a draft of some book. Cecilia squirmed as she realized that she likely should not be in possession of an unpublished manuscript.

But if Lord Neil wished for her to read it, then read it she would—even if it broke her heart. Cecilia knew in her bones that this was his goodbye to her.

~

Our world is full of small people with small minds. They don't know how little it costs to broaden one's perspective. With your continued help, I hope to change that. I love you.... Will you stay by my side?

Cecilia could have sworn that her heart stopped beating for a fraction of a second. She reread the words several times, so rapidly that they became a jumbled mess before her eyes. The tears that welled up obscured her vision and she set the remaining pages down next to her on the bed with trembling hands. She had read for hours and was long past due for a break.

"This cannot be..." she whimpered. But she knew there could be no other explanation.

She had heard that phrase spoken twice before, nearly word for word as it was written here.

The first had been at the Henshells' masked ball when she danced with her mystery gentleman. The second had been when she danced with Lord Neil. And here it appeared again, in this unpublished installment of the adventure series.

Though Cecilia's mind felt as though it swam through a

fog, there was one fact that shone bright enough for her to follow.

Lord Neil, the masked gentleman, and the anonymous author were one and the same.

Not only did that phrase appear in the book, but Cecilia did not think it a coincidence that there were many striking similarities between herself and the new heroine who accompanied the hero on this adventure. In fact, several scenes and conversations in the story closely followed her own experiences with Lord Neil.

The baron's extreme inclination to remain in his library or study made far more sense now that Cecilia knew he likely spent much of his time writing the increasingly popular series.

But the fact that Lord Neil had been her masked man shook Cecilia to her core. That truth she'd felt in her heart— though she'd been too doubtful of herself to follow it—had been correct all along. Somewhere deep inside her she'd known that such a connection as the one she'd felt with that mystery man and the one she felt in Lord Neil's presence could only come from the same source.

How often had Cecilia caught herself gazing into space, thinking about whiling away the hours of a slow, relaxing day in Lord Neil's library, perhaps having her sister or Rosamund over for a companionable dinner in the baron's dining room? Too many times to count, Cecilia knew.

Her heart ached with a deep pain she'd never known before, with the realization that all those daydreams could have been reality. Perhaps Lord Neil had shared those same daydreams as well.

In fact, he had cared for her enough to recreate her in his fictional world, or at least use her as inspiration.

Perhaps, if she had encouraged him more during their time together…. But she had been too distracted with her pianoforte troubles and pining after the mystery gentleman. She could have changed the course of both their futures.

For Cecilia loved him.

Of that she was now certain. She had been certain for longer than she realized. But it had felt too presumptuous to put it into words.

Lord Neil truly was everything she had dreamed of since she was a little girl, imagining walking down the aisle to a man she loved, becoming a wife to someone she could have genuine, deep conversation with, someone who understood her and loved her.

And now it was too late. What could she say to him if she stood before him again? Would he believe that her parents had forced her into these new courtships? Would he believe that she thought he had grown tired of her? Would he even allow her near enough, after witnessing the scene in the park, and grant her the opportunity to explain herself?

All Cecilia could see over and over again in her mind's eye was the ashen expression on the baron's face, and that expression told her that any hope she may have had was as good as dust.

Cecilia tucked the manuscript under her covers and reached for the service bell. Violet gasped when she entered the room. Cecilia must have looked a mess, but that was the very least of her troubles now.

"Miss Richards! What's happened?" Violet cried out as she picked up her skirts and ran to the bed. She settled a hand on Cecilia's arm and she collapsed under the gentle touch, curling up amongst her blankets.

"Tell Juliet that I need to see her at once. Speak of this to no one else." Her breath stuttered as she spoke and she wasn't sure if enough coherent sound had come out for Violet to understand her.

But the maid swallowed, her eyes determined, sensing the

urgency of Cecilia's request. She nodded once and flew out of the room.

Cecilia was left to her own tortured thoughts again. Her heart felt as though it were being torn apart slowly and methodically, by some evil creature who wished to prolong her suffering for as long as possible.

The baron had had feelings for her. He may have even loved her. Perhaps she could cling to that knowledge for however long she lived and it could sustain her through whatever bleak future there was in store for her.

Or perhaps that knowledge would slowly destroy her— knowing what could have been, how close she'd been to having the miraculous love she'd always dreamed of, with the most miraculous man she would ever meet.

Thinking of the future now, the years seemed to stretch forward into a cold, pitch black eternity, the only light that could have illuminated her path extinguished.

CHAPTER 16

*H*enry heard the knock on his front door from his study. It was rapid but firm. Urgent. It was almost too early for proper morning calls to be made, and Solomon rarely ever called this early.

His pen stilled over the page and he strained his ears to listen, but all he could make out were muffled voices in the foyer. He recognized the lower timbre of his butler's voice, but the other voice was unfamiliar, high pitched. Now Henry really had no idea who could be calling on him unannounced at this hour.

A few moments passed as the voices continued to deliberate back and forth, but the butler's footsteps finally sounded through the hallway.

"My lord, you have a visitor..." His face was red but Henry couldn't tell if it was from embarrassment or anger.

"And who might this visitor be?"

"I think you had best come and see for yourself."

A curious apprehension gripped Henry as he slowly stood from his desk and proceeded out to the foyer.

"Miss Juliet!" He shouted, unable to contain his shock. "What on Earth are you doing here?"

Miss Juliet Richards turned around at the sound of his voice and fixed him with a determined stare, her pale blue eyes icy. The set of her jaw, the way she held her head high and clasped her hands in front of her somehow gave the impression that she was ready for battle.

"I know what I am doing is extremely uncouth. If anyone asks, you may tell them that I visited on some sort of business. I tried to be as discreet as possible but if anyone saw me let out here with only a footman I'm sure I will be banished from Society by end of day.

"But in truth I do not give a fig about my reputation when my sister's heart is on the line. You must hear me out, Lord Neil. Please."

Only that last word betrayed the young woman's desperation. Whatever she wished to speak with him about must be of the utmost importance if she would risk coming to a man's home and ruining her standing in Society. If anyone should find out about this visit, and doubt the excuse she'd readily provided, Miss Juliet would be branded fast and jeered out of town.

"C-Come this way," Henry stammered, urging the scarlet in his cheeks to dissipate. As completely outside of the realm of decorum as this situation was, he knew that it was serious. Rules could be set aside for a few minutes, though he hoped for the young lady's sake that whatever was about to transpire would go undetected so she could remain untarnished.

Once in the drawing room, Henry waved his hand to a chair for his unexpected guest.

"No thank you. I should like to stand and face this head on." Miss Juliet took her position in the middle of the room, staring at Henry almost as if to dare him to back away.

"As you wish." Henry nodded with respect. Whatever

anyone else might say about Miss Juliet's actions, there was no denying that she was an exceedingly brave young woman. "How may I be of assistance?"

"You can undo the pain you've caused my sister," she demanded through gritted teeth. Her voice wavered with buried tears but her face remained cool and resolved.

Henry bit his lip and ran a hand through his hair. He could no longer look this audacious lady in the eye. He dropped his head and mumbled, "There is nothing else in this world I would rather do, but I cannot. The situation is complicated."

Miss Juliet snorted and glared at Henry. He took a half step back in surprise.

"You claim it is complicated yet you are the one causing the complications. It seems you've made a decision that not only affects yourself, but Cecilia as well. How is that fair? How can you banish her from you without any explanation, without giving her a chance to consider the situation?"

Henry's skin prickled. He hadn't considered that by making this choice he was also taking the power of choice away from someone else.

"I simply didn't want to entrap her or allow my own personal obligations to suffer. But why have you come to me about this? I cannot imagine that your sister even wishes to have anything to do with me now."

"Cecilia received your delivery yesterday. The one you asked Lord Overton to pass to me to pass to her. It seems she's discovered a great deal about you through that parcel. And that discovery has made her miserable."

Henry blanched. "I—I never expected that my delivery would leave such an impression. And besides, I'm sure you know she's accepted other suitors. I saw her at the park just yesterday only hours after you received the package from

Lord Overton. She seemed very happy with her companion. I cannot blame her for enjoying her life."

He kept his eyes down as he spoke, tracing the flourishing patterns on the rug. Everything from shame to dejection mingled into a nauseating rumble in Henry's stomach.

The young woman sighed and Henry looked up to see some of the tension deflate her proud and hardened form. "This is quite the predicament you two have landed yourselves in," she muttered, shaking her head as though she'd just caught two schoolchildren stuck in a tree. "Lord Neil, I cannot express to you how devastated Cecilia has been since you stopped calling. She's tried to bear it as bravely as she can, especially in those early days. She assumed you must be busy and hadn't had a chance to visit.

"But watching that hope and expectation fade from her eyes.... This was a cruel thing to do, my lord. Cecilia told me of your gift and the conclusion she came to. I cannot say I understand why you have abandoned her with a few sentences and a book. You see, she was more upset last night than I've ever seen her. She realized that you were trying to say goodbye even as she realized that you're the one she's been searching for."

Miss Juliet's voice was quiet and pained, and it cut Henry to his core. His knees felt weak and for a moment he thought he might be sick from the guilt.

He had never, ever wanted to hurt the woman he had come to love. He never expected that she would be so affected by his silence. He thought he'd done the right thing, he thought he was protecting her. But it seemed he'd made a grave error. The thought of Miss Richards weeping in her bed, confused and crushed, made Henry wish he'd never stepped foot on this Earth. How could he have done such a terrible thing, especially to someone as undeserving as Miss Richards?

"But what of the man I saw her riding with? She smiled so pleasantly at him and seemed to enjoy his company. I cannot deny that she appeared completely unaffected by what transpired between us..."

The younger Richards sister gave a wry laugh. Her eyes were cold again, but Henry could tell that he wasn't the cause this time. "My sister is a woman of many talents, not the least of which includes pandering to etiquette when required to do so. If you saw any smiles on her face yesterday, it was all a polite façade.

"I spoke with her just after she returned home from that outing. She had next to nothing to say about the gentleman she'd accompanied. She did, however, mention the way you looked at her when she discovered your presence."

"She saw me?" Henry gasped. "But Overton pulled me away so quickly, I didn't think she had a chance to see my face."

"It was only for a second, but that second shattered her. And it shattered her again after she retired to her room and found your delivery. She was already out by the time I came home with it. And now she's presently convinced that even if you did care for her at some point, you must have come to the very conclusion you just admitted to after the incident in the park.

"Cecilia has lost all hope that you might reconcile, but I have not. I'm here to entreat on her behalf, because she believes you wish to be left alone. And I hope to make it clear that Cecilia is only accepting courtships because our parents have forced it upon her. I know she's spoken to you somewhat about their greedy desires, and even if she hadn't I think it is quite apparent on its own. Since you've been gone from her life, my sister has resigned herself to finding a tolerable match at the insistence of our parents, because the match she truly wanted seems to have vanished before her very eyes, without any explanation. And though I don't know you extremely well, I sense that your heart was in the right place when you chose this course of action."

Henry's eyes snapped up and he stared at Miss Juliet unabashedly. He could hardly believe the words he heard. Could it truly be possible that the woman who had unexpectedly stolen his heart felt the same way he did?

"Does she truly miss me? She is not turned away by the quiet life I lead? Does she not think she would be eventually become miserable if she were to become shackled to me?"

The corner of his guest's mouth drew up in a small smile as Henry revealed his hesitations. "I should think that would be something better discussed between the two of you. And yes, Cecilia is an active girl. But in my long history with her, she's proven to be just as comfortable quietly entertaining herself at home as she is out on the town. Now this may be bold of me to say, but it seems to me that you rather enjoy Society activities a bit more when my sister is by your side, do you not?"

Henry rubbed his chin, mulling over that statement. He hadn't really thought about it much, but when he looked back on their meetings, whether they be dinner parties or dances or walks, he did remember that his anxiety seemed greatly reduced, partially because he was so focused on the beautiful woman in his company. Not totally banished, to be sure, but as he'd grown more comfortable with Miss Richards, her presence came to soothe him.

For the first time in weeks, Henry felt the stirrings of hope in his heart, a pinprick of light that he wanted to run toward until it grew larger and larger eventually engulfing him in its glory.

"Lord Neil..." Miss Juliet's voice dropped to a whisper. "Do you know why she's thrown off every suitor in her past three Seasons? Because she wanted to marry for true love.

She is possessed of a remarkable will when her heart is set on something, and she dismissed many opportunities for great matches because she would not let go of hope.

"You showed her that her hope was not in vain. My sister has never been happier than when she was with you. Her resolve has been challenged and nearly broken down in these past few weeks. I could not stand by and watch her become a shell of who she is, not without entreating you to reconsider."

Hope. Hope had never been something that Henry needed much of.

Being the son of a baron and eventually inheriting the barony, he had never wanted for anything in his life. He was free to pursue whatever activities he enjoyed purely for passion's sake, never needing to worry about making an income. He'd never worried about making matches because it simply didn't interest him. Therefore hope had been a useless emotion. What could a man who needed nothing need to hope for?

But since he'd met Miss Richards, hope had slowly infiltrated his heart, at first only peeking out from some dark long dormant corner. Eventually it gained courage, shining a little brighter each day until he finally admitted to himself that he did care for Miss Richards and that he could see a future with her...that he loved her. Finally, Henry had something he wanted but didn't know if he could have.

Something to hope for.

"Miss Juliet..." He addressed the young woman before him quietly, the fledgling hope that had rekindled in his heart flickering but holding on. "Do you not think it might be too late for me to apologize and win her favor back? After everything I've put her through, I can't imagine she would be too thrilled to put her trust in me again."

Miss Juliet tutted. "For as intellectual as you are, Lord Neil, you can be a bit dense sometimes."

"I beg your pardon?" Henry reeled back, surprised at her deprecating comment.

"You're trying to make yet another decision on her behalf without her knowledge, and she is so very thoroughly tired of others presuming to know what's best for her without taking her own opinions into consideration. You can't imagine what she may or may not be willing to forgive until you ask her. I can't say for certain if she will accept you again, for she has been deeply hurt, but I only encourage you now because I believe you have a chance of turning the tide yet."

"Ah..." Henry paused.

What this plucky lady said was true. He saw it plain as day now. It was entirely his fault for finding himself in this sorrowful situation in the first place. He hadn't given Miss Richards the benefit of the doubt, the chance to use her own voice. He'd had no malicious intentions, of course, but the end result was the same.

"I've been a complete fool," Henry groaned, raking his hands over his face. He suddenly felt exhausted, as if the trauma of the past few weeks had built up inside him, causing hairline fractures until it could finally burst through and hit him all at once.

"People sometimes do foolish things when they're in love," Miss Juliet shrugged her shoulders sagely. All at once she seemed far wiser and older than her eighteen years.

Henry squared his shoulders, clenched his jaw, and set his sharp gaze on the young woman. "But if you say I have hope, then I will follow that hope until the last possible moment. As your sister did for me. Even if she wishes to be done with me once and for all, the least I can do is let her know how truly dear she is to me, now and forever."

Miss Juliet's youthful face broke into an excited smile. "Thank you, Lord Neil. I knew you were made of the right stuff. Say, are you attending Lady Brunt's farewell masquerade this evening?"

"I was invited since I attended Lord and Lady Henshell's welcome masquerade, but I hadn't planned on making an appearance at this one. I haven't been much in the mood for gaiety."

His guest smiled slyly. "Well, I think you've just had a change of plans. And how fitting, since you and Cecilia met at the last masquerade."

"Did we?" Henry racked his mind for such a memory. He knew he would have remembered meeting Miss Richards. He would never have been able to forget such a thing.

Her younger sister merely looked at him with a cocked eyebrow, and he could see that she was silently calling him dense again. "Hang on.... You don't mean to say that your sister was indeed the woman I danced with at the welcome masquerade, the one who performed that incredible pianoforte piece?"

"Indeed she was," Miss Juliet chuckled. "Something in that book answered the same question that had been plaguing Cecilia since the Season began. In fact, when we first made your acquaintance, she was still so enamored with that mystery gentleman that she nearly missed her opportunity to develop affections for you. She wished desperately to discover his identity and it rather distracted her from everything else.

"But the more she got to know you, the more she let that flight of fancy dissipate. How lucky that the man she fell in love with over these past few months was the same man she fell in love with that night. Unlikely coincidences sometimes go by another name: miracles."

~

HENRY TOOK several deep breaths to calm himself as he stared in the full-length mirror at his uncharacteristically dashing figure. He didn't attempt to keep up with all the latest fashions for they often changed before he could finish tying his neckcloth. But he made sure his wardrobe was respectable, especially with Solomon's help.

But if he was going to go all out, tonight was the night. Wearing his expertly cut evening coat, his finest trousers, his most fashionable hat, and his softest gloves, Henry looked every part the well-born dandy man. He wore the same simple mask as on the night he'd first met Miss Richards.

He wasn't sure why he felt the need to dress so sharply in order to impress Miss Richards. If she rejected him, it wouldn't be because something was amiss with his outfit. But he figured it couldn't hurt, and something about putting in effort to ensure he looked nice gave him a slight boost of confidence.

His heart fluttered and his stomach flipped as he headed downstairs to meet Solomon in the foyer.

"Good Heaven!" The earl cried out when Henry appeared, the mask he wore failing to hide his glee. "I must say, when you bother to try you turn out very well. Mayhaps I'm even a little jealous. But certainly proud." He clapped his hands and grinned but Henry waved him off with a bashful smile.

"Thank you. I'm not sure if it will help me in my mission at all tonight. But if I go down in flames I suppose I might as well go down in style."

"That's the spirit!" Solomon cheered, clasping Henry's gloved hand in his and slapping his shoulder. "But I'm sure no flames will appear tonight, save perhaps for the flames of love."

Henry groaned at that outrageous attempt at wit and shook his friend off him, marching for the front door.

When Henry had sent a footman to Solomon's home requesting his urgent presence, Solomon had of course come at once. Henry wasn't the least surprised that his best friend wholeheartedly supported his quest to find Miss Richards tonight and attempt to right the situation between them.

But Henry couldn't help noticing the flicker of unease that had passed behind his friend's eyes when he mentioned Miss Juliet's surprise visit. Solomon had taken his promise to abandon his courtship with Miss Juliet seriously and had found some new female acquaintances to fill his time. He made no comment as to the appropriateness, or lack thereof of her actions, but Henry suspected that the fact that she'd contacted him at all sat poorly with him.

Henry vowed to discuss it with Solomon after tonight, however his own affairs played out.

The ride to Lady Brunt's home was not long, but Henry found himself simultaneously wishing it were longer and shorter. On the one hand, he was nervous beyond belief about what he would soon attempt to do. But on the other hand, knowing that he was just minutes away from seeing Miss Richards again ignited that familiar anticipation in his stomach that made him feel as though a hundred delicate winged creatures had taken up residence there.

Frankly, he admitted to himself, he was sick of not being with her. Hopefully he would be able to rectify that tonight.

He and Miss Juliet had agreed to keep his attendance at the ball a surprise in the event that Miss Richards balked at the idea of running into him. And her younger sister had of course lied about her whereabouts, knowing that the elder would be against troubling Henry. Perhaps his sudden reappearance in her life would have some grand and dramatic effect, giving him the opportunity to plead his case.

The ball was already in progress by the time Henry and Solomon arrived but guests continued to filter in and out at their leisure. Surprisingly, Henry didn't care about the hundreds of other people who had come to one of the most extravagant events of the Season, sending the past few months out with a bang before slowly trickling out of London to return to quiet country life.

Before he would have been in a constant state of near panic being surrounded by so many strangers. But tonight none of them mattered. His current anxiety was caused by something entirely different, and far more important. His very future was on the line.

But finding his heroine would be difficult in a crowd of this size, especially with everyone in disguises.

And indeed it did prove very difficult. He and Solomon made their way around the perimeter of the huge ballroom once with no luck despite two pairs of eyes scanning the guests both floating along the dance floor and lounging about the edges of the room.

"Drat. Do you think they haven't arrived yet?" Solomon murmured.

"The Richards family typically arrives to events on the earlier side and stays late, I've learned. Mr. and Mrs. Richards like to maximize the time they spend rubbing elbows with as many noble people as possible," Henry responded without taking his eyes away from the crowd.

And suddenly he saw her. A tightknit group must have obscured his view into the back corner of the room, but they chose that fortuitous moment to part, revealing Miss Cecilia Richards in a breathtaking pale blue dress that would surely compliment her eyes, standing idly in the corner with her sister, mother, and Miss Henshell. Though she was several yards away, Henry had no trouble recognizing her flowing movements and the grace with which she held herself. And he certainly recognized her mask. She'd worn that same one on the night they met.

Henry took the opportunity to silently observe while gathering up his courage. He now saw the truth of her sister's statement. For though Miss Richards smiled her gracious smile and laughed her delicate laugh and nodded to passing acquaintances, there was no glimmer of joy in the deep blue eyes under her white mask.

"Ah, you found her." Solomon had turned to see what Henry stared at. From the corner of his eye, Henry could see that his friend's gaze was not on Henry's target, but on the youngest woman in the group. "Well, get over there, Henry." He put a hand between Henry's shoulder blades and pushed.

He stumbled forward but as soon as he righted himself, the hostess herself approached Miss Richards and appeared to ask her a question. Mrs. Richards nodded fervently while her oldest daughter nodded and followed behind Lady Brunt.

Henry would have to wait until Lady Brunt finished whatever business she had with Miss Richards. He silently kicked himself. If only he'd been just a few seconds faster, he could have whisked her away onto the dance floor. Every moment that prolonged this experience of uncertainty was excruciating.

"Poor timing," Solomon sighed.

"It's quite alright. You need not wait around with me. Go have fun." Henry gripped Solomon's arm and smiled at his friend before nodding in the direction of the corner the Richards women occupied. "Why not ask Miss Juliet for a dance?"

The earl immediately tensed and Henry could feel his muscles flex through his coat sleeve. "I would really rather not. But a dance does sound refreshing, with the right partner." Solomon stalked off in search of a promising young lady, steering clear of that corner.

A hush fell over the crowd as the Master of Ceremonies called for attention. A special guest would be playing a piece on the pianoforte at Lady Brunt's request, he announced. It dawned on Henry that the special guest must have been Miss Richards. He was not in the least surprised that she would be prevailed upon to perform.

He slipped closer to the music platform as a curious audience gathered to watch and listen. Miss Richards took her seat at the instrument and Henry saw her take a few deep breaths as she readied herself.

Henry instantly recognized the piece. He'd played it in his head numerous times a day for weeks, the piece she'd composed herself and played in his drawing room.

But within the first few measures Henry could sense that something was amiss. The young woman played with a timid, faltering air—very unlike the standard he'd come to know of Miss Richards's talent. While most of the audience likely did not notice any missteps, Henry's memory was so attuned to the piece that he could hear a few mistakes slipping through. From Henry's vantage point of Miss Richards's side profile, he could see that her lips pressed together in a tight line.

She was not happy, Henry realized. And he had been the cause. He'd stolen her joy even as he tried to protect it.

Miss Richards had once again been reduced to the struggles she suffered when they'd first met—because of Henry.

Henry found himself slowly inching through the crowd to a position with a better view of Miss Richards's face. Even covered by a half mask, Henry wanted to see her expressions as she played. He only hoped he would blend into the crowd so as not to startle her.

But not a moment later, Miss Richards's eyes lifted from the keys and out into the crowd. Henry's heart stopped as her eyes found his immediately, as if they were drawn to him, made to seek him out amongst hundreds of people.

Her fingers fumbled as her lips parted slightly in surprise. Surely she recognized his mask from their fateful dance at the last fancy dress ball. All Henry could think to do was give a warm smile and encouraging nod. No doubt she must be upset to see him so suddenly. Henry ardently hoped that he had not ruined her moment.

Much to Henry's surprise, Miss Richards returned the smile and brought her focus back to the instrument. Her playing suddenly seemed to right itself as she floated through the rest of the piece with grace and impeccable skill.

Her expression transformed from one of strain and anxiety to delight and pride. Henry knew without a doubt that Miss Richards was indeed that same woman he'd so admired at the Henshells' ball. Watching Miss Richards play now, he felt as though he'd stepped back into that memory. His heart swelled with each crescendo and his smile grew wider as he soaked in her beauty glittering under the chandeliers.

The piece came to an end and the audience rewarded Miss Richards with enthusiastic applause. Henry clapped so loudly that a few nearby guests glared at him from beneath their disguises. But he had not a care in the world for their judgement. Miss Richards deserved accolades upon accolades.

The young lady smiled and curtsied to the onlookers before leaving the platform. Henry jumped as he lost sight of her in the throng of guests. He pushed forward, muttering apologies as he weaved through far too many bodies, his eyes darting about the room frantically.

At last, he spied Miss Richards on her way back to her family and friend.

"Miss Richards," he called, grabbing her gloved hand.

"Lord Neil! I didn't expect to see you in the audience tonight.... How may I help you?" Beneath the shock in her voice was an undercurrent of strain. She glanced around uncomfortably. Henry needed to make his appeal fast.

"In truth, I hadn't planned on coming tonight. But I needed to dance with you. Would you do me the honor?" He let go of her hand and backed up a step, bowing and properly offering his hand. He maintained the awkward position for a tense moment.

Miss Richards gazed into his eyes, but for once Henry found them unreadable. Perhaps she was thrilled to see him, or perhaps she wanted nothing more than to run away. Henry's heart felt like it might explode at any moment while he waited for her to decide, ignoring the glances from curious guests.

Finally, she nodded and quickly accepted his hand. The next set had just started so Henry wasted no time leading her back out to the floor. His heart slowed, but only slightly. He still knew that there was ample time for her to reject him once and for all.

Effortlessly, they fell into step together. They spent the first few moments of the dance in silence, collecting their own thoughts and reacquainting themselves with their movements. But Henry found that their unspoken connection was once again nearly instant.

Her one small hand in his felt perfectly in place. He barely thought about anything his feet did because he was so in sync with her that it came naturally to him. Just as it had during their first dance, when they were still strangers with hidden identities. It was as though something in their bodies, a deep essence that ran through their very blood, drew them together and matched each other step for step.

Henry couldn't resist staring down at the face he'd grown eager to see every week, the face he'd dreamed of so often these past few months. He only wished that her glittering mask could be removed so he could appreciate the perfect way her features came together to create a beautiful whole.

And he wished her eyes would catch his, the deep summer sky blue eyes he'd missed so much. But Miss Richards still seemed unsure of this unexpected encounter, and she kept them low.

As much as he enjoyed simply being in her presence again, feeling her so close, silently watching the minutest expressions pass over her face, the thundering of Henry's heart in his battered chest spurred him to speak.

"Miss Richards.... Cecilia," he whispered. It was a risk, using her Christian name so shamelessly. But he needed to convey how much she meant to him, and he had nothing to lose. He had never said her name out loud before, he realized. It felt tantalizing yet natural all at once.

Her eyes darted up to finally meet his. They were wide under her mask. "Why have you come here tonight? Why did you seek me out now after all this time?" Her breathless voice rattled something deep inside Henry. All his apprehension and shame vanished in an instant.

"I know you have no reason to believe me, and every reason to hate me. But, the simple truth is I have missed you so deeply, more than words can express. Because I love you. I've probably been in love with you for longer than I realized. As someone told me recently, I can be quite dense at times, to my own detriment."

Finally saying the words out loud felt like peace being restored...like coming home. Henry had no idea that three simple, common English words, when said in the right configuration, could have such a profound impact on him.

"But you vanished without a word. I know you do not owe me anything, but I had hoped that you held me in high enough regard to honor me with an explanation. I only received your manuscript after I returned home and I knew you were trying to close the door on us. It certainly felt closed when I saw you at the park yesterday. That expression on your face has been burned in my mind ever since. You looked as though I were dead to you."

A deep pain echoed in her voice and Henry nearly stumbled when he saw her eyes gloss over with barely contained tears. He would give anything to take back his foolish actions. But his only option now was try to forge a path forward. He used every reunion during their set to lay the groundwork for that path.

"Yes, I withdrew because I thought I knew what was best for you. But in reality I was also trying to protect myself. I wanted to protect my work, and I wanted to protect my heart from knowing that you lived beside me unhappily and resented me.

"If I saw disappointment and loneliness in your eyes every day as you yearned for better company and livelier activities, I don't know how I could live with myself. I didn't think I could give you the life you deserve because I spend so much of my time writing in my study. I was too scared to try.

"But a guardian angel of sorts came to me recently and showed me the error of my ways. By disappearing from you, I made the choice that we should not be together without taking your thoughts into consideration. And I deeply, deeply regret doing such a thoughtless thing."

As Miss Richards took her place across from Henry, she glanced to the corner of the room where her sister had been and her eyes narrowed. She seemed to have a guess as to the identity of Henry's guardian angel.

Once her hand was back in his, he continued.

"As for the park, I didn't realize you had seen me. I will admit I was shocked to see you with another suitor, especially because you looked to be your usual cheerful self. I

BEHIND THE BARON'S MASK

selfishly thought that you might be missing me, too, and when I saw you so happily living your life...I retreated even further upon myself.

"But I certainly didn't begrudge you for it. I simply hoped to show you how deeply you inspired me in our time together. That draft I gave you has turned into one of my best works yet. All because of you."

He trailed off, suddenly feeling weak. "If I can be so bold, if I can be given a chance to right this terrible wrong I've done you...

"I need you in my life, Cecilia. I need you by my side. The color in my world has been so much more vibrant since you've been in it. I feared that you would find a life with me to be boring and unfulfilling. I feared that I would lose one thing—my writing—if I gained you. But I realized that it was my life that had been missing something all along. You. Now I fear that I cannot go back to the life I used to live."

"Henry..." Cecilia gasped quietly, and now the tears did spill.

Henry's chest swelled when he heard his name, as if he'd just taken his first full breath in his entire life. The dance pattern pulled her away once more but their eyes continued to search each other from across the floor.

Cecilia took her turn to speak as they reunited again.

"I cannot promise that the future would be without hardships or disagreements," she whispered. Henry had to lean forward to hear her better, their foreheads almost touching. "But we understand each other in a truly rare way. You are someone I can speak freely with, share my passions and struggles with. Someone I can be friends with. I fell in love with you for exactly who you are. I can think of no better way to spend my time than by being wherever you are, whether it be in your study or at a dance like this one. Because I love you, too."

The words took Henry's breath away—such unimaginable, perfect, miraculous words—but he managed to muster up enough air to speak. "But Cecilia, what of my writing work? I must confess that the original draft of the manuscript I sent you fell far short of my expectations and had to be scrapped entirely. There may be times when I cannot give you the attention you deserve or cannot join you out in Society.

"This manuscript was so challenging for me because my mind is not used to sharing its space with anything else when I write. But you were always there in the background. If I had you by my side, if I knew you would always be with me, I think I could overcome this. The uncertainty is what made this process so laboriously slow and resulted in a work of poor quality. But even still, it is necessary to my being to write. Can you be happy, sharing me with my life's work?"

Despite Henry's earlier shame and reluctance to speak about his failure, he found it completely natural and effortless to speak about it now. He knew instinctively that he need not be embarrassed sharing such a blunder with Cecilia. He need not be embarrassed to share anything with her. She was someone he could trust, someone whose opinion and support he valued.

Cecilia's gaze softened from across the floor and a small smile graced her lips. It was such a look as Henry had never seen before, a look of total acceptance.

"Please don't worry about such a thing, Henry," she whispered as they came back together. "I greatly enjoyed your manuscript and I have an immense amount of respect for your passion and your desire to share it with the world. That is something I am glad to know we have in common. I consider myself exceedingly lucky to have found someone who can intimately understand my passion as a fellow artistic soul.

"I don't need to constantly be at the forefront of your thoughts, nor do I need to take up all your time and energy. I have my own interests to see to, and I think it's perfectly respectable that we have time to ourselves to pursue our desires. Though I certainly wouldn't mind sitting in while you write and I can amuse myself with a book or some embroidery. It is enough for me to share your company, to look up and see you nearby working away so diligently. That to me would be a very happy life indeed."

Such a feeling of contentment and peace that Henry had never dreamed possible settled over him, seeping into his bones from the crown of his head all the way down to his toes.

"I think I can do better than that," he said with a knowing smile. Cecilia tilted her head in that curious way Henry adored, always seeking to know more, to figure out life's puzzles and find new ways to appreciate the world around her. "There's plenty of space in my study. I can simply move the pianoforte from the drawing room. That way we can both work on our interests and still enjoy time with each other."

Henry was amazed at the words that came out of his mouth. He had pictured that exact scenario hundreds of times over the last several months, never imagining that it would come to fruition. And yet here he stood on the dance floor with Cecilia in his arms, flowing about the room with her, planning their future together. That life that had seemed so out of reach just yesterday was on the verge of becoming reality.

Cecilia beamed, her eyes swimming with visions of comfortable days in Henry's home—their home—intertwined but with the freedom to pursue their independence.

"I should like that very, very much. I should love it, in fact."

"Then it shall be so." Henry nodded seriously, and Cecilia giggled at the resolute expression on his face.

The music drifted off into the air, signaling the end of the set. But Henry kept both of Cecilia's hands in his as they came apart from the dance.

"If you could find your sister and meet me in the garden shortly, my dear, I have just a quick matter of business to attend to." Henry gave her hands a squeeze before trailing a finger down her cheek. He felt her sharp inhale and ingrained the image of her standing before him, with an expectant smile on her face, as he made his way through the ballroom. He missed her the instant he let go, but Henry knew that another moment of separation would be worth everything that was to come.

CHAPTER 17

*C*ecilia weaved through the crowded ballroom as quickly as she could.

Had all this really just happened? Had the course of her life changed in this one dance?

No, not this dance, Cecilia realized. That first dance, months ago, had changed her life. For it brought Henry into it, though she didn't know it at the time. This must be what fate felt like. This strange mixture of exhilaration, tranquility, security, the deep knowing that everything had finally fallen into place in the most natural way possible. And yes —love.

She wasn't sure how long she stood on the edge of the dance floor staring after Henry, the scene she'd just lived through already playing back in her mind. But another guest brushing past her to take the floor startled Cecilia back to her senses and she rushed forward to find Juliet and get to the garden. She had a very good guess as to what Henry's quick matter of business was, but she didn't know how long it might take. And she wanted to be in the garden waiting for him, just as she'd said she would.

"Pardon me," she mumbled countless times as she pressed through the many bodies in the ballroom. Lady Brunt's farewell masked ball always had one of the highest guest counts of any event during the Season, and for once Cecilia found herself irked by all these people who seemed not to know how to get out of her way. Not to mention it made finding Juliet a chore.

"Sissy! Wait!" Juliet's familiar voice rose above the din, shortly followed by her rosy cheeks and big blue eyes and heaving chest. "I've been trying to follow after you but it's nearly impossible getting through all these people."

"There you are! I've been looking for you. Henry asked both of us to meet him in the garden while he sees to something," Cecilia explained over her shoulder without stopping.

"Henry?" Juliet finally managed to pull up next to her sister, her eyebrow cocked knowingly. "I take it things have gone well then." The younger woman giggled, an impish smile lighting up her porcelain features.

"Yes, and I think they are about to get even better," Cecilia confessed breathlessly. "But I won't find out if I can't make it to the garden. Thank you for your help, guardian angel. I shall hear more of your side of the story when we get home." She winked at her younger sister and squeezed her hand, pulling her through the crowd.

Cecilia only stopped once to ask a footman for directions to the garden. Lady Brunt, a wealthy widow, had the largest town home Cecilia had ever been inside. Though most London residences only had very modest gardens, if they had one at all, this garden put all of them to shame.

A gasp slipped through Cecilia's lips as she paused for a moment to take in the evenly spaced lanterns that spread a soft golden light in the night air, the tall hedges with pretty blooms of all colors peeking out between the deep green leaves, the springy saplings, the quietly bubbling fountains, and the intricately wrought tables and chairs and benches that dotted the grass.

A few other guests were taking a brief respite in the soothing garden, but Juliet pointed out a relatively secluded bench partially blocked from view by a fragrant and colorful bush. The two women approached. The nearer Cecilia got the weaker her legs became. She felt as though she'd danced a lifetime's worth of dances during her set with Henry. Or perhaps her body was finally giving out under the overwhelming emotions that ran about her heart in circles.

"I'll stay within sight but I promise not to disturb." Juliet beamed and gripped Cecilia's gloved hands before finding a nearby flower to examine.

No sooner did Cecilia remove her mask and lower herself onto the cool metal of the bench than the sound of approaching footsteps behind the bush caused her to jump back up.

"Cecilia, thank you for waiting for me." Henry's warm voice greeted her as he came into sight, his face fully revealed and glowing beneath the warm lantern lighting, his dark hair threaded through with streaks of gold and his eyes shimmering brighter than the stars above.

"I only just arrived myself. It's absolutely mad in there," Cecilia laughed. She eased back onto the bench. Everything felt right now that Henry was here. She even forgot that Juliet lingered just a few feet away to keep watch over them.

He sat beside her, their bodies brushing against each other, and reached for her hands in her lap. "Indeed it was, but worth every second because you were there." His eyes gazed warmly into her face, taking everything in, reading her.

Cecilia's heart took up a deep, pulsing beat. She could feel it thundering in her neck and the palms of her hands. Though she had danced with Henry on numerous occasions and had sat near him in a carriage and at the theater, this was without a doubt the closest they had been. His leg pressed against hers through the thick fabric of her skirt, his shoulder brushing against hers. His hands kept a tight grip around hers, as if he hoped that pressing hard enough would melt their gloves away.

She stared back into his face for a silent moment, appreciating all those features that she had once thought were cold and aloof. But now she knew the truth of what lay underneath, what had come to the surface in the months she'd spent getting to know him. His surface now was only warmth and adoration and love.

"I've just had a discussion with your father," he coughed, a hint of rose coloring his cheeks.

Cecilia smiled even as tears sprung up in the corners of her eyes, the butterflies floating in her stomach bursting into a flurry of anticipation. "Go on."

"I am not a perfect man, Cecilia. I made a grave mistake in pushing you out of my life and causing you the very pain I'd hoped to avoid. But I've learned in that time that I simply cannot live without you. My world is more vibrant, more enjoyable when you're in it. Your color touches everything. And I do not wish to go back to a life without your color.

"I hope that I will be able to provide you with a similar new light in your world. For, if I can have you by my side, I promise that I will try each day to create the life of your dreams. I give you that which is mine to give. A comfortable home, a listening ear, understanding, friendship. Love.

"If you will have me, I promise to give you that which is mine to give, without reservation, for the rest of our lives. Will you marry me, Cecilia?"

Despite the tremor in his voice, Henry's words came out with a slow and steady strength. His dark brown eyes lit up, not from the lanterns above, but from the luminescence of his love for Cecilia that sprung from deep within.

He gently rubbed the back of Cecilia's hand with his thumb and let silence fall between them, patiently watching Cecilia.

How many times had she imagined this moment since she was a little girl? Receiving a proposal from her true love and becoming not just a wife but a real companion had been her dream since she could remember.

But none of her most vivid and extravagant imaginings could compare to this moment. Every fiber in her body buzzed with love, with the rightness of it all, as if everything in her sang in response to Henry's words.

She had never heard a more beautiful music than those words.

Cecilia took several deep breaths as Henry looked on. He didn't seem nervous that she hadn't responded yet. She could see in his eyes that he once again understood what her silence conveyed.

"Henry..." She managed to gasp out, still gathering her bearings. She didn't want to leave him in silence anymore. He simply smiled encouragingly and continued to rub small comforting circles against her hand.

"Yes, Henry. It would be my greatest dream come true to marry you. I love you."

The words came out so quietly that she wasn't sure if they'd made any sound at all. The tears that had held themselves back now broke free.

"I love you, too, darling," Henry chuckled as he pulled out his handkerchief and gently wiped at Cecilia's scarlet face.

She reveled in the electrifying naturalness of his touch. Unbidden, her eyes closed and she leaned her face into his hand, desperate for more connection.

Firm but gentle fingers gripped her chin and Henry tilted

PENNY FAIRBANKS

her head back slightly. She opened her eyes to find his just inches away, gazing at her with an intensity that rendered her speechless.

"May I?" He asked, sounding as breathless as Cecilia felt. All she could do was nod weakly and close her eyes again.

It was all Henry needed.

His soft lips covered Cecilia's in a sweet, tender kiss, an undercurrent of passion rippling between them.

A shiver ran down Cecilia's spine as their lips moved together for a wonderous moment, one of his hands still holding her chin while the other had become intertwined with her own trembling fingers.

All too soon Henry pulled back and the cool night air hit her lips with a shock. When she opened her eyes to look at her fiancé, she saw that some of her tears had transferred to his cheeks, or perhaps they were his own tears.

Cecilia immediately craved him again. She'd had no idea that she could crave someone's touch so deeply. But the look in Henry's eyes told her he experienced the same thing.

"There will be time for many more kisses soon, my love." Henry murmured, his voice gruff and thick with desire. "An entire lifetime's worth."

He cupped her cheek in one hand and Cecilia swore she could feel the heat from his skin through his glove. She nodded quietly, still coming out of her daze.

"Promise?"

Henry let out a booming laugh. "Promise. I give you that which is mine to give, remember?"

"I'll hold you to it. Don't think that I won't," Cecilia giggled, surprised at her forwardness.

"I wouldn't dream of it." Henry stood. She felt the loss of his warmth immediately. "Now, shall we share the good news?"

"I should think so. After all, I doubt Juliet would be able

244

to keep this a secret for very long 'even if her life depended on it." Cecilia giggled, glancing over to her sister who had given up trying to look disinterested in their conversation. Tears sparkled in her eyes and she clasped her hands before her chest. She looked ready to swoon herself.

Henry simply laughed again and reached a hand down to Cecilia.

With a bright smile, Cecilia gladly accepted her future husband's hand.

~

CECILIA RETURNED TO THE BALLROOM, this time on Henry's arm and with a blissful heart.

It seemed that quite a few guests had taken their leave as the night wore on. It was far easier to move about the room for which Cecilia was grateful.

"Sissy, I'll meet you back at our corner," Juliet announced before disappearing into the crowd.

In keeping with the theme, they'd both donned their masks again. As they walked around the perimeter of the room, searching for familiar faces among the remaining crowd, Cecilia felt as though she carried a precious secret in her chest—a secret she couldn't wait to share with her loved ones and then the whole of London and even the entire world.

"Solomon's just over there," Henry whispered to her, pointing to a footman along the wall with a tray of drinks. Henry's friend was just approaching to take a refreshment.

They quickened their pace and managed to catch him before he melted back into the group of young men he'd just left. Henry put a hand on the earl's shoulder, causing the taller man to jump slightly.

"Henry, you nearly startled me to high heaven," Lord Overton whined as he turned around.

Henry and Cecilia remained silent, waiting to see if he would catch on.

Lord Overton took a sip of his drink and looked expectantly at Henry, waiting for his friend to say something. It took him a moment to glance to Henry's side where Cecilia stood, and then to Henry and back again several times.

Suddenly he gasped, nearly splashing his drink on them all. "Goodness gracious! Has it happened?"

Cecilia could only giggle and blush, still in shock herself. Henry nodded, proudly straightening out his shoulders. "I imagine you'll be reading it in the papers in a few days."

The earl whooped, drawing half the room's attention to them. "I am so happy for you, my dear friend. I never imagined this day would come, but I'm so very glad it has. Miss Richards, I trust that you will take care of him. He is a very particular creature, you see," Lord Overton whispered conspiratorially to Cecilia.

"I am in excellent hands, Solomon, never fear. The best hands there could ever be." Henry's voice was full of pride as he drew Cecilia a little closer to his side.

"And you." Lord Overton rounded sharply on his friend, poking him in the chest. "I trust that you will do right by this miraculous young woman, the only one who could have achieved such a feat as finally bringing the unsociable Baron of Neil out of hiding."

Henry glanced down into Cecilia's face, a hopeful smile on his lips. "Of course. It is my sacred duty, one I shall cherish for all my days."

The earl shuddered at the romantic display before him, which earned him a quick slap on the arm from Henry. He took his leave of the couple to rejoin his group of friends.

Henry and Cecilia made their way across the room, to the

back corner Cecilia and her party had claimed. Juliet had rejoined Rosamund but her parents were nowhere to be found.

Juliet caught sight of them first as they approached, and her face came alive with joy once again. Cecilia couldn't help laughing, covering her mouth with her free hand. The wonder and newness of it all rendered her a giggling mess.

Her younger sister bestowed a kiss upon her cheek. When she pulled back, tears had sprung into her eyes again.

"Oh Jules, why are you crying? This is a joyous moment," Cecilia chided softly, pinching the younger woman's cheek.

"Exactly. I know how desperately you've wanted this, and I'm happier than words can express that you'll have everything you want and deserve." She sniffled before looking up at Henry. "I knew you could do it. Congratulations, both of you!"

Rosamund lingered further back, eyeing the exchange cautiously. When Cecilia caught her eye, the other young woman smiled sheepishly and came forward. "I am so very pleased for you, Cecilia. Lord Neil, I hope you know what a grand prize you've won tonight." Cecilia thought she heard a slight melancholy in her friend's voice.

"I can assure you, Miss Henshell, that I feel I am the luckiest man who has ever lived on this Earth, past, present, and future. That is how grand a prize I have won."

Henry bowed his head respectfully to Rosamund and spoke with such an eloquent gravity that even the apprehensive young lady couldn't help smiling with relief.

"But wait, where are Mama and Papa?"

"Oh I imagine Mama has already run to the newspapers," Juliet shrugged. Cecilia gave her sister's shoulder a gentle push and the younger woman laughed. "I'm sorry, Sissy, but I couldn't stop them. They're already spreading it about the room to anyone who will listen."

Cecilia shook her head. "I suppose I'm not surprised but let them do it. I can hardly contain it myself."

"Cecilia..." Everyone turned to look at Rosamund, who had a curious expression on her face. "What about the other...incident? From my parents' masquerade? Has that chapter been closed?"

An exuberant smile slowly spread over Cecilia's face, so deep and intense that she felt her cheeks might burst from the pressure.

"Yes, that chapter has closed, because a fantastic new one has just begun. You see, Henry was that mysterious masked gentlemen I met that night, the one I pined for all Season."

She gripped Henry's arm a little tighter, and when she looked up into his face she saw her own feelings confirmed. Their paths had been destined to cross, as if it were written in the stars, the way the sun rose every morning, the way the ocean always ran back to the shore.

"He's the one I've been searching for this whole time. He's the one I was meant to find. It was always Henry from the start."

Unable to contain himself, Henry leaned down to give Cecilia a peck on the cheek, a whispered "I love you" brushing against her ear as he did so.

Cecilia didn't need to say it out loud. She could see in Henry's eyes that he read her perfectly. He knew the unspoken truth in her heart.

But she said it anyway. "I love you, too, dear." The words sounded sweeter than any music she'd ever heard. At least, until they stood together before the altar and said "I will."

EPILOGUE

*C*ecilia's fingers stilled over the keys as she finished the piece, the last notes lingering in the air before drifting back into silence. She had practiced her new self-composed song numerous times already today, anticipating a request to perform it soon.

"That was lovely, darling.... Now come on, my friend, why can't you just do as you're told? How am I to write you out of this conundrum you've gotten yourself into?"

She turned so she could see her husband at his desk, his pen flying across the page, brows drawn low over his eyes, lower lip protruding ever so slightly. Cecilia giggled hearing her husband chastise his characters. They often got ahead of him to his frustration but to her guilty enjoyment. She found this habit to be one of his most endearing qualities.

"Thank you, my dear Henry. How goes it over there?" Cecilia stood from the bench and crossed the room. She stood behind her husband's chair and threaded her arms around his shoulders, resting her cheek against his.

His hand stilled and he closed his eyes, sighing contentedly. He pressed his face to Cecilia's for a moment before planting a kiss on her cheek.

"I'm making progress. I think it will turn out well. But I'm not sure how to proceed with this part I'm coming to. Will you read it later and give me your opinion?"

He scratched his temple and wrinkled his nose at the papers before him, another habit Cecilia had discovered shortly after becoming the baron's wife which she found exceedingly charming.

"I would be more than happy to. But for now we must get ready for the Henshells' ball," she chirped, massaging Henry's shoulders.

"Is it that time already? My goodness..." Henry sounded dazed as he set his pen down and stood, leaning over Cecilia's smaller frame. "Can you believe it's already been a year since we first met at this very dance?"

Cecilia wrapped her arms around Henry's torso, burying her face into his shoulder as his arms looped around her waist. "Yes and no. Somehow I can't believe that a year has already passed since that night. But I also can't believe that only a year has passed, because it feels like we've shared so much together in that time. Isn't that strange?"

"Hmm, yes and no," Henry chuckled. "It is a strange idea, but it makes perfect sense to me because I feel the same way. I wonder what life will be like this time next year?" He pulled her body away from his to give just enough room for his hand to rest gently on Cecilia's stomach.

She smiled shyly but excitedly. "I certainly hope so." She laid her hand over her husband's and interlaced their fingers. "But stop trying to distract me, Lord Neil," she said firmly. "It's high time we got ready for the ball."

Henry tilted his head back and laughed. "How can you be so sure that it isn't you who is distracting me?"

Cecilia pouted and turned away. "Me? Distracting? I would never!" She called out over her shoulder as she strode out of the room, throwing a quick wink to her bemused husband.

～

"Oh, you look just breathtaking, My Lady!" Violet cried, clasping her hands together at her chest, her eyes glowing like a child seeing her first Christmas tree.

"Thanks to you," Cecilia emphasized to her maid. She was so glad that she'd brought Violet with her when she married Henry. In addition to being very nearly a friend, Violet could button a dress and arrange curls like no one else.

And besides, Violet had indeed become a dear friend to her over the years. Not only had she borne witness to Cecilia's heartbreak, but she'd also been there for her through her triumph. The maid nearly shed a tear when Cecilia had come home from the farewell masquerade and told her that she'd soon be helping Cecilia into a wedding gown.

Violet blushed at the compliment, never fully comfortable with praise. "I've said it before, My Lady, but it is you who brings the dress and the hair and the makeup to life."

"You are too kind, my dear Violet," Cecilia tutted.

But looking at herself in the mirror, in the beautiful custom-made green dress with swirls of embroidery, and the pearls threaded delicately through her hair, Cecilia was struck by a strong sense of déjà vu.

Almost exactly one year ago, she had stood before a mirror examining a reflection that had surprised her then. But she smiled at her reflection now, thinking back on the anxious young woman who had no idea that her life was about to change in ways she'd only dreamed of.

Cecilia held her hand out to Violet for her mask. She could have had a new mask made, but it didn't feel right to let go of this one just yet. This was the mask she'd worn on that fateful night, after all. It only seemed fitting that she should wear it again on the anniversary of their meeting.

She thanked Violet and made her way downstairs to join Henry, who had likely long finished up his preparations. But the foyer was empty, to her surprise.

"Henry?" She called out, with no response. "Where could that man have gone to?" She mumbled under her breath as she turned back down the hallway. Even as the question left her lips, she already had the answer.

"How did I know I would find you here?" She asked with a hint of playful exasperation as she opened the door to the study.

Henry didn't look up as she entered the room, his hand scribbling furiously, his eyes beneath his mask darting over the papers spread before him. "I'm sorry, my love. I just had a sudden idea and needed to get it out before I lost it."

Cecilia could only chuckle as she watched her husband pour himself out onto the page.

"There!" He slammed a triumphant punctuation onto the last line.

Finally, Henry looked up from his work. His eyes travelled up his wife's figure, from the ruffled hem of her dress up to her patient eyes. Cecilia blushed, still made shy by Henry's gaze even after months of marriage.

"You're stunning..." He whispered, slowly standing from his desk.

"And you are so very handsome, my wonderful husband." Cecilia noted the tight cut of Henry's coat, a new piece he'd had ordered just for this night, and his stylish coiffure, and of course the sharp jawline and welcoming lips beneath his mask. The same mask he'd worn a year ago.

Of the rest of his face she could only see his eyes, but there was no mistaking the deep flame of love that burned in them.

When he crossed the room, he took Cecilia in his arms. She tilted her head up to receive his kiss, slow and deep and full of feeling that could not be expressed with words. True to his promise, Henry made sure to kiss her every day. Each one felt like a breath of fresh air, a rejuvenation of her spirit. Yet at the same time, each kiss felt like home, as if their lips meeting was the most natural thing in the world.

Henry pulled back and stared down at his wife. "You're even more beautiful than the night I met you. Just a year ago, I would have thought it impossible to live a life this happy and fulfilling. How can I be sure I haven't just dreamt this all up in my sleep?"

Cecilia smiled. "If you're dreaming this, then I must be sharing that same dream. But I can assure you I am quite real." She stood on her tiptoes to kiss Henry again.

She could feel his smile in the kiss. "Yes, there is no way something like that couldn't be real. That must mean you are my dream made into reality."

Henry pulled Cecilia tighter to him, nuzzling his head into the crook of her neck as she ran her hands up his broad back. Cecilia's chest swelled with pure joy and unbridled love.

Yes, here she stood, holding her dreams in her arms, both real and miraculous all at once.

***

THANK you for reading Cecilia's and Henry's story! You can read Violet's story here, or any of the other books in either of my complete Regency Romance series, Resolved In Love or The Harcourts.

If you want to stay updated on my new releases, you can sign up to my newsletter and receive my stand-alone novella, *A Lifetime Of Love,* or you can hang out with me in my private Facebook group. Happy reading!

ABOUT THE AUTHOR

Penny Fairbanks has been a voracious reader since she could hold a book and immediately fell in love with Jane Austen and her world. Now Penny has branched out into writing her own romantic tales.

Penny lives in the Midwest with her charming husband and their aptly named cat, Prince. When she's not writing or reading she enjoys drinking a lot of coffee and rewatching The Office.

Want to read more of Penny's works? Sign up for her newsletter and receive A *Lifetime of Love*, a stand-alone novella, only available to newsletter subscribers! You'll also be the first to know about upcoming releases!